THE CHARGE BLEW AND SPARKS FILLED THE AIR. THE HATCH WAS BLOWN CLEAR

McCarter thought he could hear and feel the echo of Manning's own charge as he entered the hatchway, but he had to focus on the live-or-die of going operational. He held his AK shouldered at the ready, barrel slightly lowered, as he crouch-walked through the opening. At each corridor juncture and hatchway, he shone the flashlight, moved, shone the flashlight, moved again. The key to operating in low-light conditions was never to—

The overhead lights came on, burning so brightly they hummed.

A siren wailed from the deck above. The charges had finally tripped whatever security measures the North Korean chemists and their muscle had put in place.

"G-Force," McCarter said. "Now."

He counted down in his head. Vibrations traveled through the metal of the ship, footsteps, as armed men within the vessel marshaled to repel boarders.

The freighter shuddered and the hull rang like a bell as Grimaldi, at the Cobra helicopter's helm, opened up with the Gatling cannon....

D0181208

Other titles in this series:

#60 DEFENSIVE ACTION
#61 ROGUE STATE
#62 DEEP RAMPAGE
#63 FREEDOM WATCH
#64 ROOTS OF TERROR
#65 THE THIRD PROTOCOL
#66 AXIS OF CONFLICT
#67 ECHOES OF WAR
#68 OUTBREAK
#69 DAY OF DECISION
#70 RAMROD INTERCEPT
#71 TERMS OF CONTROL
#72 ROLLING THUNDER
#73 COLD OBJECTIVE
#74 THE CHAMELEON FACTOR
#75 SILENT ARSENAL
#76 GATHERING STORM
#77 FULL BLAST
#78 MAELSTROM
#79 PROMISE TO DEFEND
#80 DOOMSDAY CONQUEST
#81 SKY HAMMER
#82 VANISHING POINT
#83 DOOM PROPHECY
#84 SENSOR SWEEP
#85 HELL DAWN
#86 OCEANS OF FIRE
#87 EXTREME ARSENAL
#88 STARFIRE
#89 NEUTRON FORCE
#90 RED FROST
#91 CHINA CRISIS
#92 CAPITAL OFFENSIVE

#93 DEADLY PAYLOAD
#94 ACT OF WAR
#95 CRITICAL EFFECT
#96 DARK STAR
#97 SPLINTERED SKY
#98 PRIMARY DIRECTIVE
#99 SHADOW WAR
#100 HOSTILE DAWN
#101 DRAWPOINT
#102 TERROR DESCENDING
#103 SKY SENTINELS
#104 EXTINCTION CRISIS
#105 SEASON OF HARM
#106 HIGH ASSAULT
#107 WAR TIDES
#108 EXTREME INSTINCT
#109 TARGET ACQUISITION
#110 UNIFIED ACTION
#111 CRITICAL INTELLIGENCE
#112 ORBITAL VELOCITY
#113 POWER GRAB
#114 UNCONVENTIONAL WARFARE
#115 EXTERMINATION
#116 TERMINAL GUIDANCE
#117 ARMED RESISTANCE
#118 TERROR TRAIL
#119 CLOSE QUARTERS
#120 INCENDIARY DISPATCH
#121 SEISMIC SURGE
#122 CHOKE POINT
#123 PERILOUS SKIES
#124 NUCLEAR INTENT
#125 COUNTER FORCE

DON PENDLETON'S

STONY

AMERICA'S ULTRA-COVERT INTELLIGENCE AGENCY

MAN®

PRECIPICE

A GOLD EAGLE BOOK FROM

W✦RLDWIDE®

TORONTO • NEW YORK • LONDON
AMSTERDAM • PARIS • SYDNEY • HAMBURG
STOCKHOLM • ATHENS • TOKYO • MILAN
MADRID • WARSAW • BUDAPEST • AUCKLAND

Recycling programs
for this product may
not exist in your area.

First edition August 2013

ISBN-13: 978-0-373-80440-5

PRECIPICE

Special thanks and acknowledgment to
Phil Elmore for his contribution to this work.

Printed in U.S.A.

PRECIPICE

CHAPTER ONE

Somewhere in the Philippine Sea

The pitching deck of the "Taiwanese" freighter slapped David McCarter's boots hard enough to rattle his teeth. As he unhooked and shrugged out of his rappelling gear, bending his knees to absorb the rolling of the ship, he unlimbered the AK-pattern rifle and chambered a round. The Chinese copy was functional but was as legitimately a Kalashnikov assault rifle as the vessel was from Taiwan.

The lean, fox-faced Briton frowned into the spray washing over the ship's deck. Behind him, the larger Gary Manning finished his descent, landing heavily and nearly dropping to one knee. McCarter resisted the urge to reach out to steady the Canadian, holding his position instead. Manning could find his sea legs himself; he couldn't both descend and return fire should a guard discover the two Phoenix Force commandos. McCarter scanned the deck and the superstructure ahead of them, watching for movement.

McCarter and Manning stood at the bow of the ship. Above them, the Boeing CH-46 Sea Knight—with a borrowed Navy pilot at the controls—headed for the stern of the boat. There the pilot would offload Calvin James, Rafael Encizo and T. J. Hawkins, the other members of Phoenix Force. It took longer for the team's leader, McCarter, to think it than it did for the men to carry out their orders. They were already rappelling, silhouettes visible against the night sky of the South Philippine Sea. As for Grimaldi, the premier Stony Man pilot, he wasn't flying the Sea Knight. He was instead behind the stick of a Cobra attack chopper, flying support for the raid. The Cobra was not visible from this side of the ship, but McCarter believed he could hear its rotors, which sounded markedly different from the double rotors of the Sea Knight.

McCarter and the rest of the team wore blue tiger-stripe camouflage of Russian manufacture, perfect for nighttime operations. Their rifles were Chinese, their sidearms Bulgarian Makarov clones, with the exception of McCarter, who had pulled rank as team leader and insisted on a Browning Hi-Power. The Farm's armorer, John "Cowboy" Kissinger, had supplied him with a FEG, a Hungarian copy of the 9 mm pistol. Kissinger had also seen to it that each AK was fitted with a tactical light clamped to its barrel. The lights were American-made, easily available throughout the world and over the internet. This last, Kissinger had said, winking, was to throw people off as much as it was to make sure the team had appropriate equipment. It would look suspicious if every nation *but* the United States were represented in the team's gear.

Hal Brognola, director of Stony Man Farm, had insisted on plausible deniability. The members of Phoenix Force comprised many nationalities, which made that easier. Encizo was a Cuban-born guerilla fighter; Manning was Canadian; Calvin James was from Chicago's South Side, while Hawkins was Georgia-born and McCarter, obviously, was from England. Their equipment, from their web gear to the Ka-bar-style fighting knives on their belts, was sterile, traceable to no country of origin.

Phoenix Force was operating in international waters for the most part, passing in and out of jurisdictions as they neared ports of call. Dispatched from covert assets in the Subic Bay Freeport Zone, they were committing an act of war by boarding this vessel. That might worry David McCarter and the men and women at the counterterror facility of Stony Man Farm…if, in fact, the ship was Taiwanese. It wasn't. The Taiwanese government had confirmed, through channels, that the ship was not theirs. The false-flag operation had been ongoing for some time.

The Farm's intelligence network had confirmed multiple sightings. It hadn't taken much cross-reference work and data sleuthing—in the words of Aaron "the Bear" Kurtzman, head of Stony Man's cybernetics team—to find records of the equipment purchased and loaded onto the ships, or to trace the true registries of the vessels. There were multiple freighters, all of them under fictional nationality, and every one of them linked to North Korea.

The region had experienced a surge in drug traffic in the past year. That, coupled with the other data, pointed to a scheme the North Koreans had deployed before. The nation was perpetually cash-strapped and had increasingly turned to state-run criminal ventures to generate income. Predictably, the money found its way into the pockets of North Korean government officials, never trickling down to the starving masses.

The ship was a floating drug lab.

There was more than one ship, and that was part of the problem. As more than one vessel was operating in international waters, few nations were willing to take direct action, lest this touch off military action by the North Koreans. It was likely, in any event, that North Korea's dictator would blame the United States and the CIA when his little floating chemical sets were sunk.

What was the little fellow's name again? McCarter wondered to himself, moving quietly behind the barrel of his

Kalashnikov, trying not to wish for a cigarette. Bloody hell but I've forgotten, he thought. Sounded just like the last one. Can't blame a fellow for not keeping them straight.

Given that a fully armed commando team had just been dropped on the deck of the drug ship, the forces belowdecks couldn't be running the tightest possible operation. The night was working to the intruders' advantage. The crew was probably largely asleep, drunk or high or sleeping off either. This possibility was why McCarter had elected a night insertion despite the added risk of rappelling from the chopper in the dark.

McCarter signaled to Manning with a chop of his arm. Manning took up position near a hatch on the starboard side. McCarter, moving so that Manning remained just within his field of view, took the port side.

"Right lads," the Briton whispered. "Black, set," he said, employing his code name for the mission. His words were picked up by the microelectronic transceiver he wore in his ear. This device connected all of the Phoenix Force counterterror operatives, as well as Grimaldi in the Cobra chopper overhead. For the duration of the mission, the Navy pilot in the Sea Knight could also monitor their operations, but only if Grimaldi permitted it. The Stony Man pilot had a master override to the patch from their communications gear to the Sea Knight. The covert nature of Stony Man's missions meant that the less people knew exactly what was happening, even among those military personnel the Farm "borrowed" to support its various missions, the more secure everyone was overall.

Manning was in sight of McCarter. He nodded to the former SAS man as he said, "Blue, set."

"Red, set," came Rafael Encizo's voice in McCarter's transceiver.

"Green, set," said Calvin James.

"Brown, ready," T. J. Hawkins confirmed.

"G-Force, standing by," Grimaldi added from the cockpit of the Cobra. The Stony Man pilot was flying broad loops around the ship, staying well above, biding his time until he was needed. More than once Grimaldi and a gunship had saved the lives of the Phoenix Force commandos. It was a lesson McCarter would not forget; having Jack Grimaldi as their guardian angel was often a game-changer.

From the satchel slung over his shoulder, McCarter produced a magnetic shaped charge. He placed this on the hatchway, pressed the switch on the small timer and stepped back against the bulkhead.

"Go," said McCarter.

The charge blew. Sparks filled the air. The hatch was blown clear.

He thought he could hear and feel the echo of Manning's own charge as he entered the hatchway, but McCarter's mind was focused now on the live-or-die of going operational. He held his AK at the ready, barrel slightly lowered, as he crouch-walked through the opening. At each corridor juncture and hatchway he flashed the light, moved, flashed the light, moved again. The key to operating in low-light conditions was never to—

Every overhead light switched on, burning so brightly they hummed.

The wail of a siren began to peal from somewhere on the deck above. The charges had finally tripped whatever security measures the North Korean chemists and their muscle had put in place.

"G-Force," McCarter ordered, "now."

McCarter counted down in his head. Vibrations traveled through the metal of the ship, and these weaker sounds were numerous. They were footsteps, as armed men within the vessel marshaled to repel boarders. The fact that the crew had switched on the overhead lights meant they weren't prepared to operate in darkness.

The freighter shuddered.

The hull rang like a bell as the Cobra's General Dynamics 20 mm Gatling cannon opened up. Grimaldi would be targeting the portion of the superstructure through which the ship's primary power was routed. The freighter was an old but relatively common model, its schematics and particulars easily ferreted out by the team at the Farm. Grimaldi and Phoenix Force had planned for just this contingency.

On his head McCarter wore a dark blue watch cap. Over this he wore Japanese-made night-vision goggles. He lowered the NVGs over his face as the lights went out again, the ship's power knocked out by the attack chopper.

David McCarter smiled.

"Thank…you!" he said in his most clipped British accent.

"De nada," Grimaldi said in his ear.

In the dancing green monochrome of the NVGs, McCarter gauged his position and then stationed himself at the end of a long corridor. There was a manway leading down, and he would take this into the lower portion of the ship in a moment. The rest of the team had similar orders: move through the ship, neutralize hostiles and make their way to the hold, where the drug lab was surely to be found.

There was, McCarter knew, at least a chance that their intelligence was mistaken, that this ship was not, in fact, a floating North Korean manufacturing platform for illicit narcotics.

But it probably is, McCarter thought as the first of the uniformed North Korean soldiers boiled out of the hatchway at the opposite end of the corridor.

The cramped space came alive with the buzz saws of

multiple bullet ricochets. The North Koreans were armed with AKs equipped with folding metal shoulder stocks. They fired the moment they saw McCarter, who simply stepped back and behind the corner. A ricochet came dangerously close to his face, leaving a dent in the bulkhead near him, but he was unharmed.

Wankers, McCarter thought. Once more he counted down in his head.

The North Koreans had no fire discipline. They ran out more or less simultaneously, as the fusillade died off and the ringing of Communist-bloc steel shell casings rattled in time to the ringing in McCarter's ears.

The Briton swiveled, angled his rifle around the corner with his body still behind cover and triggered a long spray of 7.62 mm rounds. The corridor was filled with blood and—briefly—screams.

Before his magazine was empty, McCarter hauled the rifle back behind the bulkhead and swapped it out. There was nothing but silence from the bloody corridor beyond.

From where he now stood, in the green blobs of his augmented vision, he could see a galley to his left. To his right was some kind of storage room, possibly for dry goods and other items for the galley. The crates and boxes on the metal shelves were visible, but their labels were not. He did not believe the North Koreans were hiding their heroin in the pantry, however.

Heroin. The poison had killed countless men, women and even children through the years. There was nothing good about it, and McCarter—who had his share of vices—had no patience for it. It was heroin trafficking specifically that had plagued the region since the North Koreans set up shop. According to the mission briefing, a copy of which was on the secure satellite smartphone in McCarter's pocket, there was renewed interest and therefore profit in the opiate. McCarter supposed that meant the drug lab was less a lab than a refinery. Not that this mattered one bloody bit.

McCarter checked each of the fallen men. One of them was barely alive. He would linger for some time if not attended to. The Briton could see no reason to let him suffer.

The Phoenix Force leader slipped the knife from his belt sheath and thrust it quickly between the man's ribs, waiting as the last of the life ebbed from the fallen soldier. He wiped his blade on the dead man's clothes, resheathed it and took the manway down.

McCarter could hear sporadic gunfire from elsewhere in the ship. Each member of the team could take care of himself; there were no more experienced a group of counterterrorism operatives than Able Team.

How far we've come, McCarter thought. Then he smirked at his own inner dialogue. I am getting bloody old, he thought, cracking jokes to myself.

He wished, briefly, for a cigarette.

The ship's deck plan indicated crew berths beyond the galley. He headed for these, sweeping the small cook's station to make sure no one was hiding there.

He saw the sole of the rubber sandal before he saw the body that wore it. The dead man also wore an apron. There was a bullet hole in his forehead and a much larger exit wound at the back of his skull. McCarter tracked the angle of the body, glanced back and gauged the distance. The bullet could not have come from his weapon. The trajectory was wrong. The man had obviously been the victim of a stray round, ricocheting from the bulkhead after it was fired by one of his own crewmen.

They've shot their own bloody cook, he thought. Seems a harsh criticism.

There was a large pot on the stove. He put his hand

against it; it was cold. Apparently the gunfight had broken out before the man had begun preparing the evening meal. Or maybe whatever was in the pot was served cold. He bent slightly and sniffed at it.

McCarter wrinkled his nose. Then again, maybe the bastard had it coming, he thought.

The galley opened into a corridor with a facing hatch. The Phoenix Force leader made for this and tested it. It was not locked.

Probably a trap, he thought.

He knelt by the bulkhead and pushed the hatch with one hand.

Bullets rang from the collar around the hatchway, buzzing past his face and legs. At least one managed to find the corpse of the Korean cook. McCarter winced.

Definitely a trap, he thought. To hell with it. He pulled a grenade free from his webbing.

From beyond the hatch, Kalashnikov fire rattled like gravel in an oil drum.

McCarter flinched slightly. More bullets found the corpse in the galley. "You're doing that on purpose, you bastard!" he called out, and popped the pin with his thumb.

The answering shout, in Korean, was meaningless to him. All he needed, however, was the pause in the gunfire that accompanied it.

He let the spoon on the grenade spring free and tossed the bomb.

"Break's over," he whispered. The explosion pushed a column of superheated air and chunks of meat into the galley.

McCarter took the corner, then the hatchway, snapping the AK to his shoulder. The bunk room beyond was cluttered. In his night vision, he picked out first one, then another, then a third target.

The man on the left, hiding behind one of the double bunks, fired blindly into the darkness. The muzzle-flashes created a temporary green-and-white-out effect as McCarter's goggles struggled with the changing levels of ambient light. He dropped to his belly. Targeting the first man's feet below the level of the bunk, he triggered his AK.

The bullets chopped the man's ankles out from under him. He fell, screaming, and when his head struck the deck, McCarter put a bullet in it.

The Briton rolled. The second and third men were moving now, stumbling into each other, trying to find the hatchway that led from the rear of the bunk room. McCarter fired, missed and just avoided an answering blast of Kalashnikov fire that clattered off the deck next to him. They were trying to track his muzzle-blasts in the dark.

McCarter pushed to his feet, took careful aim and shot the closest man in the head. The spray of blood that splashed the last man's face brought him up short. He threw his rifle to the ground, started to put his hands in the air and then froze. Through his NVGs, McCarter actually watched the man's expression change from fear to one of blank resignation.

"Don't you dare, you filthy bugger," McCarter muttered under his breath.

The North Korean soldier went for the flap holster on his belt. Before he could tug his pistol free, McCarter shot him in the throat. He toppled, clutching at his neck, gurgling and trying to call out. Then he was still.

McCarter shook his head.

"Green, clear," came the voice in his earbud. He glanced at the analog face of the military chronograph. The first leg of the mission had run as planned. Opposition on the decks leading to the hold had been eliminated.

"Brown, station," reported Hawkins, the team's youngest member.

"Red, station," the Cuban stated.

Hawkins and Encizo had been instructed to eliminate hostiles in their areas of the ship, then assume guard positions to watch for contact from behind. McCarter hurried on to the next manway. The ladder leading down would take him to a chamber leading to the hold, if his memory of the deck plan was accurate.

"Blue, clear." The voice was in McCarter's earbud but also in the chamber with him. Gary Manning and Calvin James were waiting for him on either side of the hatchway to the ship's hold. The chamber was a secondary cargo area.

"Green. Right in front of you," said Calvin James, grinning.

"Very funny," said McCarter.

"The hatchway's not sealed," reported Manning. "They closed it just as we took the ladder. I saw a total of three men, wearing chemical suits and respirators. Refinery technicians, would be my guess."

McCarter took a good look at the crates of equipment behind James and did a double take. When he stepped closer, he could feel heat rising to his face. "Wait a moment. What's this?"

James turned.

Manning looked over his shoulder. "David," he said. "Are those what I think they are?"

McCarter lifted one of the components free of the crate and rolled it end for end in his hand. "I think it is," he said. "You don't run into so many that they're familiar, but…" He rummaged around in the crate. "There's no documentation. We'll need to snap photos of these, lads, and send everything to the Farm for analysis. I hope we're wrong."

A shot rang out from the other side of the hatchway. It was followed by several more.

"Go, go!" McCarter instructed.

Manning kicked the hatchway in with his combat boot. The heavy metal door opened on well-oiled hinges. The three Phoenix Force commandos came through in standard cover formation, sweeping the deck in front of them, the barrels of their rifles moving urgently as they checked for targets.

The smell hit him first. McCarter almost gagged. Around them was arrayed the drug lab's complex refining equipment, some of it haphazardly jerry-built, some of it still gleaming in stainless-steel and chromed fittings. That was the North Koreans. Whatever technology they had they adapted, and if they couldn't build an integrated system from what was available to them, they would graft junk to professional gear and think little of the Frankenstein contraption that resulted.

"Mind your breathing, lads," McCarter said. He threw his free arm over his mouth and nose, using his sleeve as a filter, holding his AK to his shoulder by the pistol grip alone. They would not want to spend too much time in the hold. There was no telling what chemicals might be in the air.

"I'll let you know if I start to feel really revved up," said James.

"Over here," Manning said. He was on the opposite side of the cluster of refining equipment that dominated the center of the hold. "I found them."

When McCarter could see what Manning was looking at, he lowered his rifle. On the deck, lying in spreading pools of blood, were the three technicians. There were also two dead uniformed North Korean soldiers. One of the soldiers still held a Tokarev-type pistol. McCarter was no forensics expert, but as he had in the galley, he could surmise what had happened. The man with the Tokarev had shot the three technicians and his fellow soldier, then turned the weapon on himself. There were scorch marks on his temple where the muzzle-blast had burned the skin around the entry hole.

The dead man still bore a resigned, almost horrified expression. It was precisely the look the man in the bunk room had given him, the man who'd dropped his rifle only to try for his holstered sidearm.

"North Korea," said Manning. "A country that tortures and kills its Olympic athletes when they lose in the Games. These men knew the price for being captured would likely be reprisals against their families. Or slow deaths should they be deported home. That one—" he jerked his chin toward the corpse with the Tokarev "—was either acting on behalf of these others or following standing orders from his superiors."

"Works out to be the same thing," said James.

"Bloody hell," said McCarter.

CHAPTER TWO

Stony Man Farm, Virginia

Barbara Price entered the briefing room at Stony Man Farm and ducked as a disposable cup flew past her shoulder. The honey-blonde mission controller, wearing a conservative blouse and thigh-length skirt that nonetheless hugged her curves, shot Hermann "Gadgets" Schwarz a withering glare.

"Sorry, Barb," said Schwarz, who promptly threw another cup from the plastic sleeve. He was aiming for Rosario Blancanales, whom the other teammates called "Pol"—short for "Politician." Blancanales was reading a newspaper and doing his best to ignore the cups that bounced off the front page.

In his wheelchair on the opposite side of the table, Aaron Kurtzman was working on the controls built into the briefing room table. These were wired through the walls to the flat-screen televisions throughout the room. The main screen, sitting on the wall facing one end of the briefing table, was dark.

"I told you that system was going to be trouble if we had to perform maintenance on it," Schwarz said, casually lobbing another cup at Blancanales's paper.

"Shaddap," Kurtzman said without looking up. He was intent on the circuit inside the square housing built into the table. In one large hand he held the enormous coffee mug that Blancanales had once called a "flagon." In the other he held the soldering pen that was his weapon of choice for the task. A wisp of smoke curled up from the circuit board.

"Modular, I said," Schwarz went on. "Make it modular. Sound replacement theory, really. I remember during that mission to—"

"Shaddap," Kurtzman said again, still not looking at Schwarz.

Price rolled her eyes and took her seat. Like any equipment at the Farm, the systems they employed in the briefing room had been state of the art when installed. Like so many of those systems, however, time worked against them. As the days, the months and then the years passed, systems that were not mission critical, like the cameras and screens in the briefing room, were left alone provided they were not malfunctioning. This never sat well with Schwarz, Able Team's electronics specialist. The slim, bookish-looking man was, she knew, not the harmless nerd he might first appear to be. Schwarz, like his teammates on Able Team and their counterparts on Phoenix Force, was a veteran counterterrorist operative.

If Schwarz had a character flaw, it was that he never knew when to leave well enough alone. That included his penchant for bantering with and teasing his teammates. Carl Lyons, Able Team's leader, had already excused himself to get more coffee from the Farm's break room, probably because he was getting annoyed with Schwarz's improvised game of foam-cup basketball. Schwarz was trying to hurl the lightweight cups, and Blancanales was shifting his newspaper to prevent his teammate from landing one behind the barrier the paper created.

Schwarz had also been assisting Kurtzman with repairs to the briefing room's video systems. They were waiting for a transmission from Hal Brognola, Director of the Justice Department's Sensitive Operations Group and the one man most responsible for directives given to the Farm. Brognola had been delayed, however, due to some meeting or other in Washington. It was after he text-messaged Price to inform her of the delay that Schwarz and Kurtzman had started arguing about electrical interference and the quality of the briefing room screens. That had prompted a long string of verbiage from Schwarz that Price could not follow, with Schwarz referencing screen resolution and pixels as often as teasing Kurtzman about the system's outdated wiring.

"We could run HDMI," Blancanales put in from behind his paper.

"You don't even know what HDMI *is*," Schwarz said. "You just heard me say that."

"Ten-eighty pee," said Blancanales. "Plasma. Refresh rate."

"See!" Schwarz pointed. "He's just rattling off terms."

Kurtzman took another swig from his coffee mug. "Shaddap," he said again.

"This is why you can't remember the name of the movie," Schwarz said. "You have to have seen it. It's only one of the best action movies that has ever been made. It defined a genre, Pol. It signals the beginning of a new era in action cinema."

"So I'm not into movies like you are," Blancanales said. The two men were continuing a conversation they had been having since they arrived for the briefing. Frankly, Price thought there was a good chance Schwarz had read a review of the film and was just pretending to like it so much. It was the sort of thing he did to annoy Carl Lyons.

Come to think of it, thought Price, a lot of the things he does are to annoy Carl.

"Come on, you have to remember the name," Schwarz said.

"The one where the guy says he's sick of those snakes on his mother—"

"No," Schwarz said, interrupting. "Not that one at all. This is the one about the balding guy in the skyscraper. You know, the one where thugs take over the building and one New York cop has to fight them all."

"*One* guy against an army of terrorists?" Blancanales said from behind his paper. "That doesn't sound realistic at all."

"So you *have* seen it."

"No," Blancanales said. "I'm saying it doesn't sound realistic."

Schwarz threw another cup at him. "There's this great scene where the bad guy pretends to be a hostage and fakes an American accent, and when he goes to betray our hero, he says—"

"Cock a doodle doo, Mother, may I," said Carl Lyons, walking into the briefing room. The burly Lyons, once an L.A. cop himself, held a pot of coffee in one fist.

"No," said Schwarz. "No, that's not it at all." He pointed to the coffeepot. "Did you bring enough for the rest of us, Carl?"

"Funny thing about that," said Lyons. He reached across the table and snatched the plastic sleeve of foam cups from Schwarz's grasp. "Some joker took all the cups out of the break room." He shook a cup out of the package and began filling it from the pot.

Kurtzman activated one of the video feed pickups. His image appeared on the main flat-screen monitor. Schwarz immediately reached into his pocket and produced a remote control.

"What's that?" Blancanales asked.

Schwarz pressed a button on the control. On the flat-screen, Kurtzman's head-and-shoulders image suddenly appeared behind a superimposed image of a clown car, making it appear as if the Stony Man cybernetics team leader were driving the little vehicle.

Kurtzman glared at Schwarz.

"Okay, okay," said Schwarz. He pressed the remote again. The video feed of Kurtzman, also glaring, switched from the superimposed clown car to a superimposed spaceship, complete with shooting stars whizzing by to simulate movement.

Carl Lyons looked over. "Lemme see that thing."

Schwarz handed Lyons the remote. Lyons switched it off, clearing the graphics from the flat-screen, and then snapped it neatly in two. Small fragments of the remote's internal circuit fell out onto the table. Lyons brushed them aside with the edge of his hand.

He handed the pieces back to Schwarz without comment.

Kurtzman harrumphed under his breath. He finished his work and closed the housing on the table's control box. The flat-screen switched off. Schwarz started to say something, but Kurztman held up a single finger.

"Not a word," he warned.

Price felt her wireless phone vibrating. She checked it and nodded to the others. "Hal says he's on his way to his office."

"I don't envy him the battleground he walks every day," said Blancanales. "Compared to the work we do, Wonderland is far more treacherous."

"I spend a little time there myself," said Price, who frequently fielded calls from the various agencies and other governmental entities on whose toes Stony Man walked to accomplish its goals. "It's one of the reasons I keep pestering Hal to take better care of himself."

"At least he chews the cigars more often than he smokes them now," Schwarz said.

The flat-screen came to life again, this time with the image of Hal Brognola. The big Fed looked as though he had slept in his clothes in the office again, which he very well might have.

"Have we got Phoenix online?" Brognola asked.

"Bringing them up now," said Kurtzman. He pressed a switch on the control panel. The flat-screen monitor opposite Kurtzman and Price activated, bearing a secure satellite feed of the members of Phoenix Force crammed into a crew berth aboard what could only be a ship. Price knew that meant they were aboard the Navy ship the Farm had reassigned for what had been described, to the Navy brass as a joint drug task force interdiction. This it was, in effect, but the nature of Stony Man Farm as an organization had not been disclosed. Too many people knew of the existence of the Farm, indirectly, than Price would have liked as it was. Their efficacy rested in large part on their ability to operate outside the regulations that hindered other, more mainstream parts of the government, law enforcement and the military. Secrecy was integral to that.

"We can hear you," said McCarter. "There's some delay but it's not bad."

"All right, then," said Price. "Let's get started. As is obvious to everyone, Phoenix is on assignment in the Philippine Sea. They have been running drug task force raids on floating refineries operated by the North Koreans in international waters."

"Where we've no authority to interdict them," Blancanales said.

"Yes," said Price. "That's correct. Initially the region came under scrutiny because drug traffic, mostly heroin and methamphetamine, quadrupled in the region during the second half of last year. When Bear and his team traced the false-flag operation back to North Korea, however, the Man decided it was time we get involved."

"But why does the President care if North Korea sells drugs half a world away?" Schwarz asked.

"It isn't the drugs," said Brognola. "It's the money. Or rather, it was. North Korea is poverty stricken. It always has been. Its leaders border on insane. They build giant housing projects that are little more than facades, designed to 'prove' to the rest of the world that their nation is prosperous even as they starve and suffer. North Korea's citizens are brainwashed slaves, whose media outlets fill their heads with ridiculous myths about how great their dictator of the moment is."

"Where does the money go, then?" Schwarz asked.

"Military projects," said Brognola, "and more state-sponsored terror against the West. Cut off from most of the free world and sitting uncomfortably on the border with its southern counterpart, North Korea has very real financial problems. Solving those financial problems makes it much more dangerous. Every dollar of disposable income the North Koreans have is another dollar of guns and bombs that will find their way to someone or something that is acting against Western interests. The drug refineries are one way to generate a great deal of cash relatively quickly. They've already done so in the last six months. With the protection of operating at sea beyond national boundaries, they can keep doing it indefinitely if we don't stop them. The Farm is one of the few agencies that can take on this operation, given its…extralegal…status."

"That's a polite way to say it," McCarter put in.

"The operation seemed simple enough in the planning stages," Brognola said. "Under the aegis of plausible deniability, we sent Phoenix in to track and raid the drug ships we know are operating in the area. We smash the operation. We confiscate any drugs or cash we find. In so doing, we cut off the flow of funds to North Korea and send a message that this won't be tolerated anymore."

"But they've done it before," Blancanales said. "I remember reading a news article about the North's floating drug labs."

"They have," said Brognola. "That's yet another reason Phoenix was deemed the appropriate response. A decisive military operation is as unambiguous as unofficial international warnings get."

"I sense there's a 'but' coming," Schwarz said.

"There is," said Brognola. "As I said, the operation as planned was simple enough…but it hasn't stayed that way. David?"

McCarter held up, visible to the satellite camera pickup, one of the components Phoenix had recovered from the North Korean drug ship. A full photographic catalog had been uploaded to the Farm's computers following the raid. The parts had been analyzed by Kurtzman and his computer team. The results were not encouraging.

"Hal," Schwarz said. "I can't be looking at—"

"You are," said Brognola. "That is the guidance system to an intercontinental ballistic missile. Phoenix has recovered a shipment of ICBM components that were aboard the North Korean drug ship. We theorize the components were dropped at the drug vessel for eventual transport back to North Korea, to be included in their missile program."

"Just how extensive is this program?" Carl Lyons asked.

"We know they've been working for some time on ICBMs capable of reaching Hawaii and California," said Brognola. "So far, the technology required to do that has eluded them. Honestly, we haven't been too worried about them—they aren't known for their technological prowess."

"Were these the blokes with the flying fighter-boats?" asked McCarter.

"I think that was Iran," said Schwarz. "The fighters were a kit ordered from the back of a magazine."

"North Korea," said Brognola, "isn't much better off, although militarily they do enjoy the support of communist-sympathetic international concerns. What we are seeing in this shipment of parts, if it is not unique, is the establishment of a supply pipeline in contraindicated technology. If the North Koreans develop an ICBM, we can hit them, hopefully take it out. If they continue to develop and build them, that's going to get harder and harder. We can't have them building these missiles in quantity. We need to root out the other end of this pipeline and destroy it utterly."

"What did your check on the parts produce?" Gary Manning asked through the satellite feed.

"That's where things start to get interesting," said Price. "The parts are, as near as we can tell, produced right here in the United States. The manufacturer is TruTech."

"Wait a minute," Schwarz said. "TruTech is Claridge Clayton's company."

"That's right," Brognola confirmed.

"That's hard to believe," said Blancanales.

"Who the hell is Claridge Clayton?" Lyons asked.

"Claridge Clayton," said Brognola, "is one of the more famous contributors to the political action committee that helped put the Man in the Oval Office. He owns several firms, the largest of which is TruTech. TruTech is a contractor to the Department of Defense. Clayton also sponsored the Rally for Independence Day last year, an event in Philadelphia featuring a variety of Hollywood stars and musicians."

"I remember that," Blancanales said. "They donated the proceeds to a fallen soldiers' fund."

"Wait," said Lyons. "*This* guy is selling ICBM parts to rogue nations? He's practically wearing American flag underwear."

"It does indeed seem far-fetched," said Brognola. "And in Clayton's defense he may have no idea that his products are finding their way into this pipeline. For that matter, the pipeline is itself in contention. We have strange reports of private concerns, as yet unidentified, battling it out with foreign elements peddling ICBM parts. At least, that's the online chatter. It's very sketchy and we don't know who's involved."

"There are supposed to be fail-safes in place to prevent component smuggling," Blancanales said. "Import and export restrictions. Chains of custody. These components are sensitive technology and therefore wouldn't simply be shipped out of the country. There are a lot of legal and record-keeping hoops the firm would have to jump through to send ICBM components to a legal trading partner."

"I doubt these went through official channels," said Brognola. "We've queried Clayton and asked him to turn over the appropriate inventory records. He believes he's dealing with either the FBI or the NSA, depending on which contact identity we used to speak with his representatives. Inventory records sent from TruTech, and verified by Clayton himself, show no missing items. Everything the company has produced for the Department of Defense has been accounted for."

"Obviously not," Lyons said, jerking his head toward the flat-screen. McCarter nodded and put down the component, placing it out of the camera's field of vision.

"What's Clayton have to say for himself?" McCarter said.

"He says he invites government scrutiny," Brognola said. "I spoke with him myself this morning and he reassured me that his corporation welcomes our involvement.

He says he doesn't want his products used against this nation any more than we do."

"So either he's a snake," Lyons said, "or he's incompetent."

"That's our Ironman," Schwarz said. "King of the false dichotomy."

Lyons shot Schwarz a warning glare. Brognola ignored the exchange and called up a set of maps, which temporarily replaced his image on the flat-screen. "TruTech's headquarters is here, in Atlanta," he said. The map showed Atlanta as a red icon. "Its primary competitors, whom Clayton seems to think might have a stake in discrediting his company, are also located in that region of the country."

"So what's the plan?" Lyons asked. He emptied his coffee cup and placed it on the table.

"Able Team will travel to Atlanta," said Brognola. "There you will interview Clayton and inspect the grounds of the TruTech facility. Treat Clayton with respect. He does, after all, have the ear of the President, after a fashion. But assume he may be involved nonetheless. If he can assure you otherwise, fine. He is supposed to provide us with the names of those firms he considers most directly in competition with his own. These will become your priority targets for follow-up. If TruTech isn't the source of the components, then a source within in the industry, one possessing the same manufacturing capacity and capability, must be to blame. There are no other options. These weren't cobbled together in a cave by unwashed, bearded men carrying RPGs. They're the result of a very intricate process and contain several controlled and delicate parts."

"I don't like Clayton's chances," said Lyons. "The simplest explanation for all this is that his company is involved, even if it's at a level below him."

"The right hand doesn't know what the left hand is doing?" Blancanales suggested.

"Yeah," Lyons said. "That."

"Our photographic analysis of the components, including some interiors that I had Phoenix take, shows that the ICBM parts conform to the precise design and, in some cases where it's apparent, the manufacturing process we know TruTech uses for the DoD," Kurtzman said. "But that's still not *proof,* as such. We know the Chinese have become masterful at manufacturing near perfect reproductions of everything from civilian automobiles for the world market, to former Communist-bloc hardware. The Russians are up in arms over the MiG fighter plane copies the Chinese are turning out, to say nothing of the small arms market."

"Your task, Able," Brognola said, "is, despite the diplomatic niceties, to put the screws to Clayton. Find out what he knows. Figure out what's going on. And when you track the problem to its source, burn it down."

"But be respectful," Lyons said. He snorted. Brognola let it go.

"And us?" McCarter asked. The Phoenix Force leader had been reasonably quiet, Price thought. It was usually McCarter who gave Brognola the most flak in a briefing. She could understand why, in this case, Lyons was agitated. Carl Lyons was as patriotic a man as it was possible to be. The idea of an American turning traitor, a wealthy man famous for his jingoism, would be turning Lyons's stomach.

"Phoenix will continue its drug interdiction raids in the Philippine Sea," said Price. "We've only begun to interfere with the pipeline itself. The primary mission is no longer the drugs, however. While disrupting drug traffic in the region will remain a significant benefit, we have to operate on the assumption that these ships are also acting as transit drops for the ICBM pipeline. Cutting that link makes it that much harder for the North Koreans to get the parts they want. Everything we do that delays them works in our favor. As we've already covered, it's manufacturing ICBMs in quantity that is the real threat. The North Koreans will know that, too. They'll be looking to build an arsenal as quickly as they can. Beyond a certain size, it becomes its own deterrent and provides some protection from future operations to neutralize them."

"Then we're back to the Cold War," Blancanales said. "Mutually assured destruction. With North Korea's crackpot leader flexing his thumb over the button."

"Not a good thing," Schwarz said.

"Not a good thing," Brognola agreed, nodding. "Barb has your mission briefings and will have them transmitted to your satellite receivers. Good hunting, gentlemen."

"Phoenix out," said McCarter. The flat-screen monitor with his team's satellite feed went dark.

"Brognola out," said the big Fed. His screen, too, went blank.

"Let's move, Able," Lyons said. He stood to go but stopped himself. As if remembering something important, he paused just long enough to flick his mostly empty foam cup at Schwarz, bouncing it off the man's forehead, splattering him with droplets of coffee.

Price tried not to laugh. Lyons left the briefing room without another word.

Schwarz stared after him, speechless.

CHAPTER THREE

Atlanta, Georgia

The pretty blonde behind the counter was wearing a skirt so tight and so short, Carl Lyons wasn't sure how she walked. Maybe she didn't walk at all; maybe she just took her perch on the chair behind her desk and stayed there until someone rolled the chair out of the room at closing time. When Lyons, flanked by Schwarz and Blancanales, entered the lobby of TruTech headquarters in Atlanta, the woman began chattering at them at full speed and volume. She was, Lyons thought, practically shouting at them almost before the doors had closed behind the men of Able Team.

"Good morning, gentlemen. I trust you have an appointment? Welcome to TruTech, the leading name in high-tech solutions for military and civilian applications. We are prepared to supply you with tailored solutions for industry that meet or exceed all requirements of local and international—"

"Dial it back, honey," said Lyons, which earned him a reproving glance from Blancanales and a rude expression from Schwarz. Realizing he was, perhaps, being a bit hard-nosed, even for him, he did his best to smile. "We don't have an appointment, but your boss is expecting us. My name is Weaving. That's Fishburne—" Lyons nodded at Schwarz, then to Blancanales"—and the other fellow is Reeves. We're with the Justice Department."

"Oh," said the blonde. Her face fell for just a moment before she regained her composure. "Of course, sir. Just one moment, please. I'll need to get someone upstairs on the intercom."

"Take your time, miss," Blancanales said politely. He nudged Lyons and Schwarz to move away from the desk, grabbing each of them by an elbow.

"Getting a little grabby, aren't you, Pol?" Schwarz asked.

"Are you seeing this?" Blancanales whispered.

Lyons looked around the elegantly appointed lobby. The ceiling was at least three stories tall, featuring a gigantic crystal chandelier. The walls were accented with lustrous hardwoods whose origin Lyons could not guess; the floors were polished marble. The elevators at the rear of the lobby, on either side of the blonde receptionist's marble-fronted desk, were constantly in motion, as men and women in suits and ties hurried this way and that. Classical music lilted from hidden speakers. Everything about the building bespoke wealth and taste.

Except for the armed guards.

They wore custom uniforms and stood almost completely immobile, like statues. They were spaced around the perimeter of the lobby in specially designed alcoves, as if security this heavy had been part of the building's design from its conception.

"I count at least six," Lyons said. "Which seems heavy, even for a Department of Defense contractor. But I'm more interested in their sidearms."

"Brugger and Thomet TP-9 pistols," Blancanales said. "That's serious hardware."

"It's a far cry from a .38 wheelgun and a sap," said

Lyons. "Maybe Clayton just likes outfitting his people with the latest toys."

"Maybe," said Schwarz. "He sure didn't skimp on the lobby decorations. He jerked his chin almost imperceptibly, calling their attention to the high ceiling. "I count what looks like at least ten different cameras with either thermal imaging or infrared intruder detection."

"How can you tell that from here?" Lyons asked.

"He sleeps with the catalog under his pillow," Blancanales said.

"Do not," Schwarz said. "Dead-tree product catalogs are so 1990. But the cameras aren't all. This place is wired for light-optics at the floor level. The apertures are supposed to look like tastefully shrouded power outlets, but I can tell the difference. At night this place must be blanketed in security lasers.

"High-tech tripwires," Blancanales affirmed. "Walk across one and set off every alarm in the building."

"Of which there are probably several," said Schwarz. "Also, those fancy doors we walked through to get in here?"

"Yeah?" said Lyons.

"The hinges have small hydraulic motors built into them," Schwarz said. "The only reason to do that is for an automatic handicapped door, which those aren't, or so that you can trigger a lock-down remotely."

"What would you like to bet," Lyons said quietly, "that all those panes of glass—" he nodded at the perimeter of the lobby "—aren't glass at all."

"Bullet resistant," said Blancanales. "There's a good chance. So what does all this really tell us?"

"Either TruTech and Clayton are just nutty about security, or there's something they're not telling us," said Lyons. "That might be that Clayton is more than just a little worried about his competitors stealing his designs. He's rigged to repel an invasion."

"So what's he not telling us?" Blancanales asked.

"Maybe he's been hit before," Schwarz said. "It's not unheard of. There's a lot of money in this market, which means a lot of power and more than a few inflated egos. Clayton wouldn't be the first guy who decided he could fight his own battles rather than be muscled over. The kind of guy who'd hire a private army before he'd bring in the cops or the FBI."

"Funny thing about private armies," said Lyons. "The guys that own them are almost never altar boys."

"It's a lifestyle thing, Ironman," said Schwarz. "Have you ever read the Evil Overlord list on the internet? It's almost exactly like that. See, the first thing you do when you become a super villain is—"

"Gadgets?" Lyons said, interrupting.

"Yes, Carl?"

"Stop talking."

The receptionist was eyeing them from behind her desk, looking agitated and gesturing for them. Lyons nodded to her. "Come on," he said. "Before she pops a button or something."

"Heaven forbid," said Schwarz quietly.

"Mr. Clayton will see you now," she said. "Take the first elevator on your left and go right up."

"Thanks," said Lyons. "Which floor?"

"Why, his own floor, sir," said the receptionist. She sounded surprised.

The men of Able Team filed into the elevator. Once there, Lyons realized what the gag was supposed to be. The elevator buttons were numbered except for the very top one. That button was metallic gold, surrounded in gilded scrollwork. Instead of a number, it bore the engraved image of Claridge Clayton himself.

Lyons stabbed the button with one large thumb. The doors closed silently and the elevator began to ascend. In speakers hidden in grillwork in the ceiling of the elevator car, a saxophone-heavy version of "Garota de Ipanema" began playing. Schwarz opened his mouth to speak.

"So help me," Lyons growled, staring at the elevator doors and not once turning to his teammates. "Don't start."

Schwarz thought better of whatever it was he had been about to say.

When the elevator finally stopped, Lyons suppressed the urge to go for the .357 Magnum Colt Python in the shoulder holster under his brown leather bomber jacket. There were more guards here, two per side on both walls flanking the elevator. They eyed the men of Able Team with frank suspicion. Lyons walked brazenly past them, pretending they weren't there, but he was grateful for the firepower his teammates bore. Blancanales carried a Beretta M-9 pistol in his waistband and, for this operation, a full-auto MAC-11 submachine gun strapped under his right arm. Schwarz was only slightly less heeled, wearing a custom shoulder holster that carried his Beretta 93 R machine pistol. At a command from Lyons, the other two men could fill the corridor with a swarm of 9 mm bullets.

It occurred to Lyons that of the three of them, he looked the least like a government agent. His black sports shirt was more appropriate to the gym, while the steel-toed hiking boots he wore would never be appropriate gear in white-collar halls of power such as this one. Schwarz, in a windbreaker, T-shirt and jeans, at least seemed nerdy enough for the tech part of things. Everybody expected electronics geeks to dress down, after all. Blancanales was the most appropriately attired; he wore a light canvas jacket over a shirt and slacks. Add a tie to Blancanales and change his jacket for a blazer and you could stand him behind any podium. It was for the sake of appearances that they had been forced to leave their heavier weaponry—a pair of M-16 rifles for Blancanales and Schwarz, and Lyons's beloved Daewoo USAS-12 automatic shotgun—behind in the for-official-use-only Chevy Suburban they had "borrowed" from a government motor pool.

Another pair of guards, these as large, as stone-faced and as heavily armed as the others, awaited them at the end of the marble-tiled corridor. The light fixtures along the hall were gold-plated, as were the actual double doors to Clayton's penthouse office.

"Tasteful," said Schwarz. Lyons glared at him. Schwarz simply pointed upward. There was another camera mounted in the corridor ceiling, where it overlooked the doors.

The clack of an electronic lock releasing confirmed that someone within was aware of their presence. The doors opened automatically on hydraulic hinges.

"Gentlemen!" Claridge Clayton said, spreading his arms wide. "Come in, come in! Thank goodness you're here."

Lyons took an instant dislike to the famous patriot-businessman. Clayton was a big man, with a ruddy complexion and a prow of gel-laden black hair that might have been an acrylic helmet. He wore a suit that was probably as expensive as most families' cars, cut to conceal what Lyons suspected was a broadening paunch. The gold cuff links at his wrists sparkled with inset diamonds; his silk tie, which seemed almost too tight around his thick neck, was held in place with a gold-and-diamond tie clasp.

His desk was a gold-leafed horror. Whatever burnished hardwood had been used to build the massive piece of office furniture was lost under gilded corners and sculpted golden ivy. A glass surface had been used to make the top of the monstrosity functional as a desk, and on this was perched a high-end laptop, a desk phone and a tablet computer. Clayton was just slipping his personal wireless phone—the brand and make that people had been standing in line to get just a week previously—into an interior pocket of his sharkskin jacket. Lyons wondered, for a moment, if that's what sharkskin jackets really looked like, and realized he was guessing. Then he tabled the entire inner dialogue as unimportant.

Clayton was giving his thirty-megawatt smile a workout as he turned to each of them and shook their hands. His grip was strong and firm, which surprised Lyons; he had been expecting a limp wrist or clammy palms. On the wall directly behind Clayton, the businessman could be seen shaking hands with a former President known for his inspirational, patriotic speeches. Smaller photographs arrayed around this one showed Clayton with various celebrities, including a generous allotment of Hollywood starlets in skintight dresses. A few were even in bathing suits aboard what Lyons took to be Clayton's yacht, the *In Excess*. The name of the boat, and its specifications, had been in Stony Man's briefing files.

"Mr. Clayton," said Blancanales. "Thank you for taking the time to meet with us. Your government understandably appreciates any cooperation you can provide. As I'm sure you can imagine, this is a potentially very serious matter."

Clayton's winning smile immediately transformed into a tragic frown. There was a gigantic set of American flags on poles at either side of the desk, behind where the man sat. Lyons got the impression Clayton would have wrapped himself in one of them, had he the option.

"Yes. Yes, of course," Clayton said, sounding very

sober. "I can't imagine the danger our men and women in uniform must have endured, to safely secure the samples of this hardware from hostile territory."

Schwarz and Blancanales exchanged glances. Lyons resisted the urge to perform a face-palm.

"Are you implying that you have sources within the Department of Defense, Mr. Clayton?" Schwarz asked. "Sources who've told you the circumstances under which the components were recovered?"

The smile that came to Clayton's face broadened too easily. "I could not officially admit that," Clayton said. "Just as I know you gentlemen would prefer I not ask exactly which of our government agencies you happen to be with. I know it's not the Justice Department, as you told Claire downstairs. That means it's likely what the boys downstairs call No Such Agency. The NSA. Am I right?"

Blancanales smiled. "We could not officially admit that," he said.

Clayton nodded. Lyons clenched his teeth. It wouldn't do for Clayton to see him smirk at how easily Blancanales was playing him.

Blancanales took a legal-size envelope from within his jacket, smoothed its crease and removed the hard copies from it. These were prints of the images sent by Phoenix to Stony Man Farm, showing the recovered ICBM parts and, in several instances, the interiors of disassembled portions. Blancanales spread the photos across the glass tabletop of Clayton's desk.

Clayton didn't speak at first. He took each photo, examining the shots one by one, carefully, from every angle. Then he leaned back, clucking his tongue and humming.

"Hmm," he finally said. "Yes. I can see why you were concerned. These appear, at first glance, to be TruTech components, produced by my factory and with my tooling."

Lyons looked at Blancanales and Schwarz, then back to Clayton. "And...?"

"And...they're not," said Clayton. "I can say with certainty that these are brilliant forgeries."

"How can you tell from the photographs alone?" Schwarz asked. ·

Clayton smiled again. "Because I have taken precautions against just this sort of thing." He pressed the intercom on his desk. "Janet, you can bring that in now."

An auburn-haired woman, as attractive as the blonde receptionist and just as tightly clothed, somehow managed to walk into the office on stiletto heels. She entered through a side door that was concealed as part of the paneling in Clayton's office. Lyons could see a workstation in the smaller room beyond.

The woman carried a cardboard carton whose seams were taped with TruTech seals. Clayton accepted the box, looked her up and down and nodded to her. She left through the same concealed door, pressing her fingers against a portion of the paneling to make it pop free.

Clayton reached into his center desk drawer and removed an expensive custom knife. The pearl-inlaid handle bore a silver button, which he pressed, causing the spring-loaded blade to snap out from the front.

Lyons could feel his eyebrows go up.

Clayton cut the seams on the carton and removed the heavy component from within the box. Placing his knife on the desktop, he held up one of Blancanales's photographs. The two parts were identical to the casual eye.

"These are the same part, yes," Clayton said. "Except for this." He turned the component over and showed the Able Team members the shimmering holographic seal set in the base. "This holographic seal is remarkably difficult to counterfeit. I chose it for that reason. In the photographs,

I can see that the seal turns flat and drab when reproduced. My own image remains vibrant and displays a watermark image of my company's logo in the correct lighting. These parts are fakes. They are fakes deliberately created to make it look as if TruTech is involved."

Schwarz took the component when Clayton gestured with it. The Able Team electronics expert examined the holographic watermark carefully.

"Agent, uh, Fishburne?" asked Lyons.

Schwarz looked up. "He's right. He's absolutely right."

"Gentlemen, I assure you, I would never work with the North Koreans, nor any enemy of my country. I love this great nation. This is the greatest country in the world. The arms and arms components I manufacture are dedicated to one and only one purpose. That is preserving our way of life, and saving the lives of as many American soldiers as possible."

Pardon me while I hum the "Battle Hymn of the Republic" behind you, Lyons thought. Aloud, he said, "We were informed that you could give us some insight on those companies that would be able to produce ICBM parts with the same precision."

"In other words," said Clayton, "you were told that I could give you the lowdown on who among my competitors might be trying to ruin me. And I can." Going once more into his desk drawer, Clayton pulled out a legal pad and ripped off the top sheet. "You won't have to go terribly far, relatively speaking," he said. "We're something of a new Silicon Valley for the military-industrial complex down here in these parts." Clayton exaggerated his Southern accent as he said the last few words. He handed the sheet of paper to Lyons. "I've ranked them in order of what I consider greatest capacity to reproduce TruTech's designs," he said. "I believe you may indeed find what you're looking for if you knock on those doors, gentlemen."

"The government will take your input under advisement," Blancanales said smoothly.

"Please, Agent…?"

"Reeves," Blancanales supplied.

"Agent Reeves," said Clayton. "You, Agent Fishburne here—" he indicated Schwarz with a nod "—and Agent Weaving hardly strike me as deskbound types. I would imagine men such as you would be on the front lines of any…direct action…that takes place."

"Thanks," said Lyons, standing. "We'll be leaving now. You've…been a credit to your nation." Lyons hoped he sounded more convincing than he felt.

"That's all I ever want," said Clayton. "Please see Claire at the front desk on the way out. She'll supply you with some marketing literature and other paraphernalia we give out for sales calls. That way it will look like you're just making an ordinary business call, should anyone be, you know, watching as you leave."

"Do you have reason to believe someone is watching your offices, Mr. Clayton?" Blancanales asked.

"No, no," Clayton said quickly. "I just want to make sure I do whatever I can to help you. Thinking of every contingency is something I, you know, something I do. My specialty. It's how TruTech became so successful so quickly."

"Yeah," said Lyons. "Got it. Come on, er, agents."

The trio backtracked, taking the elevator and stopping at the front desk as suggested. When Able Team hit the sidewalk in front of TruTech's headquarters, Schwarz could contain himself no longer.

"You forgot my damned name," Schwarz said.

"What?" Lyons asked as they walked toward their Suburban.

"Agent Fishburne," said Schwarz. "That's the lame moniker you hung on me in the lobby. But when you went to use it in Clayton's office, you forgot who I was supposed to be, didn't you?"

"I did not," Lyons said.

"You did," insisted Schwarz. "You so totally did."

They passed a trio of Harley-Davidsons parked near the front of the employee parking lot across from TruTech. A man dressed in a leather jacket and formal business clothing was preparing to start one. He wore a backpack over his shoulders and was probably taking his bike out on his lunch hour.

"Beautiful Fat Boy," said Lyons.

"Thanks, man," said the employee.

When they were out of earshot of the would-be biker, Lyons said to Schwarz and Blancanales, "Maybe there's something else we should be worried about. Like how he knew I was supposed to be Agent Weaving when I never told him that."

"You think he's got the lobby wired for sound?" asked Schwarz.

"That, or the receptionist simply told him our names," Blancanales pointed out.

Lyons snorted. "Something's not right. I don't like it. I don't like it at all. I feel like I've got crosshairs painted between my shoulder blades."

"Oh, good," said Blancanales. "I was worried it might just be me." The trio had reached their parked SUV. Blancanales tossed Lyons the keys; Lyons unlocked the rig with the push of a button on the electronic fob.

Schwarz's voice held no hint of humor when he said, "No. You're right. I feel it, too. Clayton's definitely hiding something. There's a good chance he's worried his competitors are looking to use force. Muscle him out of the market the old-fashioned way."

"It would explain the high-tech ordnance his little army is wearing, all right," said Lyons. He climbed into the gray Suburban, feeling slightly more secure behind its bullet-resistant armor. The vehicle was an executive-protection model, intended to resist small-arms fire. It wore run-flat tires and had plating beneath the undercarriage to prevent damage to vital engine components. A massive wrap-around steel bumper guarded its grille and headlights.

"Let's call the Farm and bring them up to date," said Lyons. "Pol, pull that map out of the glove compartment, would you? I want to plan the most efficient route."

"Or we could just use the GPS application in our secure phones," said Schwarz. "I mean, since we're not driving a stone carriage pulled by a team of dinosaurs."

"Gadgets," Lyons started to say, swiveling to talk to the electronics expert from the driver's seat. "Why don't you—"

"Guys!" Blancanales shouted. He pointed.

"Is that a rice burner?" Lyons had time to ask.

Automatic gunfire sprayed across the windshield as the whine of multiple motorbike engines enveloped them.

CHAPTER FOUR

Atlanta, Georgia

"Oh no, you did *not*," said Carl Lyons, kicking open the door of the Suburban, leaving the keys in the ignition. The armored windshield was scarred but intact. As Lyons slid from the front seat he dragged his Daewoo shotgun out from behind him. The massive weapon had its drum magazine in place. Using the armored door for cover, he took aim and triggered a blast from the automatic weapon. A gout of flame leaped from the Daewoo's muzzle.

There were five gunmen, all dressed in black fatigues and all driving sport motorcycles. Lyons had lined up on the last of these with the Daewoo, aiming low, letting the big shotgun buck upward with each discharge. The gunman's motorcycle disintegrated beneath him.

So did the lower portion of his spine.

Lyons looked back at the Suburban, then at the speeding sport bikes. He shouted, "Pol!"

Blancanales stuck his head out from the passenger side of the truck. Lyons launched the shotgun at him like a heavy spear. Blancanales caught it, his expression one of bewilderment. Lyons pointed after the bikes and said, "Go!"

Carl "Ironman" Lyons, for his part, ran for the employee parking lot.

"Justice Department!" he roared, bearing down on the

employee with the Harley Fat Boy. "Justice Department! This is an emergency!"

"Uh," said the biker. "What?"

Lyons pushed the man off the bike as gently as he could, which was not very much so. The biker shouted in outrage, but Lyons could only call over his shoulder, "Official business!" With practiced movements he urged the big Harley forward, tearing off in the direction the motorcycle-riding gunmen had gone.

Oh, he was going to hear it from Brognola and Price over this.

He passed the Suburban easily, despite the fact that Blancanales, behind the wheel, probably had the accelerator to the floor. All that armor made the truck too heavy for a truly high-speed pursuit, especially against crotch-rockets like these. The Harley might itself not be up to the challenge, but it was at least a better option than the Chevy.

"Come on, baby," Lyons muttered into the wind. "Faster."

Two of the bikes' owners looked back to see their comrade blown from the saddle of his sport bike. They peeled off from the other two and circled back, aiming for the flanks of the speeding Suburban, coming close enough to the armored SUV that their hands reached out to touch its flanks and steady their bikes.

Lyons withdrew his Colt Python and jacked back the hammer.

Schwarz and Blancanales could deal with the pair circling the SUV. He could hear more automatic gunfire behind him. The sport-bike riders wore black bandannas tied over their mouths and noses to conceal their features. The Czech Skorpion machine pistols in their fists were full automatic models, illegal for most mere mortals to possess in the States. Whoever these killers were, they were clearly an organized kill team. They had targeted Able Team and were using defined team tactics in an attempt to eliminate their targets.

"Should have sent more guys," said Carl Lyons. He extended his gun hand while guiding the Fat Boy with his off hand. The custom-tuned action "broke" like a glass rod, sending a .357 Magnum hollowpoint round rocketing from the barrel.

The round punched one of the two bikers in the back of the neck, tearing out his throat and dumping him from the seat of his motorcycle. The bike was moving fast enough that it flipped end over end and crashed into a parked car. The nearly headless body rolled into a crumpled heap near the car's rear bumper. Blood was everywhere.

Lyons poured on the speed.

The Fat Boy's engine bellowed its fury as he pushed it to its absolute limit. The outlying commercial district in which TruTech's facility was located had given way to Atlanta suburbs. The streets here were not as wide and they were filled with civilian bystanders. That was not good. Lyons jammed his revolver back in his shoulder holster and focused on dodging and weaving through traffic without dumping the bike.

The gunman on the sport bike was not as experienced a rider and was forced to slow as he took each new corner. This gave Lyons a chance to gain ground, despite the fact that his borrowed hog was not as maneuverable. He considered taking a shot, but with the number of pedestrians and other bystanders they were passing, not to mention civilians in their own cars, he did not dare.

The gunman on the sport bike appeared to be reaching around with his Skorpion.

Don't you try for it, Lyons thought. Don't do it.

He was going for it. Lyons could not allow innocent

people to be caught in the cross fire. His only option was to draw the gunman's fire at a trajectory that would put only one person in peril: himself. Lyons gunned the Harley and pulled forward in traffic as the enemy shooter slowed down, angling for a shot.

"Come on, you bastard," Lyons shouted. "Right here. I'm right here!"

The gunman shouted something Lyons couldn't understand through the black mask over the shooter's face. The Skorpion came up, the barrel tracking toward Lyon's midsection. The two motorcycles were now abreast of each other.

Lyons leaned hard to one side. His Harley nosed in near the sport bike. Kicking out with his leg, the Able Team leader smashed the shooter's thigh with the sole of his steel-toed hiking boot.

"Road rash, bast—" Lyons roared. The last word was cut off by the sound of the sport bike careening into the curb and scraping across the sidewalk, sending its rider tumbling over the handlebars and onto concrete. He left a red streak to mark his path.

Lyons braked his Harley and laid down rubber skidding to a stop. His Colt Python was back in his fist before he had left the Fat Boy. The gunman lay still. As Lyons approached, lawn sprinklers began chugging away, drenching the fallen shooter.

The former LAPD officer resisted the urge to pump a hollowpoint round into the prone man. They needed at least one of these guys alive if they were going to learn anything about how and why Able Team had come under fire. Who was the shooter working for? How had he and his people known to hit Able Team? Was it a coincidence? Had they blundered into a street war between Clayton and a competing high-tech interest?

I miss the old days, Lyons thought. When gangbangers had funny hair and drove tacky cars. You could spot 'em more easily.

Lyons planted the toe of his boot in the gunman's flank and shoved.

The injured would-be killer rolled and surged to his feet. A knife flicked open in his hand as he came up. Lyons dodged the spear-point blade and laid the barrel of his Python across the man's face. Blood spurted from the shooter's nose. He went down on his back, then rolled, coming up with his Skorpion again, which he'd apparently rolled right over.

"Damn it," Lyons said, and pulled the trigger.

The bullet snapped the man's head back and laid him down once more. He would not get up again.

I guess I know what the last thing was that went through his mind, Lyons thought. He shook his head. There had been no choice; he could not have the man shooting without restraint in a residential neighborhood. He checked the Skorpion, pulling its bolt back just far enough to verify that there was a round in the chamber. The little squirt gun was neither the most accurate nor the most powerful weapon available, but terrorists and Third World hitters loved the things. They fired fast, were small and light, and made it easy for the operator to spray and pray. This one was chambered in 9x18 Makarov.

For all the good it would do, Lyons snapped a picture of the dead man with his secure satellite phone. Images taken by the phone's camera were automatically encoded and transmitted to the Farm for analysis. It was understood that any dead men so photographed were being documented for analysis and background checks. You learned a lot about your enemy by examining the ranks of his fallen.

Somewhere in the distance, Lyons could hear police sirens. They were a long way off yet. Lyons went to one knee and patted down the corpse. He found another magazine for the Skorpion, a gas-station-brand condom sealed in its wrapper and a pewter money clip with two hundred dollars in twenties. There was no identification. He secured the money and tossed the prophylactic.

The knife was a commercial, production model with a blade the length of his palm and an aluminum handle. It was a quality knife, not dissimilar to blades "Cowboy" Kissinger had issued the team on past missions, complete with an automatic safety catch that blocked the locking mechanism when the blade opened. The cross-guard was integral to the blade and allowed it to be snapped open with a flick of the finger. Lyons pocketed the knife, as well. He went to the Harley and prepared to fire it up again.

The Skorpion had a black nylon strap attached to its folding metal stock. Lyons slung it over his shoulder and tucked the spare magazine in his back pocket.

"Carl!" The voice was Blancanales's, and it came from the earbud transceiver he wore in his left ear. "Carl, Gadgets says, per the GPS locator in your phone, we're coming up on your location. Fast."

"What? Where?" Lyons had time to ask, just as the gray armored Suburban thundered past him. It was trailed by the two sport-bike gunmen who remained, and this time their guns were blazing. Fortunately, the rounds were being absorbed by the massive target that was the SUV. Lyons prayed the ricochets stayed on the asphalt and found no passersby.

The Harley rumbled to life beneath the big cop. He pushed it hard, pursuing his teammates and the other two gunners.

"What happened to your guy?" Schwarz said through the transceiver connection.

"Sidewalk poisoning," said Lyons.

"And that first guy had lower-back problems," said Schwarz. "Had."

"Yeah, yeah," Lyons muttered. "Take the side street up ahead. We want to lead them away from this neighborhood."

"On it," said Blancanales. The SUV's engine was loud enough, as Blancanales goosed it, that Lyons could hear it over the connection. "My foot's getting tired."

"There's always cruise control," said Schwarz.

The bikers were having no trouble keeping up, but Blancanales led them on a merry chase anyway, using quick turns and skidding, sliding, rubber-burning maneuvers to make the Suburban as elusive a target as the big vehicle could be. Every now and then one of the bikers would trigger a short burst from a Skorpion, but they were being sparing with their ammo now. Reloading while also trying to chase the SUV would prove problematic. It was occurring to them that the longer they chased the truck, the fewer rounds they would have at their disposal should they catch it.

Lyons shifted left, then right, trying to line up a shot. Twice Blancanales took hard turns that put the Suburban squealing across lanes and over curbs, bringing angry honks from civilian drivers. At least some of those drivers would be using their wireless phones to call police, reporting armed men speeding through traffic. The sirens of approaching law-enforcement vehicles were getting louder. Despite the moving target, the officers would home in on the action, and that was something Lyons wanted to avoid. He did not want local police driving into a stream of full-auto bullets. As a former cop he had nothing but respect for his fellow law-enforcement officers, but the average patrolman was not prepared for submachine gun battles in the midst of commuter traffic.

The surrounding area shifted from residential to commercial. Lyons came up so close behind one of the two gunmen that his front wheel almost touched the rear tire of the man's sport bike.

Too late, the black-clad hitter realized he had become the quarry. He tried to swivel in his seat, causing his sport bike to wobble dangerously, but could not manage to maintain pursuit and fire behind him at the same time. That bespoke, to Lyons, a fairly mediocre level of training, but he wasn't going to punch a gift horse in the face. Or whatever the saying was supposed to be.

Carl Lyon shoved the Skorpion to full extension on its sling, using the nylon strap to brace the weapon. He triggered a blast that emptied the squirt gun's magazine. The hitter was sprayed all over the back of the Suburban as bullets pocked the armor of the truck's rear doors.

"Hey!" Schwarz said over his transceiver. "You're shooting us."

"Know your backstop," Lyons said, narrowly missing the dead hitter's fallen sport bike. He paused, then said, "Pol. That parking lot up ahead. Looks like a pick-and-pull yard."

"I see it," said Blancanales. The Suburban swerved and headed for the empty lot. A sign on the corrugated metal fence fronting the junkyard listed the place's hours. It was closed today.

"Hit the brakes," said Lyons. "Now."

Brake lights flared. Lyons broke right, skirting the flank of the SUV.

The remaining sport-biker crashed into the back of the Suburban. He was thrown from his crotch-rocket and rolled several times on the cracked asphalt, shouting something indecipherable as he went.

Lyons stopped, kicked out the Harley's stand and dismounted. He unslung the recovered Skorpion he carried and swapped out the empty magazine for his lone spare. He was too far away to reach the fallen shooter in time, but Schwarz, piling out of the passenger seat of the Suburban, was not. The Stony Man electronics expert carried his 93-R machine pistol. As the enemy hitter tried to bring up his own Skorpion, Schwarz kicked him in the face.

"I'd like to get your insurance information, sir," he said.

"Sock it," growled Lyons. He grabbed the man by the collar of his fatigues with his free hand and hoisted him to his feet. "I'm going to shove the barrel of this stupid little machine gun in your mouth," he warned. "You're going to tell me who sent you or I'll blow your childhood memories out both your ears."

"Carl!" Schwarz shouted.

Lyons hit the ground. He dragged the gunman with him. He was fast, but the physics of it was against him. The bullet—fired from a rifle, judging from the heavy crack of its passing—tore through the hitter's skull and left a white pockmark on the Suburban's armor.

"There!" said Blancanales, rounding the driver's side of the Suburban and bringing his M-16 to his shoulder.

There was a sixth man, apparently. He had followed them, holding himself in reserve, and now stood bracing a bolt-action rifle on top of a public mailbox. Behind him was a cinder-block building, evidently some kind of commercial building supply house. There was no traffic on the narrow side street. Lyons looked left, then right, and snapped open his borrowed Skorpion's wire stock.

Blancanales began firing single shots from the M-16.

A second rifle bullet tore a hole in the asphalt by Lyons's feet. It should have been an easy shot, but Blancanales's cover fire was having the desired effect. The sniper had rushed it and was now hurrying to run the bolt of his weapon.

"I can see him shaking from here," said Blancanales. He fired twice more. The shots were intended to unnerve the sniper, not kill him. "Help me herd him, will you?"

Without a word, Lyons fired his Skorpion empty, focusing on the right side of the mailbox. The sniper dropped his rifle and went left, trying to make the end of the street, which was exactly what Blancanales had been going for. He took careful aim, let out a breath and punched a 5.56 mm round through the running man's left calf.

The sniper fell.

"Let's collect him," said Lyons. "Gadgets, watch our backs."

Schwarz nodded. He took up a trailing position as Blancanales and Lyons advanced on the sixth shooter.

As they approached, the gunman was reaching for something in his fatigues.

"Hands!" Schwarz shouted. He held his 93-R in both hands, his support hand wrapped around the trigger guard and the metal fold-down forward grip. "Let me see your hands!"

The gunman held out his hand triumphantly. He was holding a grenade.

"You will grant me safe passage!" he started to say, his voice heavily accented. Lyons placed him as Middle Eastern, but figured he'd have to be blind, drunk and stupid not to pick up on that. "I will kill us all! Back away! Back away!"

The gunman tried to stand. His leg was injured and would not take his weight. He stumbled.

The spoon slipped from beneath the man's fingers and sprang free.

"Uh-oh," said Schwarz.

The hitter tried to chamber his arm for a throw. His injured leg collapsed completely. He dropped the grenade—and promptly fell on it.

The men of Able Team flattened themselves to the sidewalk.

The unmistakably wet explosion was muffled by the hitter's body. Lyons rolled to avoid the worst of the debris and found himself facing Schwarz. The electronics expert propped his head up on one arm.

"So we're up against some kind of suicide squad," he said, deadpan.

Lyons glared. The only sound, apart from the ringing in his ears, was that of approaching local cop cars.

"Too soon," said Blancanales.

"Just for that," said Lyons, "you get to photograph what's left."

"Thanks a lot," said Schwarz.

With Schwarz so occupied, Blancanales and Lyons returned to the Suburban. "We're going to have to find the ones who fell along the way," Blancanales said. "And we're going to need a cleanup crew."

"Call the Farm," said Lyons. He bent and retrieved first one, then a second Skorpion. Tucking one of the weapons under his arm, he began disassembling the other, throwing the parts onto the parking lot. Then he repeated the process for the second. As the first of the squad cars rolled toward Able Team with lights and sirens spun up, he held up his hands, palms out, to show he was not holding a weapon.

"Stop where you are! On the ground! On the ground!" came the shouts from the police.

"Justice Department," Lyons countered. "I have credentials in my pocket. I'm going to remove them and hand them to you."

"Slow!" said the nervous officer, who was climbing out of his squad car with what looked, to Lyons's eye, like a .40 caliber Smith & Wesson pointing in the Able Team leader's direction.

It took some time to get matters straightened out. Eventually the local cops accepted that the men of Able Team were federal agents of some kind. They were none too happy about the dead bodies. After working out an agreement wherein the corpses would be turned over to the medical examiner's office after their photographs and fingerprints were taken, Lyons, Blancanales and Schwarz climbed back into the Suburban. Blancanales established a connection with the Farm and put his secure phone on speaker, placing the phone on the dashboard of the battle-scarred SUV.

"Price," said the Farm's mission controller.

"Able," said Lyons. "We have made contact. Six dead, no prisoners. Unfortunately."

"Understood, Ironman," said Price. "Bear and his team are running facial recognition now."

"Were the macro images of the fingerprints the locals took of sufficient detail for you to run them?" Schwarz asked.

"Bear said he enhanced them. They should be sufficient. What did you get from Clayton?"

"He's hiding something," said Lyons. "I'll put money on it. He's got a lot of security on hand, even for somebody who makes missile parts. Heavily armed bruisers lining the walls."

"You think he's dirty?" asked Price.

"I think maybe he's involved in a turf war," Lyons said. "The whole thing smells. We're going to follow the list he gave us in the order of his priorities. Shake the tree, see what falls."

"A tried-and-true strategy."

"It is that," said Lyons. "Any updates for us?"

"Not at this time," said Price. "I'll let you know when we've sifted through your body count."

"Understood. Able out." Lyons nodded to Blancanales, who closed the connection.

"Now what?" said Blancanales. He looked at the windshield and then out the window on his side. The gray Suburban was covered in gouges and scars from bullets striking its armor.

"We should probably find a car wash," Schwarz said.

Lyons rolled his eyes, started the Suburban and sent them rolling into traffic.

CHAPTER FIVE

The Philippine Sea

The Zodiac F470 Combat Rubber Raiding Craft, or CRRC, was typical of its type, equipped with a powerful but quiet fifty-five horsepower motor. The CRRC's high-pressure deck system, coupled with a rigid aluminum frame, made it possible to support the motor's weight. The motor itself incorporated a high-pressure impeller, not an exposed propeller, and the entire boat was coated in a skin that made it resistant to tearing. All in all, Phoenix Force was riding in style. Calvin James hefted his Kalashnikov-pattern rifle and jacked the bolt back far enough to check the chamber. His teammates did likewise.

The disguised cargo ship was a modified multideck vessel capable of acting as a passenger craft, too. Powered by two Wärtsilä 12V46C diesel engines, its deadweight tonnage was 6,500 and it boasted 1,750 lane meters of deck space. Its generators produced 25,200 kilowatts and its service speed was a workmanlike 23 knots. James knew all this because the data had been sent to his secure satellite phone by Stony Man Farm. The intelligence was the result of satellite imaging cross-indexed with transit data from the vessel's ports of call. This ship, too, flew a Taiwanese flag, which was as false as the vessel's name of record: *Plumage Bird,* roughly translated.

"All right, lads," said McCarter. "Ready."

James slung his AK and prepared the grappling hook. Rafael Encizo did the same. They would be the first up the lines, followed by McCarter and Hawkins. Manning would come up last, guarding their ascent until the team covered his own from the weather deck of the ship.

Balancing carefully in the CRRC, James prepared to hurl the hook. Grimaldi would be up there somewhere, and James thought, as he half crouched to make his throw, that he could hear the rotor blades of the Cobra somewhere in the distance. The acoustics of the ocean were funny that way. It was hard to judge distance at all. Sound traveled farther than it had any right to do, sometimes, and at other times seemed almost to be swallowed whole by the waves. While their Navy transport was not too far off, it had nonetheless seemed like a long, lonely trip in the little rubber combat craft. It was at times like these that James's respect for ancient mariners—men who traveled the seas in tiny, fragile wooden sailing ships—increased greatly.

"G-Force to Phoenix," said Stony Man pilot Jack Grimaldi in their earpiece transceivers. "Getting ready to make a racket."

"Go," said McCarter. "Green light."

"Roger."

It took a moment for the noise to register over the sounds of the sea, but when they did, the explosions were unmistakable. Grimaldi was using the Cobra's guns and missiles to attack…nothing at all, creating a lot of commotion and light. The distraction was necessary to facilitate the daylight raid.

From the F470, the men of Phoenix Force could hear footsteps on the weather deck above. Grimaldi was calling attention to the opposite side of the ship, by design. It was all the opening Phoenix needed. James threw his grapple.

The hook caught on the railing high above. The hull of

the ship was painted a bright red, but the paint was fading, giving way to the mottle of rust and an accumulation of seagoing debris. James heaved himself up and noted, in the corner of his eye, Encizo paralleling him on his own line.

This is some serious ninja action right here, thought James. I don't care how many times we do it. I will never feel like I'm not in a comic book.

Once on the deck, James found himself beneath the ship's twin exhaust stacks, which could only mean he was close to the vessel's engines. He unslung his rifle and covered the deck beyond while Encizo covered the CRRC. It was only moments before McCarter, Hawkins and Manning had joined the two commandos. Manning carried a cable tied to his belt, which led to the F470. He and Hawkins hauled the craft onto the deck.

McCarter gave the signal. James and Encizo went left, skirting the perimeter of the deck in what would be a clockwise rotation once they reached the rail. The other three Stony Man operatives went right. They were covered by the stacks and those portions of the ship's superstructure that stood between them and the North Korean soldiers whom James assumed were massing on the port side of the ship. The pops and cracks of semiautomatic gunfire could be heard. The crew of the *Plumage Bird* was shooting blindly into the sea. Grimaldi would be stationed, per their raiding plan, much too far out for them to really see him, much less effectively target him with small arms. It did occur to James to worry that the North Korean drug ship might be equipped with anti-air hardware. The briefing did not indicate that this was likely; the first ship, which had been well equipped, had not held aboard it anything that the Cobra's countermeasures could not handle even if it had been deployed.

Hard to worry about shooting down enemy air support,

James thought, when you're more concerned with eating a bullet so your family back home isn't tortured. He shook his head. Phoenix Force had faced some truly dangerous adversaries. Some of those had been worthy foes. Others had been vicious, murderous, even evil men and women. These North Korean drones weren't evil. They were simply dangerous tools, obstacles thrown in their path by a corrupt government. James took no pleasure in taking them down.

Which did not mean he would hesitate for a second to do so.

The two Phoenix Force men covered each other in turns as they moved from one portion of the deck to the next, always careful to avoid placing themselves in the line of sight from the elevated bridge at the bow. The *Plumage Bird* was relatively steady at anchor. Sporadic gunfire continued to echo across the water.

As they neared the bow of the ship they saw the clump of crewmen reacting to Grimaldi's diversion. These men did not wear uniforms. They were dressed as civilian sailors.

"If those are Korean military," James whispered to Encizo, "I'm with the Commodores."

"Something's up," Encizo whispered back. "This isn't standard procedure at all."

The sailors, if that's what they truly were, stood armed with SKS carbines. The forerunner to the Kalashnikov family of assault rifles, the SKS was a workmanlike weapon chambered in the same 7.62 x 39 round that the AK-47 fired. Its internal magazine held ten rounds and was loaded with stripper clips from the top. It was not a battle rifle so much as it was a scouting and even hunting piece, in James's opinion, but such weapons were cheap and readily available on the international market. It was just the sort of thing with which the North Koreans might equip second-line or backup operators. It was also what James would choose were he to arm the crew of the ship to free soldiers for other duties.

The group of gunmen continued to pop rounds blindly at the horizon with their carbines. The pace of the firing tapered off as Grimaldi's own noisemaking tapered off. The gunmen argued with each other, probably about whether the threat posed was significant. James frowned. Had their intelligence been wrong? Were these men no more than in the wrong place at the wrong time?

"Mark," said David McCarter through the transceivers. "Eyes on hostile contacts."

That was McCarter, indicating that the rest of Stony Man Farm was in position. They would be appropriately stationed to catch the gunmen in a cross fire. The question now was whether to engage.

The shooters were tiring of firing at something they couldn't see. One of them said something that extracted ugly laughter from the others. He moved out of sight for a moment, into a gap in the superstructure. When he emerged, he was dragging a girl by the hair. Her skin was darker than theirs; she appeared, to James, to be a Pinay—a Filipina.

One of the shooters stood guard with his SKS held casually in both hands. The rest began to loosen or unbuckle their pants. One man used his own rope belt to tie the frightened girl's hands behind her back. She was screaming. He took a filthy bandanna from his back pocket and shoved it into her mouth.

Oh, that's engage, thought James. Definitely engage.

"Hold," said McCarter in his ear. James knew why. They had a very real, very simple logistics problem. The girl was surrounded by a circle of the enemy. If Phoenix Force took them down from either vantage point, there was a very real risk of hitting the girl. There wasn't much time before things got very bad for her, however. Phoenix Force had worked together for many, many years; there was very little communication required among the team members. Every one of them was capable of assessing the situation and determining the available options.

"I got this," said James.

"Go," said McCarter without hesitation. James looked at Encizo, who nodded. Encizo brought his Kalashnikov copy to this shoulder, ready to cover James should things go from bad to worse.

James put his rifle on the deck.

He stepped out and walked across the deck, moving slowly and deliberately. The would-be rapists saw him and, astonished, stopped speaking. James put his hands out, palms forward, and smiled.

"Can anybody tell me how to get to East 56th Street?" James asked. "I am *so* lost."

The gunmen exchanged glances before one of them shouted an angry command. The words were, if James were any judge, Korean. The veteran Phoenix Force warrior simply kept advancing, counting off his steps, judging the distance between himself and the nearest "sailor." The girl, meanwhile, was on her knees on the deck amid the clump of men, her eyes wide, looking quickly this way and that. The terror on her face was plain enough. She was certain something horrible was going to befall her. Only the direction from which the horror would come remained in question.

"I think I got off the train at the wrong stop," said James. The closest of the gunmen was within arm's reach now. His hand snaked to his belt, reaching for the butt of a rusted revolver tucked there.

Calvin James ripped his combat knife from his belt and

brought it across the man's neck in a single fluid movement. He spun as he did so, moving inside and to his left, avoiding the spray of blood that followed. Without hesitation, he spun and stepped past the dying man, into the next soldier, then the next, cutting a path through the enemy. His blade moved like a sewing machine as he thrust it, reversed, into the neck of the next man.

He had just carved an exit route.

Grabbing the screaming girl by the wrist, he pulled her with him, slashing at yet another of the enemy before reaching the rail on the opposite side of the group. Careful to hold the blade of his bloody knife away from his body, he tackled the girl to the deck, covering her with his body.

"Now!" he said.

Encizo, McCarter, Hawkins and Manning opened up from their positions. The remaining armed men fell dead around James and the girl, all of them shot through the head.

The girl finally stopped screaming.

Footsteps rang on gangways leading to the adjoining hatches in the superstructure. There were more hostiles coming their way from within the ship, drawn by the noise of the action on the deck. McCarter pointed to his own eyes and then to the hatch opposite where they stood.

"Gary, see to the hostage," McCarter ordered. "The rest of you lads, on me."

McCarter was up then. Manning came to his side and gestured; he took the girl from James and ushered her in the opposite direction.

Encizo whistled through his teeth. James looked to his teammate, saw Encizo with the rifle and tossed it to James, who caught it and ran the bolt back.

Time to go to work.

James took his position on Encizo's flank. The team

broke into pairs and stood at either side of the hatch. From a pouch on his web gear, McCarter produced a shaped charge—little more than a lump of plastic explosive with a detonator stuck in its mass. He pressed the switch on the detonator as he slapped the charge on the hatch.

The four commandos edged away from the hatch against the bulkhead.

The timing could not have been better. The lock bar on the hatch was just starting to move when the charge blew. The hostiles on the other side of the hatch walked into the concussion of the blast followed by the steel hatch itself. The door was blown inward and crushed one man to the deck inside. Dark red blood was everywhere.

The man beneath the door was wearing a North Korean military uniform.

McCarter, in the lead, positioned himself above a manway that led down. Whatever he saw prompted him to spray the passageway with the contents of his rifle's magazine.

James took a grenade from his web gear, yanked the pin and rolled the bomb down the manway. McCarter stepped back. The explosion in the close quarters of the ship made James's ears ring, but the screams from below were proof enough of the success of his throw.

There was no time to wait. If they allowed the men belowdecks to regroup, the initiative would be lost and they would be climbing down into a firestorm.

James found himself staring into the eyes of a naked girl.

Like the Filipina on deck, this girl was young, probably early twenties. The North Korean soldier standing behind her held her in a chokehold. The barrel of his Tokarev was pressed to her temple. The girl said something, probably a plea for mercy. The soldier barked a reply. The barrel of his gun wavered as he spoke—

James fired, blowing the man's ear off, turning his head in that direction. He lost his grip on the hostage and dropped his pistol as both his hands went to his bloody head. James caught the girl as she tried to run past and handed her off to Hawkins, who was behind him in the corridor.

"Don't you move," ordered James. The North Korean soldier looked up at him, muttered something, and reached with one blood-covered hand for the Tokarev on the deck.

Calvin James shot him dead.

"What the hell was that about?" said James. The soldier and his hostage had come from a side corridor. He checked his secure phone; according to the ship's plans, as obtained by Stony Man Farm, this was an auxiliary bunk room, smaller than the main crew compartments. He went to this hatch and, after a nod from McCarter, wrenched the lever to open the mechanism.

The smell that hit him made his eyes water. The chamber within reeked of human waste. Chained to the metal supports of the berths in this bunk room were two more women. No, James thought, there were three. The third, however, was slumped on the floor. Her head hung at an unnatural angle.

Hawkins covered the hatch. The rest of the team waited in the corridor beyond. James went to the prone woman and placed two fingers against her neck. Her head shifted. Two dead, glazed white orbs stared back at him.

Damn, he thought. Too late. Far too late.

"She died two days ago," said one of the other women. She was the oldest of the three, possibly in her thirties. She wore only a towel wrapped around her body. All three women exhibited signs of having been beaten. James went to her and checked her chain. The multitool he carried in his web gear was all he needed to pry open the lock. He did the same for the second woman, who looked at him fearfully. The one who had spoken said something to her in Spanish.

"She has no English," said the older woman. "No education, poor thing."

"What happened here?"

"We are prostitutes," she admitted. "We were aboard a fishing boat. The *Magandang Umaga*. We were at anchor. You know. To party."

"Where's the crew that, uh, hired you?"

"Gone, with the rest of my girls. Taken by the Koreans when they boarded our vessel."

"Taken? Taken where?"

"I heard them speak of Calayan Island," the woman said. "I know nothing else. You are American?"

"Something like that, yeah."

"Then I thank you. Unless you wish me to...?"

It took a moment for James to realize what she was saying. "Uh, no, lady. No thank you, I mean. You two stay here. It ain't over yet."

"We will do as you say." James turned to go and she called after him. "There was another girl. Inez."

"Pretty young Filipina girl?" James asked.

"Yes."

"She's fine," James said. "When the shooting's over we'll get you somewhere safe, get you checked out."

"That is all I ask."

McCarter nodded to James.

"Let's move out," the Briton said.

Descending to the lower decks, they had time to take cover in the corridor leading to the cargo hold before the enemy mounted another offensive. Shells rang from the bulkheads. The air was close and thick with gun smoke.

Pressing the advantage produced by their bold assault, Phoenix Force breached the hold and found themselves in the midst of another drug refinery. This one was haphazardly stacked with crates and barrels, boxes and cartons. A handful of uniformed North Korean soldiers were hunkered down amid the machinery at the opposite end of the laboratory. They fired Kalashnikov rifles and Tokarev pistols at the invaders.

Without prompting, the men of Phoenix Force split up. McCarter and Encizo fired on the high line, while James and Hawkins went flat on their bellies and began shooting low. Soon James had tagged one, then a second soldier, by shooting their feet out from under them. Skimming bullets along the deck on full automatic proved surprisingly easy. Phoenix Force's enemies lay at the end of a wide metal funnel.

Then the shooting stopped.

"Report," said McCarter.

"Clear," said Encizo.

"Clear," repeated Hawkins.

"Manning here. All quiet on deck. The hostage remains secure."

"I'm clear," James said. "And I've got the jackpot." He went to one of the bins on the floor nearby. The plastic packages of meth and what he presumed was heroin were obvious enough, but the machine parts were of greater interest. He took one of them out of the packaging. "Look at this."

"That's a holographic seal, all right," said McCarter, nodding. "The very one that's supposed to be hard to counterfeit, according to the updates from the Farm. Rafe, get a shot of this."

Encizo nodded and took out his phone. He keyed up the camera application and snapped several shots for scrambled transmission to the Farm.

"Does anyone see a pattern in these dead guys?" Hawkins asked, pointing to the corpses of two North Korean soldiers.

"They're all North Korean," said James.

"Very funny," Hawkins said. His drawl was thicker than normal when he said, "Look at these two, and those over there." He pointed. "I was checking rank tabs on the ones we met along the way. Did anybody notice something odd?"

"Let's have it, T.J.," said McCarter. "What is it?"

"There isn't a single one of these fellers with any rank to him," Hawkins said. "No officers."

James nodded. "That makes sense. The higher-ups are off enjoying themselves and they left the grunts to keep an eye on the shop here."

"Which," said McCarter, "leaves us with…"

"Calayan Island," said James. "The briefing files said that's one of the possible ports of call for the drug ships."

"If hostages are involved, our timetable must advance," said McCarter. "Gary?"

"Here," said Manning.

"Place a call to the Farm. Ask them to go through channels, see if there's a ship missing. What was it she called it?" he asked James.

"Magandang Umaga," said James.

"Right," said McCarter. "Ask them if they're looking for a vessel by that name and, if so, how many are presumed missing with it."

"Got it," said Manning.

"The rest of you, let's split up and police the ship. We need to secure any other stragglers, tie up any loose ends before we get Barb back on the blower and plan our next move."

"And then?" James asked.

"Then we pay a little visit to Calayan Island."

CHAPTER SIX

Outside Mobile, Alabama

"According to the travel company's trip index," said Schwarz, pretending to consult the glossy flyer he had picked up at a roadside rest stop, "this five-hour drive took us just under four hours. You were speeding so hard I think we almost went back in time, Ironman."

"Shut up, Gadgets," said Lyons.

Blancanales looked out the passenger-side window. "'Engineering Consulting Synergies.' Sounds bland."

"Sounds like a shell corporation," Schwarz said. "You know, give the company a boring name that sounds like every other business name and buzzword you can think of. That way, nobody remembers it."

Lyons connected his secure satellite phone to the truck's wireless network. He tapped a button on the touch screen and waited as the call was routed through the Farm's scramblers. The voice that answered was that of Barbara Price.

"Able Team," she said, "we were just about to ping you. Bear and his team have updates for us."

"Hello, Barb," said Blancanales. "Go ahead."

"Transmitting full dossiers to your secure phones now," said Price. "The preliminary findings are...unexpected, to say the least."

"How so?" asked Blancanales.

"Your dead men are all Iranian black-bag operators," she said. "We've traced the majority of them to a some-time terror outfit called the Revolutionary Path of God. It styles itself as your typical radical jihad-style group, but in reality it's a guns-for-hire circle that uses radical terror ties to market itself."

"Never thought I'd see that used as a hiring plus," Lyons said. "The obvious question then becomes, how did the Iranians know to target us? And was it us specifically they wanted? Or anyone seen talking to Clayton?"

"We're doing what we can to trace the shell corporations and holding companies that Revolutionary Path of God uses to transfer funds," Price told them. "As you can imagine, it's slow going. There are a lot of transactions to untangle. If we can find a link, we'll follow it."

"We may have more information for you," Lyons said. To Schwarz, he asked, "They still with us?"

"Just circled the block," Schwarz said. "Three of them, conspicuous as a hot blonde at a science fiction convention."

"Remind me to have a long conversation with you sometime," Lyons muttered.

"What is that?" Price asked.

Lyons raised his voice so the Farm could hear him. "We were followed. They're not exactly doing a good job of staying under the radar. Three identical black SUVs, late-model domestics, riding practically in each other's tailpipes and on our bumpers the entire ride here. It's not a coincidence."

"Do you want me to scramble backup?" Price asked. "We may not be able to get a blacksuit contingent in place in time, but I can pull a special operations team as well as local law enforcement, even a SWAT team."

"No," Lyons said. "Until we have more information,

our tail may be the only lead we're likely to get. I'd rather wait for them to come at us and then bust them open, see what falls out."

"Bad guy piñatas?" Schwarz whispered. Lyons shot him a venomous look.

"Where are your traveling companions now?" Price asked.

"Melted away," Blancanales replied. "They broke in two directions, two west, one east. Could be hiding around the block or even in the parking garage under the ECS building." The parking garage signs were clearly marked. Able Team had passed several of them before parking directly and illegally in front of the main entrance.

"Be careful, you three," Price said.

"We won't," said Lyons. "But we'll get the job done."

"Understood," said Price. "Farm, out."

"Able Team, out." Lyons cut the connection.

"I could be wrong," said Blancanales, "but it looks like there's a lot of security in there. Enough to make Clayton's building look undefended."

"What have you got?" Lyons asked.

"At least four or five uniformed security personnel," said Blancanales. "Moving around like they're nervous or something."

"Gadgets," said Lyons, "get one of the duffel bags."

Schwarz nodded. The heavy gear bags they carried in the truck's cargo compartment were long enough to conceal even Lyons's Daewoo 12-gauge. Without prompting, Schwarz began filling the bag with the team's heavy weaponry and spare magazines.

"Let's go see if we can't cause a ruckus," Lyons said.

"I love it when he talks like that," said Schwarz.

Blancanales shook his head.

They entered the lobby of the ECS building. Lyons immediately took the initiative. "Federal officers," he announced loudly. "We're here to inspect the grounds of your facility in an effort to satisfy a national security condition. You are hereby ordered to comply with this Justice Department investigation."

The lobby was indeed full of uniformed security men. They looked at each other silently, then back at Able Team, glaring. They wore holstered pistols on their belts, although nothing as exotic as the high-tech hardware Claridge Clayton's people sported.

The guards began to close in on them.

"Excuse me," said the receptionist. She was an older woman, a brunette, and had probably been attractive enough in her day. Lyons took out the Justice Department credentials he and the rest of the team carried for these occasions. Flashing the engraved badge and identification did not faze the woman. "You can't just walk in here and —"

"Lady," said Lyons, "I *can* just walk in here. And if your lobby goons don't back off a few paces, I'll be happy to hold a conference on the many *ways* in which I can just walk in here, starting with a grand opening sale on asskickings." In one large hand he grabbed the telephone on the desk and slammed it down in front of her. "Get me somebody in upper management who can walk us through this facility."

The receptionist looked horrified. "Just what is this about, sir?"

"It's about whether your corporation is shipping missile components abroad, in violation of federal export restrictions," said Blancanales. "I suggest you do as he asks, miss. It would be the fastest way to resolve this."

Her hands shaking, the receptionist dialed a number on her phone. She cupped the receiver with her hand and turned her body away from them as she spoke.

"Five bucks says the weasel she calls leaves a slime trail when he walks," Lyons whispered to Blancanales and Schwarz.

"You're mixing your scumbag animals," whispered Schwarz.

The guards continued to mill around, doing their best to look intimidating, shooting hard glares at the three Stony Man operatives. Lyons could feel himself rising to the bait, at least at an emotional level. Something here wasn't right. He could smell it. There was too much aggression from these men, and there were too damned many of them for a legitimate manufacturing operation, even one as sensitive as a defense industry contractor. The big former cop flexed his fists. It would be *so* satisfying to smash the tough-guy look off the faces of each of those thugs...

The elevator at the east end of the lobby chimed. The doors opened and a spindly man in an ill-fitting business suit oozed out, shooting a three-hundred-watt grin at them through obviously capped teeth. His hair held enough gel to grease the drive screws on a battleship. His tan came out of a bottle and left him looking slightly orange.

Schwarz slipped a five-dollar bill to Lyons, who tucked it quietly in his pocket.

"Gentlemen," he said. His voice held a hint of an accent that Lyons couldn't place. "I am Hector Lafontaine, vice president of operations here at Engineering Consulting Synergies. Let me say first of all that I'm happy to provide any and all necessary cooperation to the United States Justice Department. Of course, I'll need to see a warrant."

Lyons shoved his credentials under Lafontaine's nose. "I could get a warrant," he said. "But that would take time. It's time I'd rather not spend with my thumb up my butt in your lobby. And if you make me spend that sort of time—"

"Perhaps you don't understand," said Lafontaine. His

voice had turned to steel. "I'm not just vice president of operations. I'm also head of this corporation's legal team. Unless you'd like to see just how miserable I can make your life, Agent—" he glanced at Lyons's identification "—Weaving, I suggest you back down. The power I can bring to bear on you will make you wish you'd never set foot in this office."

Lyons looked at Blancanales and Schwarz. "Gimme a minute," he said.

"Huh?" Schwarz asked. Blancanales had time to look questioningly

Lyons grabbed Lafontaine by the elbow. He started walking. The goons in the lobby looked questioningly at the vice president, but he shook his head at them, obviously thinking he had the situation covered. There was a small anteroom leading from the lobby, the corridor to which probably led to an executive washroom. Lyons dragged Lafontaine through the doorway and closed the heavy wooden door.

"What is the meaning of—"

Lyons grabbed Lafontaine's necktie in his right hand and jerked the man off his feet.

Lafontaine squawked like a frightened bird. Lyons put his free hand on the man's chest and forced Lafontaine to his knees. The Able Team leader pulled the fabric taut, choking vice president of operations with his own necktie. Lafontaine promptly turned bright red.

"Let me tell you about power," said Lyons. "By the way, I should add that I'm in a bad mood. Have been all morning. Probably still going to be tomorrow. And one of the reasons I'm in a bad mood is that every time I turn around I'm dealing with some self-important piece of crap like you who thinks he's got power."

Lafontaine managed a sound that was midway between a groan and a squeak.

"Sleazebags like you I could buy in bulk," said Lyons. He wrapped the tie around his fist a couple of times, pulling it tighter. Lafontaine turned from red to purple. "Cheap suit. Botox. Probably work out in the gym every other day and hit on the hotties there for good measure. You drive an expensive car and you think you're the man. You figure people ought to be afraid of you."

Lafontaine hissed something unintelligible.

"Well, you're not the man, Hector," said Lyons. "*I'm* the man. And you want to know something? I could choke you to death and leave your body on this floor. I could walk out to my car and drive away with my friends. And when your secretary out front tells people who killed you, you know what she'll say? She'll say it was Agent Weaving from the Justice Department."

"Please," Lafontaine managed to plead. The word was a croak.

"Only there isn't any Weaving from the Justice Department," said Lyons. "He's a ghost. Doesn't exist. Wasn't here. So basically I can kill you for free, you little worm, and the only reason I'm not doing so is because that's *not* what we do. We're Justice, Hector. But so help me, if you don't drop the attitude, I will squeeze the life out of you. And that, you little schmuck, is *power*."

Lyons opened his hand.

Lafontaine collapsed to his hands and knees on the floor, gasping for breath. He sucked air desperately, wheezing and coughing. Slowly, his color receded to something that, while not normal, was at least not livid purple.

"Now you're going to take us on a tour of your manufacturing floor," said Lyons. "You *do* have a manufacturing floor here?"

"Yes," said Lafontaine. His voice was little more than a stage whisper.

"Then let's go, Hector. Let's go while I'm feeling generous." He grabbed Lafontaine by the shoulders and hauled him to his feet. Then, with great care, he smoothed the front of Lafontaine's shirt, loosened his tie and patted the tie into place.

The two men returned to the lobby.

"Gentlemen," Lafontaine croaked. "If you'll just accompany me and…Agent Weaving…here, I will take you to where we assemble components."

Lyons saw Blancanales slip Schwarz what looked like a five-dollar bill.

The shaken vice president guided them through the anteroom, down a corridor and past what appeared to be offices. Several side rooms full of fabric-walled cubicles contained men and women typing at workstations. Lyons stuck his head into each of these, glaring at the people working there, obviously checking for anything that seemed out of place.

The armed guards certainly were.

In each of the office areas there was a single guard standing in the corner of the room. They passed several more uniformed goons in the corridors they walked until finally, at the rear of the large ECS complex, they came to the manufacturing floor. Here workers in antistatic boots, some connected to their workstations by grounding wrist straps, were bent over a variety of circuits and piece parts. Some of the workstations held mechanical fixtures that were used in preparing the components, such as vises and presses. Lafontaine stood back and kept his mouth shut as Able Team walked the rows of workers, peering at each of the components under construction.

Blancanales moved up behind Lyons, then beside him.

"More guards," he whispered. "A few are filtering in from other entrances. They're converging on us." Lyons had seen them, too. They were moving in what they probably thought was a casual fashion, stacking themselves two and three deep around the perimeter of the manufacturing area.

Lyons's secure phone began to vibrate. He touched the earbud transceiver he wore.

"Not a good time," he said.

"Price here," said Barbara Price. "I just got a call from Hal. He says someone from a corporation in Alabama just called the Justice Department, screaming about 'police brutality' or something like that."

Lyons looked around. "Where's Lafontaine?"

"Don't see him," said Blancanales.

The vice president had slipped out one of the doors, obviously. Lyons swore under his breath. The little slug was probably still on the phone.

"What was that?" Price asked.

"Nothing," said Lyons. "Barb, something is very wrong here. I decided to take the most direct approach."

"By directly provoking a retaliatory assault," said Price. It was not a question.

"How did you know?"

"You forget," Price said. "I know how you operate. Are you reconsidering my offer of backup?"

"If we didn't have time before," said Lyons, "we really don't have time now. But there is something we need."

"Standing by."

"Send a cleanup crew," Lyons said.

"Wait," said Price. "What?"

"It's about to get bloody," said Lyons.

"Are you sure?"

"Count on it." He tapped his earpiece, closing the connection.

Lafontaine emerged suddenly from a doorway to their left. He had hit the metal fire door at a run, apparently, because the door banged against the wall behind it. The vice president looked furious. He marched straight for Lyons, but not before giving his armed security forces an almost imperceptible nod.

Able Team stood in the center of the manufacturing floor, in an area of floor space that was free of equipment and workstations. Around them, the ECS factory workers continued at their tasks, although now and again one or another would eye the newcomers with curiosity or fear. Whenever a worker looked up from his labor, it did not take long for one of the uniformed security men to pass by, prompting the employee to work very hard at looking busy.

The factory floor was very bright, lighted by banks of fluorescents in the high ceiling. The only windows were set high above along the perimeter of the space. These were covered in grime. Below the fluorescents, Lyons felt like he and his men stood in a spotlight. No, he corrected himself; it wasn't a spotlight. It was a bull's-eye.

"Gadgets," Lyons said quietly.

Schwarz still carried the heavy duffel bag containing their long guns. He hefted the bag and nodded.

Lafontaine walked directly up to Lyons. "Weaving!" he bellowed. "I've just been on the phone with Washington. Your career is over. I'll have you brought up on charges. I'll sue you into poverty. If you've got a family you better start—"

Lyons held up a finger.

"You just watch your mouth about my family," he said. "You're not going to be suing anybody. There's nothing you can do to any of us, Hector. Maybe you're forgetting the different kinds of power already."

That brought Lafontaine up short. He looked around

as if seeking support from his guards. The security men continued to edge closer, their hands drifting for the pistols on their belts.

"I'll let you in on another secret, Hector," said Lyons. "You spend enough time around bad men doing bad things, you get kind of a sixth sense for these things. I could tell the moment we set foot on the property something wasn't right."

"Your psychic powers are hardly admissible in court," said Lafontaine.

"True," said Lyons. "But what you've got to ask yourself is, just why it is you think the bunch of you can take down three Federal agents and get away with it."

Lafontaine sputtered. "What? I never... We wouldn't..."

"Wouldn't what? Wouldn't think of assaulting government agents? What's going on here, Lafontaine? When we really analyze the components you've got in the works here, when we start taking photos and handing them upstairs, what are we going to find? You're dirty, aren't you? You're involved in illegal arms exports."

Lafontaine flushed. He raised his hand and pointed to the men of Able Team. Around them, the security guards started to withdraw their weapons.

"I wouldn't," said Lyons. "I really wouldn't."

The guards hesitated. They looked to the vice president, who looked from Lyons to Schwarz to Blancanales.

"You don't understand," said Lafontaine quietly. "I don't make the decisions here. I'm just doing what I'm told."

"You can follow orders," said Lyons, "or you can walk out of this place."

The vice president shook his head. "I should never have let you in here," he said. "You're putting me in an untenable position."

"How about putting you on a slab at the morgue?" Lyons asked. "How untenable a position is that?"

Lafontaine went pale. "There's nothing I can do."

"Call your bosses," said Lyons. "Call 'em now. We can negotiate something. You and your buddies can testify, answer our questions. You'll cool your heels in some federal minimum security joint for white-collar pukes. It'll be a lot better than being dead. I'm telling you, Hector. Call your bosses."

Lafontaine reached into his jacket. Lyons's hand twitched. The vice president removed a smartphone from his suit, pressed a quick-dial button on the touch screen and put the device to his ear.

"It's me," he said. "We have a problem."

"Do the right thing, Hector," said Lyons.

The vice president watched Lyons as he listened. Finally he said, "What assurances can you give me? Immunity from prosecution for ECS management. Guarantee of safe passage out of here for our security forces."

"No way," said Lyons. "I can't make those kinds of deals. I can only promise your life, Hector. Your goons here…I'm getting the impression they're not exactly solid citizens. They're not going anywhere. Surrender peacefully or die violently. Those are the choices."

"You're a federal agent," Hector said. "There are rules. There are standards of conduct. You can't do this."

"Don't make me choke you with your tie again, Hector."

The man in the suit winced. He spoke a few more words into his phone and then waited. As he listened, he grew more pale. Finally he put the phone away. "I'm sorry," said Lafontaine.

"So am I, Hector," said Lyons. "So am I."

Carl Lyons whipped his Colt Python from its holster and shoved the barrel in Lafontaine's face.

CHAPTER SEVEN

Sibang Cove

The purpose-built yacht, which reminded Rafael Encizo of a large PBR patrol boat, lay at anchor in the tropical paradise of Calayan Island. From the shore, concealed in a stand of trees and scrub, the Cuban-born guerilla expert watched the yacht through a compact monocular. The spotting scope was powerful enough that he could see the expressions on the hookers' faces.

"At this point I think we can say that naval discipline has gone *all* to hell," drawled T. J. Hawkins.

He watched the boat through a ten-power Unertl scope. The optics were mounted to the Remington M-40 A3 sniper rifle snugged to his shoulder. The powerful 7.62 x 51 mm NATO weapon was the rifle used by the Marine Corps, widely regarded as one of the better sniper weapons in the world. Hawkins lay prone behind the weapon's McMillan Tactical A4 stock.

"What's that music they're playing?" Encizo asked. "I can just hear it from here."

"Beats me, man," said Hawkins. "If it isn't Hank Williams Jr., I couldn't say."

"Since when?" Encizo said, laughing. "No, seriously. I think it's 'Soul Finger' by the Bar-Kays."

"You've been talking to Calvin," said Hawkins.

"What *is* it with these bad guys? Do they trade mix tapes?"

"Element One, in position," said McCarter over their transceivers.

"Roger," said Encizo. "Element Two is also in position."

A man wearing most of a North Korean military officer's uniform—his uniform shirt hung open, unbuttoned, and he was barefoot—emerged from belowdecks. He brought handfuls of long-necked brown-bottle beer to the other two men on deck. One of these men wore his uniform, while the other only his combat boots and pants. The man with the open shirt distributed the beers and all three had a good, long laugh over whatever it was he said to them. Then the shirtless one returned to what he had been doing before the beers arrived, which was running his hand over the backsides of the pair of bikini-clad Filipino working girls standing at the deck rail.

"Report," McCarter's voice echoed in the recon team's ears.

"We've got a party on deck," said Encizo. "Two noncombatants, possibly more belowdecks. Three North Korean military, officers by their tags. Given that this group broke away from what must be a much more boring assignment aboard their courier-slash-lab ship, it stands to reason these are the higher-ups. It's good to be in charge, and all that."

"Every Commie Party system is a party for the Party," said Hawkins quietly, shielding his earbud so his voice would not carry over the open channel. Encizo grinned and had to stifle a laugh. McCarter had no sense of humor these days; the burdens of running the team, ever since they'd lost Katz, weighed heavily on him. Occupational hazards of leadership, and all that.

"Belowdecks?" McCarter prompted.

"Hard to say," said Encizo. "Definitely at least one or two people down there, possibly a lot more, depending on how stationary. We've seen some indications of movement, but nothing specific enough to give us a head count."

"Give me the count-off," said McCarter. "We will go on your mark."

"Roger," said Encizo. "From my mark in five…four… three…two…one…*mark*."

Hawkins fired.

The 180-grain shock-point bullet, intended for big game, punched an exit wound the size of a fist in the head of the shirtless man, whom Hawkins had selected for his target. The noise, the spray of blood and the messy collision of the dead man with the deck of the yacht all captured the attention of the people on the boat, as they were meant to.

Grappling hooks hit the deck railing. A pair of arms reached up, grabbed the string bikini tops of the two hookers and yanked the women overboard.

Clawing for a pistol in his waistband, the North Korean with the open shirt went to the railing. Through the spotting scope, he looked as if he expected just about anything to be waiting for him over that rail, from a sea monster to the devil himself.

What he got was the barrel of McCarter's Hi-Power, which punched a 9 mm hole through his left eye. He fell back and collapsed on the blood-washed deck.

"Element One, go—" McCarter started to say.

"Element One, no go! No go!" Encizo shouted.

The two men who burst onto the deck of the PBR had obviously planned their maneuver. The first carried an RPK-type light machine gun with a bipod. He used it to rake the railing with full-auto fire, spraying out the belt of his weapon.

The second man carried an RG-6 grenade launcher.

"Uh-oh," said Hawkins.

"Get the second man! Get the second man!" urged Encizo.

"Little problem," said Hawkins. "Our friend with the belt-fed RPK is in the way."

"T.J.," said Encizo. "We are about to have a very serious problem." The man in uniform was now moving to flank the RPK gunner, effectively screening the machine gunner as a target from the shore.

"Give me a minute to line it up," said Hawkins. "Wind's picking up."

The machine gunner was keeping the rest of the team from moving up out of their positions along the yacht's hull. The chopper that had inserted Encizo and Hawkins had dropped a quick-inflate rubber patrol boat with the rest of Phoenix Force. They had used that to paddle up on the yacht, nice and quiet, unnoticed even in broad daylight. Then they had simply played barnacle, waiting for the chance to come up over the side. The only problem was that they would now get their heads blown off if they stuck them above the rail.

The man with the Russian-surplus revolving grenade launcher turned toward the shoreline. In Encizo's spotting scope, he appeared to be looking straight at the sniper team.

Hawkins shot the man in front of the RPK gunner. The bullet punched through the man's neck, causing blood to geyser as the North Korean soldier went down. The heavy 7.62 mm round then struck the machine gunner in the face, leaving a crater where his nose had been. His weapon chattered as he clenched the trigger in death. The bullets flew skyward, destined to come down somewhere over the ocean.

"Here it comes," said Encizo.

The grenadier raised his weapon skyward and fired once, then again, then again—

Hawkins pulled the trigger once more. The man with the grenade launcher joined the growing pile of corpses on the deck of the yacht.

Encizo pushed himself to his knees and landed on top of Hawkins as the rounds smashed into the shoreline just beyond their position. The explosions rocked the ground beneath them and sprayed them with dirt and debris. To Encizo it felt as if a giant, invisible, fiery palm had smacked them both into the earth, grinding them under with its tremendous heat and pressure.

"Element Two!" McCarter shouted through the transceiver link. "Element Two! Come in!"

"Element Two," said Encizo, coughing. "We are intact—"

"You have contact, your six," McCarter informed them.

"Wait," said Hawkins, "aren't *we* spotting for *them?* And get off me, Rafe."

Encizo rolled off his teammate. He unslung his dirt-caked Kalashnikov clone and, from his back, pointed the barrel of the weapon between his own legs. An ancient jeep, possibly old enough to be World War II vintage, was rumbling toward them. It was full of armed men. Encizo couldn't see them well from his position, but he would swear they were wearing North Korean uniforms.

"Not the Sibang Cove tourism committee," said Hawkins. He rolled, twisted his body and positioned the sniper rifle toward the oncoming gunmen. "By the way, Rafe, I didn't know you cared."

"Sniper support is mission critical, or can be," said Encizo. "Observers are optional."

"You're as good with a rifle as I am," said Hawkins. The enemy jeep was moving closer.

"You had the rifle," said Encizo. He fired a short burst from his weapon, which caused the men in the jeep to veer left and take cover in a stand of trees not far from shore. Encizo busied himself leaving bullet holes in the rear of the jeep, trying to find the fuel tank.

"So you were shielding the *rifle,* not me," said Hawkins.

"Yep," said Encizo. He fired again. "We should probably find cover. We're exposed here."

Bullets struck around their position, but few of them came very close. "North Koreans," said Hawkins. "Not much for fire discipline or trigger control. I think we're okay unless they come closer."

The muzzle-flashes in the tree line picked up in frequency. The gunners were starting to walk their shots in on the two Phoenix Force soldiers.

"*That's* going to become a problem," said Encizo.

"You figure that character with the grenade launcher really thought he could hit us?"

"You know that old saying," said Encizo. "'Close enough' only counts in horseshoes and hand grenades." He fired a long blast and then paused to change magazines, pulling another thirty-rounder from his web gear. "But no, unless there's a streak of incurable optimism in the People's Glorious Jerkwater Dictator Republic of North Koreastan, I think he was warning his buddies stationed beyond those trees somewhere. I think they were far enough out, or asleep on the job, or just plain drunk, stoned and high, that they didn't realize their pals on the boat were in trouble." He fired again. "So he blew his wad in our general direction and figured he'd wake up reinforcements in the process."

"I've always admired your poetic bent," said Hawkins without a hint of a smile.

"And I admire your sense of humor," said Encizo. "I'd have missed you if you got killed."

"I'm glad it wasn't just the rifle you were trying to save."

"No," said Encizo. He pushed to his knees and then went prone on his stomach, his AK firing in short, measured bursts. "Well. Mostly the rifle."

"I'm going to tell David you said that," said Hawkins. He triggered the Remington once and dropped a man with a perfectly placed shot through the eye socket. "They say the eyes are the windows to the soul," he drawled.

"See?" Encizo said. "Sense of humor."

"I don't think we've got the angle on this," said Hawkins. "I may be able to line up another of those guys, but there's a nest of 'em back in there behind the jeep. Every minute we spend messing around with these jokers is a minute we're not supporting the others."

"Time to call in our guardian angel," said Encizo, keying his transceiver. "G-Force, you hanging around up there?"

"Express elevator's on the way down, Element Two," said Jack Grimaldi over the communications link.

It was not long before they could hear the whirl of Grimaldi's chopper blades. The Cobra descended with speed and precision, a flying monster whose teeth were sharp.

"You've got a fix on us, G-Force?" Encizo asked.

"Roger," said Grimaldi.

"That-a-way." Encizo pointed. "Ten degrees to our left and ahead about—"

"About so," said Grimaldi, walking his chopper laterally across the face of the tree line. The 20 mm Gatling cannon howled, producing a gout of flame. The trees disintegrated, creating a wooden blizzard whose shrapnel tore through the contingent of North Korean soldiers. It might have been possible to hear their screams, if the cannon itself were not so loud.

"And one to grow on," said Hawkins quietly as Grimaldi unleashed a volley of Hydra 70 rockets. The high-explosive "ten-pounders" pounded the tree line flat, annihilating anything that might have been standing after the rotary cannon fusillade.

"Element Two," said Grimaldi through his radio, "you are clear. I repeat, you are clear. Recommend you rejoin Element One."

"Roger that," said Encizo. He nodded at Hawkins. "Keep that rifle dry."

"Har, har, har," said Hawkins. He was already zipping up the Remington in its waterproof container. "I've been thinking all morning it would be nice to take a dip."

"That's only because you were looking at girls in bikinis all morning," said Encizo.

Grimaldi maintained station high above, probably watching for any further incursions from farther inland. Encizo had to admit to himself that it wasn't likely. He had been surprised enough that the North Koreans posted part of their number off the boat to serve as a rear guard. It wasn't truly that he underestimated their foe so badly. You couldn't do that, not in any engagement, and stand any chance of survival. Even the most ill-equipped and untrained Third World child soldiers, such as the fanatical conscript forces fielded in the worst regions of Africa, could surprise you with their ferocity. Many of them made up for in sheer meanness and desperation what they lacked in training and weaponry.

No, it was simply the nature of this hare-brained maneuver. The North Korean drug ships were, presumably, very important to the leadership of North Korea and to the isolated Communist regime. For the officers of one of those ships to decide to take a private vacation, make a "separate peace," even a temporary one, endangered the entire operation. It also made the North Koreans look like the rogue thugs that they were. Taking hostages, hijacking prostitutes, probably murdering fishing boat crews… it made the North Korean military no better than pirates.

Pirates had a long history of swinging in public for their crimes.

The pair made their way to the rubber boat in which Calvin James sat with the two prostitutes from the deck. He had somehow managed to charm them both. They were speaking in broken English and he was responding with mostly sign language, his voice no louder than a whisper. The women had caught on and were doing their best to stay quiet, as well. Both prostitutes looked wide-eyed at the two men who came aboard and grabbed the lines of the grappling hooks.

"Calvin," said Hawkins.

"Calvin," echoed Encizo.

"You two finish blowing up the island yet?" James asked.

"That wasn't us," said Encizo.

"Yeah, yeah," said James. He held his Kalashnikov at the ready, his eyes scanning the water and the shoreline. He sounded relaxed, but he was anything but. He was coiled and ready for more action. "Watch yourselves up there. We've got a situation."

The transceivers were designed to screen gunfire and other sounds of sufficient decibels. They also operated on a complicated local network algorithm that isolated chatter from the nearest elements when keyed by a thumb. Mc-Carter and Element One had apparently been isolating their communications while Element Two made driftwood of the trees nearest the beach. Encizo realized the second his boots hit the deck that there was some kind of hostage situation going on.

McCarter and Manning were waiting by the hatch leading to the lower decks. The hatchway was set up like a landing; there were stairs leading down. At the bottom of that landing was a single North Korean officer. Judging from the medals and braid on his shoulders and chest, he might have been the highest ranking of all of them, possibly a unit commander.

It was also likely he had been belowdecks enjoying the favors of yet another of the prostitutes, for he was holding one at gunpoint. He had what appeared to be a chrome-plated Makarov pressed against the head of a very frightened, very naked Filipina. The girl had long, dark hair and the North Korean had wrapped the fingers of his left hand in it. The gun was pressed against the base of her skull. Shooting him would almost certainly result in her death.

"Helicopter!" shouted the officer in English. His accent was thick, but he continued. "You bring me helicopter!"

"You don't want our helicopter, lad," McCarter said. He pointed skyward. "That's the gunship that just chewed up the only reinforcements you had. Weren't they?"

Manning duck-walked over to where Encizo and Hawkins were crouched, careful to stay out of the line of sight from the hatchway.

"What's the story, Gary?" Hawkins asked.

"We searched the lower decks after you eliminated the resistance up top," Manning said. "Nice work, by the way. Although next time you might want to move more quickly. Prevents localized global warming."

"Prevents *what?*" Hawkins asked.

"Grenades going off overhead," said Manning, with the barest hint of a smile.

"Everybody's a comedian today," said Hawkins.

"We found the cabin they were using to entertain themselves with the fishing boat crew," said Manning. His face turned dark. "They were into sex and violence. I guess torturing the crew to death was their idea of fun, too."

"You found the crewmen from the fishing boat?"

"No," said Manning quietly. "Just evidence that they were here. We figure the North Koreans played doctor, in more ways than one, and dumped the bodies over when they were done with them. James reports that there is at least one prostitute missing, according to the two he pulled off the deck. The others think she was used up, killed and dumped in the ocean on the way here."

"Hard men," said Hawkins.

"Vicious men," said Encizo. "It doesn't take strength or will to be a venal, murderous bastard. You just have to be vicious. They didn't take the hostages to take hostages. They took them because they figured they'd get bored."

"So now their pirate captain wants to negotiate a way out for himself," said Encizo.

"Looks like it," said Manning. "There's more."

"And?" Hawkins asked.

"Before we got to the master cabin and interrupted Don Juan down there, we found a lot of drugs, probably skimmed from the lab ship. We also found quite a bit of documentation. They were hauling intelligence data gathered for someone higher up, probably because our guy belowdecks is in charge of the overall operations of these ships."

"Figured he deserved a sabbatical for all his hard work," said Encizo.

"It looks like he was getting ready to make a report," said Manning. "We recovered maps and a pile of stuff in

Korean. But there were also English-language brochures for a company called Sapphire."

"What's it do?"

"International security," said Manning.

"Data?"

"So the brochure claims," said Manning, shaking his head. "But it reads like a cover-op for hired muscle. We've seen enough of those types of firms over the years. Everything's been photographed and shot to the Farm for analysis."

"Then that just leaves Blackbeard down there," said Encizo.

"Yeah," said Manning.

"Too bad for him," said Encizo. "David's going to get bored any minute now."

"He's always had a temper," said Hawkins.

Manning, who was the picture of calm most of the time, may have rolled his eyes just then. Encizo could not be sure. He also knew that if he asked, Manning would not reply.

"All right, all right," said McCarter. "You can have your chopper. But I think you're laboring under a bit of a misconception, friend. We don't know that girl. We don't care about her. She's disposable. Another is easily bought to take her place."

"I said I want helicopter—" said the North Korean.

McCarter's hand shot out. He was fast—deadly, rattlesnake fast. He snatched the hooker by the wrist and jerked, pulling her forward. The movement took the man off balance, for his off hand was tangled in the girl's hair. The sudden jerk spun the North Korean's body, bringing the barrel of his chrome-plated Makarov up and away from the girl's head.

McCarter shot him.

The bullet traveled up under the man's jaw and erupted from his face just beneath his nose. The girl screamed. She was covered in gore, but she was alive.

The body hit the deck.

"Sorry for the harsh words, miss," McCarter told the girl, who stared up at him in shock. "I didn't mean them."

She leaped forward and put her arms around the Phoenix Force team leader, hugging him and saying something repeatedly in a language none of them knew.

"I'm betting that's a thank-you," said Hawkins.

That time, Encizo was quite certain he saw Manning roll his eyes.

CHAPTER EIGHT

Outside Mobile, Alabama

"Wait," said Lafontaine.

Lyons pulled the trigger.

The back of Lafontaine's head exploded. Droplets of blood flecked Lyons's face. The tiny .25-caliber pocket pistol Lafontaine had been pulling from his waistband, behind his back, clattered to the floor.

Chaos enveloped them.

Lyons and the rest of Able Team dived for the floor as the guards around the room opened up with their weapons. First one, then another of the workers was hit by fire from the guards' pistols. The staccato blasts from handguns were soon joined by ripping auto-fire bursts. Several of the guards had what were probably illegal submachine guns. Empty brass began to jingle on the sealed concrete floor.

Lyons rolled to the duffel bag. Schwarz was already unzipping it.

Time to go to work.

Carl Lyons pulled his Daewoo automatic 12-gauge from the bag. Schwarz handed Blancanales his M-16 and, from the bag, he took a second Beretta 93-R that matched the one he was already carrying.

"Let's clean house," said Lyons. He held the Daewoo at waist level and swung it from left to right, squeezing off a barrage of double-aught buck that blazed a ring of destruction through the nearby machinery. He was careful to avoid the workers; unlike the guards, he fired behind them, scattering them, driving them onward, as the machines spewed smoke and oil and whatever else ran their hydraulics or electrical systems. As fumes and clouds of black vapor began to form a fog bank over the manufacturing floor, the guards moved in, shooting wildly.

The fog of war, Lyons thought. It isn't just figurative, sometimes.

Crouched low, Lyons, Schwarz and Blancanales began to stalk through the aisles of workstations, which were now a deadly maze. The rattle of repeated gunfire, both full-automatic and semiautomatic, was deafening within the enclosed space, even as large as it was.

Lyons raised his shotgun to his shoulder as he swapped out the box magazine. The next magazine was loaded with slugs—each one capable of blowing a hole the size of a quarter in its target, while burrowing a gaping exit wound on its way out. Slugs were, at short range, the only way to make precision shots with the Daewoo. You could never be certain how the pellets from the buckshot would spread, not to the degree that you could take shots in and around nonhostile targets.

Lyons was lining up just one of those shots.

One of the ECS guards was trying to shield himself behind a young man in a pair of ECS coveralls. The worker was terrified. The guard had one arm wrapped around the young man's throat. He held a MAC11 submachine gun in the other, the barrel pointed at his hostage's temple. That was bad. The full-auto MAC11 was an open-bolt design. It wouldn't take much to cause its magazine to empty into the victim's skull.

"Hey!" shouted Lyons. "Hey! Over here!" He stood at

his full height, lowering the Daewoo to his side, the barrel still pointing forward.

The guard saw him. The MAC11 wavered, then swung toward Lyons.

Lyons triggered a single slug from the hip. It was no kind of point-shooting his instructors had taught him, back in the ancient days of the LAPD, but it was effective. Lyons knew that shotgun better than he knew himself.

The slug blew off the guard's jaw and took a good portion of his brain through the rear of the man's head. The ECS shooter hit the floor like a sack of wet grain.

"Fan out!" Lyons ordered, knowing that Schwarz and Blancanales could hear him through his transceiver. "We don't stop until this floor is empty of hostiles."

To his left, Schwarz triggered triple burst after triple burst from his two Beretta 93-R machine pistols. Men fell this way and that. The employees of ECS, the unarmed workers, were largely clear of the battleground now, at least as far as Lyons could see through the smoke and—

"Fire!" Blancanales shouted. One of the machines, some kind of industrial loader, blazed bright orange as flames licked up from it. Now the three Able Team soldiers were backlit by a demonic orange glow. The silhouettes they made instantly turned them into targets.

Lyons hit the deck as a renewed burst of fire chopped the workstations around him. He began to crawl, working his way along the floor, angling to put the blaze to his side and not behind his back. In so doing he managed to trip up an ECS guard, unseen in the smoky pall. The guard fell on him.

"Who is that?"

"Not your boss," said Lyons. He slammed a heavy fist into the man's gut.

The ECS guard was a big man, a muscular bulk who

smelled of tobacco and sweat. The punch didn't stagger him. Instead, it flipped his combat switch, something Lyons had seen before and would see again.

He was wired much the same way.

The big man thrashed and fought, doing his best to hammer away at Lyons with his own balled fists. Lyons shrugged off most of the blows. They were too close to each other for that type of thing to be effective.

He thought about drawing his Python and blowing the man off him, but as hard to see as it was now, there was no telling where his bullets might go after they exited his adversary. He could hit a stray worker or, worse, shoot one of Able Team. Around him, the battle raged on. Between the adrenaline coursing through his veins and the constant battery of gunfire on his eardrums, the fight had started to sound as if it came through a tunnel from far away. He barely processed it. It wasn't his immediate concern.

The guard had trained in mixed martial arts, or thought he had. He was coming in for the ground-and-pound, trying to mount Lyons and then punch him senseless. Lyons rolled onto his back and managed to get his feet up under the man's chest, where he worked both arm joints at the shoulders, pressing with his combat boots. As his opponent tried to shift and come in, Lyons bobbed his feet, keeping the attacker off balance and struggling. It wasn't hard to do, but it was the sort of game that could get tiring fast, especially because his attacker was a big, heavy man. Lyons was forced to support the other man's weight as he fought.

The guard apparently realized that he still had a weapon on his belt. His hand went for the sheathed knife on his hip. Lyons pushed hard with his right leg and retracted his left, shoving the man's right arm over hard as he did so. The guard landed heavily to one side of Lyons, who rolled and reversed their positions. He came up on top of the ECS man just as the guard managed to pull the knife from his belt with his left hand.

Lyons's Python was already pressed against the man's neck.

"Don't," said the guard.

"Sorry," said Lyons. He pulled the trigger.

Lyons was up again, then, holstering his pistol, marching forward with the Daewoo in front of him, at the length of its shoulder sling.

"Follow me!" he shouted.

Schwarz and Blancanales fell into step on his flanks. The three men formed a wedge of firepower that pushed through the remaining floor space of the manufacturing area. Armed ECS guards dropped in their tracks. Blood was everywhere.

Lyons's ears were ringing when, finally, he ripped open the door leading out of the assembly room. His boots left bloody footprints on the corridor floor.

Blancanales and Schwarz were right behind him. Schwarz slammed the fire door and, looking around, found a wooden chair in the corridor against the wall. He raised it above his head and dropped it on the floor hard enough to break one leg free. This he wedged under the doorway, forming a makeshift doorstop. The barrier would not last long, but it would give them some time if anyone came up behind them.

Able Team burst into the lobby.

The receptionist behind the desk screamed. Several of the armed ECS guards went for their guns.

Lyons snapped his shotgun up to his shoulder. He fired once, then again. Next to him, Schwarz blasted away on semiautomatic, punching 9 mm rounds through the men that Lyons's shotgun slugs did not annihilate. There was one man unaccounted for, and he began to aim a revolver at them, dropping to one knee for a steadier shot.

Blancanales calmly and methodically punched a single 5.56 mm bullet through his eyeball. His M-16 bucked lightly against his shoulder, once.

"Clear," said Blancanales.

"You don't know what you've done!" shrieked the receptionist. "You don't realize what you've done! They're insane! They're insane and now you've given them a reason to—"

"Grab her," Lyons ordered Schwarz.

Schwarz tucked away his machine pistols and ran for the receptionist, who was running for the door. She almost made it. At the last second, the Stony Man electronics expert grabbed the collar of her blouse, spinning her and bringing her back to slide across the lobby floor and collide with her own receptionist desk.

"Nook!" she screamed. "No! It's only minutes! It's only minutes before it…" She stopped, pale, and looked up at them in nearly catatonic terror.

"I don't like where this is going," said Schwarz.

Lyons knelt in front of the woman. She was shaking with fear. "Listen to me very carefully," he said. "Whatever you're talking about, you are going to have to make me understand it before we can help you."

"The…the Iranians."

"Yes?"

"They own the company. They run everything. When they came in they installed all their own people, people loyal to them. When they bought ECS."

"Tracking you so far," said Lyons. "Go on."

"They told us they had the names and addresses of our families," said the woman. "They said if we didn't do exactly as we were told, our relatives would be murdered.

And they said if anyone ever called in the government or the police, ever tried to invade the building here..."

"What? What did they threaten?"

"They said there was a bomb," the receptionist said. "They said it was right beneath my desk. They said the timer would start if anyone tried to interfere with operations here. We're all going to die! We're all going to die!"

"Reeves," said Lyons, using his pseudonym.

Blancanales nodded. He took the hysterical woman by the arm and led her across the lobby to the outer doors, then into the parking lot.

"You think she was lying?" Schwarz asked.

"If she was, she's wasting her talents in administration," said Lyons. "Because she should be in Hollywood."

"I was afraid you'd say that."

The door connecting the lobby to the manufacturing area burst open. Three of the ECS guards still mobile were coming straight at them. Schwarz turned, took one of the Beretta 93-Rs and triggered a burst that stitched the lead man in the chest and throat.

As the first man went down, exposing the man behind him, Lyons's Python boomed. The .357 Magnum bullet punched through the man in the middle and then wounded the man behind, tagging him in the shoulder. Schwarz finished the last man off with another triburst.

The three bodies hit the floor.

Schwarz let out a breath. "That third guy counts as mine," he said.

"Whatever," said Lyons. He went back to the desk. "Pol," he said through his transceiver, "I'm going to call in an evacuation of this building. Keep an eye on the parking lot out there. Don't let anybody come in."

"Roger," Blancanales returned.

Lyons used the desk phone to inform the building's

occupants, via loudspeaker, to leave. When he was done, he said to Schwarz, "Help me take this thing apart. If she was right and the Iranians weren't just blowing smoke, we need to know it."

He began removing drawers from the desk. The structure was really two desks: one the workstation for the receptionist, the other a podium-like wooden shell behind it. Schwarz tapped on the shell with his knuckles, trying to see if it was hollow.

"Anything?" Lyons asked.

"I'm not sure," said Schwarz. "Nothing we can get to like this." Lyons looked left, then right. He spotted the glass case on the far wall next to a fire extinguisher.

It was a fire ax.

Schwarz followed his gaze. "Holy crap," he said. "I thought stuff like that was only in movies."

"Bring me that," said Lyons.

Schwarz nodded. He ran for the ax and returned with it. Lyons handed Schwarz his Daewoo. The electronics expert shouldered the weapon and took up a position to guard his team leader.

Lyons brought the ax high overhead.

The heavy blade tore into the receptionist's desk. Lyons hacked away as if the desk had made him furious. He reduced the wood veneer to splinters, revealing cheaper compressed particleboard underneath. The desk came apart easily and he nearly waded through it, crushing papers and office supplies under his heavy combat boots.

"The shell," said Schwarz.

"The shell," said Lyons. He tore into the taller structure with the ax. It came apart beautifully; it was indeed hollow within. It was then that Lyons saw it: in the midst of the particleboard scraps, deep within the podium, was a series of wires connected to metal cylinders.

"What is this thing?" Lyons yelled. "Are we in trouble?"

"I think we're boned," said Schwarz. He scrambled over and knelt by the device, actually climbing into what was left of the podium shell to do it. "This is a wireless detonator antenna," said Schwarz. "Whoever has the button for this can press it and blow us all to—"

Lyons reached in, slapped Schwarz's hand aside and ripped the antenna out of the device. It came away trailing wires.

"Uh," said Schwarz. "Okay. That problem's solved. But this probably has a backup timer. And there's no way to know if it's been tripped or not."

"No LED readout?" Lyons asked. "I was looking forward to watching the numbers count down."

"That really *is* in just the movies," said Schwarz. He indicated conduits radiating from the device. "I'm going to go ahead and call this a bomb," he said, "but I'd love to know where these conduits go."

"Let me see if I can't sleuth that out," said Lyons. He took the ax and began smashing away pieces of the floor. When he had enough leverage he dropped the ax, reached in and started tugging on the cables.

"I'm not sure we should be—" Schwarz started.

Lyons pulled. The cable pulled up from the floor in an explosion of plaster dust. The polished veneer of the lobby floor was just a coating, intended to conceal the work that had been done laying the cables. Lyons traced the conduit he was pulling on all the way to a support column at the lobby perimeter. When he reached it, he took out the folding knife he had taken earlier, snapped open the blade and probed the column. It wasn't long before he found a seam, made of the same plasterlike cover that had been used on the floor.

Lyons chipped away at the column. He revealed, eventually, a square cavity the size of a shoebox. The top of the cavity lifted away in a single piece of phony plaster. He tossed it to the floor, where it shattered.

The cavity was filled with plastic explosive.

"Are we boned?" Schwarz asked.

Lyons bent to the hole and breathed in through his nose. The smell was unmistakable. Semtex.

"We're boned," said Lyons.

"There are three more of those cables," said Schwarz. "Based on the amount of explosives…this is enough to level the building. Bring it down completely."

"And you said the timer could already be running."

"There's no way to tell," said Schwarz.

Lyons came over and took his shotgun from Schwarz. "This building goes, and a lot more than us get killed. There's no telling how many people in neighboring buildings might be affected.

"I'm ahead of you," said Schwarz. "You better get the Farm on the line." He knelt over the bomb hub once more, taking out a penlight, a bandanna and a multitool from his pocket. The multitool he snapped open and placed on the floor beside him. The bandanna he tied around his forehead. Then he switched on the penlight and tucked it under the bandanna, creating a makeshift headlamp.

Lyons took out his secure satellite smartphone and dialed the Farm. When the connection was made, he set the phone to video and propped it on what remained of the podium. It would now send a video feed to the mission control center at Stony Man. The cross-connection to the team's earbud transceivers was made automatically. In the parking lot, Blancanales would be able to hear everything said.

"Are you getting this feed?" Schwarz asked when the call connected.

"We are," said Barbara Price. "What am I looking at?"

"An employee at ECS claims 'the Iranians' have purchased a controlling interest in the company," said Lyons. "It would explain the Iranian mercenaries we've encountered to this point."

"It does and it doesn't," said Price. "It's a possible reason for the mercenaries you encountered. We still don't know exactly what the connection between the Iranian element and the ICBM smuggling is, or how it was made."

"Giant bomb here," said Schwarz. "Really giant bomb."

"I have you," said Akira Tokaido on the line. Tokaido was one of Kurtzman's cybernetics specialists. Through the connection, despite the distance between them, Lyons could hear Tokaido's fingers flying over the keyboard at his workstation. "We are overlaying schematics now. I need you to free the housing so we can see the board connecting all of those wires."

"Is it likely to have an antitamper?" Schwarz asked.

"Very likely," said Tokaido.

"We're boned," said Schwarz. "Everybody get ready to explode."

"I hate you when you do bomb disarms," said Lyons quietly. "I really do."

"I'm a lot of fun," said Schwarz. "People always say so."

Schwarz used the needle-nose pliers of his multitool to lift free the antitamper wire from its contacts. Then he snipped them, tossed them as far from him as he could and set about removing the casing of the bomb hub.

"What kind of sick bastards even think up something like this?" said Schwarz. "Wiring the entire building to explode. And no bright red LED readout so I know how many minutes I don't have."

"Seriously," said Lyons. "Hating you right now." More seriously, he said to Price, "We're going to need that cleanup team. Containment in spades."

Schwarz made exploding-bomb noises with his mouth.

"The circuit design supports four ignition wires, a ground and a cross-connect switch," Tokaido said. "You need to isolate the cross-connect and sever it before you can cut the others."

"So this is a red-wire, blue-wire, green-wire kind of thing?" asked Schwarz.

"Yes," Tokaido said.

"Well, that's a problem," said Schwarz. "Because all these wires are gray. Our bomb-maker wasn't terribly user friendly. I'll bet the ground wire isn't even brown. Oh, wait. Now I can't remember. Is standard color convention for ground brown or black?"

Sweat was beading on Schwarz's forehead. His wise-cracking was an attempt to keep his cool in the face of extreme stress.

"On the count of three," Lyons said. "I'll grab you and yank you to your feet. We'll run for the doors."

"No," said Schwarz. "I can do this. I just have to follow the circuit board back to the cross-connect. It's small, but I can eyeball it."

"You're sure?"

Schwarz clipped one of the wires. "Okay," he said, after a pause. "There's good news and there's bad news. The good news is that the circuit to the Semtex has been cut. This building isn't going anywhere."

"And?" Lyons demanded.

"And the bad news is that the hub has a primer explosive that's big enough to destroy this lobby. Cutting the cross-connect starts the fuse—"

Lyons grabbed Schwarz by the collar, yanked him from the debris of the podium, and all but threw him toward the lobby entrance. The two Able Team members ran for all they were worth, shouting, "Clear the front of the building! Clear the front of the building!"

The explosion, when it came, shattered the building glass at the lobby level. The wall of heat that came up behind them knocked Lyons and Schwarz to the ground. Pebbles of safety glass pelted them. The black smoke that swept over them smelled of burning insulation.

Blancanales was standing over them as the smoke cleared. He held out his arm. "Help you guys up?"

"Two more bomb disarms and my punch card is full," said Schwarz from his back on the pavement. "Then I get a free sub sandwich."

Lying next to him, Lyons ran a palm over his face. "Seriously," he said. "I hate you."

CHAPTER NINE

Berlin, Germany

Diana Deruyter fought for her life.

It *had* to be a fight for her life, had to contain real danger, or the fight was meaningless. Andre had been given explicit instructions in this. He was to use full contact, fighting as if he meant to kill her, and if she were injured, so be it. Only the element of real danger, the knowledge that if she faltered, if she showed weakness, she would suffer true injury, made the sparring session worthwhile. The only way to learn to fight was to fight; there were no substitutions. All other martial arts training was theory alone. She wouldn't waste her time with mental exercises. She had worked many long years to hone her edge. She wouldn't allow time or complacency to dull it.

The massive studio, which was in fact the great room of her apartment in Berlin, was divided into zones. On the hardwood floor were placed removable adhesive markers, which could be configured to her taste. The perimeter of the room, which still bore the lavish paintings in gilded frames that had been hanging there when she bought the place, was designated the running track. She would run laps around the perimeter of the great room until her heartbeat was sufficiently elevated, then diverge on any of several paths marked on the floor.

The zone at the end, the largest of these, was the spar-

ring zone, where Andre always waited. Should any part of
her body cross into the sparring zone, he would immediately attack her, doing his best to injure her badly. He was
a head taller than she, despite her height, built of muscle on
muscle that tapered to a trim waist and widened to powerful legs. He wore a black GI uniform and simple wres-
tling shoes, but no padding of any kind. His face was hewn
from granite, his blond hair shorn in a chiseled flattop. He
was a creature of beautiful, perfect severity, given to silence most of the time. It made him all the more fearsome.
Andre had beaten to death no less than six men with his
bare hands, the last four on Diana's orders. His knuckles
were callused knobs, for he conditioned them regularly.

Andre threw a series of kicks that whipsawed through
the air fast enough to make the leg of his uniform crack
with the force. She blocked each of these and hammered a
knuckle into his thigh in retribution. For all that he moved,
he might not even have felt the blow, but Deruyter knew
him better than that. The barest flicker in his gray eyes
told her she had stung him. He punched and missed as she
danced out of the sparring zone, continuing on her circuit
of the room. If Andre knew any disappointment that she
was now beyond range, he didn't show it. He merely folded
his hands in front of his body and stood, relaxed and ready,
waiting for her to come near again.

She ran to the chin-up block, which was a series of
bars that rose high above her head. Pulling herself up to
the first one, she reached up and performed a single-arm
pull-up to the next. Then she switched arms for the next,
and so on, finally reaching the top and then reversing the
pattern back down. Her arms were screaming by the time
she was done, but she did not relent.

The next section of the room, in her circuit pattern, was
the wooden dummies. These were kung fu appliances, built

in the traditional manner and of fine hardwoods. Wooden "arms" and "legs" jutted from them at various angles. She worked her way from the first, to the second, to the third, punching and striking, chopping and blocking, her arms and legs weaving an intricate pattern of blows and kicks as she moved from dummy to dummy.

Those who knew nothing of the martial arts bragged of breaking the wooden dummy with the force of their attacks. This was ignorance. The dummy trained the structure of one's techniques, allowing the practitioner to hone the exact angles of a block, a punch, a kick. The precision of the exercise was what she found most appealing.

She left the dummies and went to the weight bench, where the weights were preset for her leg lifts. She worked in sets of eighteen repetitions, then twelve, then six. The weight was perfectly set; she almost, but not quite, failed the last set of reps. Now the muscles of her lower body howled in protest. She was up again and running as if to silence them.

Mirrors were set at intervals along the walls. Had the room been smaller, each of these could have been a full floor-to-ceiling model, wide enough for the average ballet studio. Deruyter permitted herself the vanity of appraising her own appearance as she ran.

Her hair was jet-black, maintained by dye. This was, so far, her only concession to advancing years. She was forty-two, but her toned body, her taut stomach, her sculpted legs were those of a woman in her late twenties at most. In the black sports bra and yoga pants she wore, her feet bare, her hair tied back with a length of black silk, she could see the sweat beading on her exposed flesh, see the evidence of the morning's workout.

Andre watched her as she ran the room's perimeter, perhaps admiring her body, perhaps thinking about something entirely irrelevant. It was impossible to know with him.

She was nearing the sparring zone again when she came to the low table with the long knives on it. These were a matched set, custom built for her, each blade as long as her forearm. The knives were single-edged, with the draw-cutting tips of Japanese swords. Each bore a genuine temper line. She picked them up and worked an elaborate pattern drill through the air. The blades flashed and whirled.

Not for the first time, she thought of all the work it had taken to get to this place. Berlin was not, in her opinion, an ideal city in which to live. Oh, yes, from a business perspective, it was well suited to her needs, providing her with a means to direct her company's operations throughout the world. Berlin was just modern enough to offer all the conveniences she preferred, yet just corrupt enough that she could grease the wheels of local law enforcement and government. The balance was just right. It was far preferable to, say, Colombia, where she had once tried to establish Sapphire Corporation's headquarters. Everything was for sale in Colombia, which appealed to her, but she had spent so much time haggling with greedy officials that it had begun to grate. Here in Berlin, they took what you gave them once and did not constantly try to renegotiate better terms. It was much more civilized.

She found Berlin a depressing, morose city, however. Something about the place simply played with the minds of its inhabitants. Only recently, yet another death cult had been cleared out of the city. It was not the first time. The gloom of the place drove people to extremes. She would put money on it.

She struggled to remember, sometimes, the many lifetimes she had been forced to live before her plan—to form her own security firm and achieve independence—could come to fruition. An avowed American expatriate, she had married several times to wealthy men, in Paris, then in Germany, and once more in Paris. Her socialite ties were immensely helpful in working her way up in international business; she had selected her mates for their connections, directly or indirectly, to the worldwide security industry.

Her efforts had not come without pain, without hardship. She had made enemies. When first building her customer base, she had inadvertently poached customers from an English firm. The owner of the firm was an old bastard who had served in Rhodesia. Her mind always recoiled at the thought of Benjamin Hillock. He had paid her a visit late one night to explain to her what she had done wrong. He was going to teach her the meaning of respect, he'd said. He was going to make her pay for slighting him. She would come to know the value of paying deference to her elders. And, he'd promised her, he would show her why women should stay well clear of what was a man's business. It was the same reason women did not belong in combat, according to Hillock.

Because they could be raped.

He had tied her to her own bed and proceeded to have his way with her for four hours. He'd kept taking her, leaving to recover and then returning to assault her again. He'd grinned like a madman as he did it. She'd known, then, that his attentions were as much about him desiring her body as they were about supposedly teaching her a lesson for crossing him.

She'd learned something else about herself, then: she did not care as much for sex as she did for the power it gave her over men. She'd made it clear to Hillock, after a time, that she was enjoying herself. He had finally untied her. She had taken him from the bed to the couch in her office.

Rough sex she could endure. It was of no consequence. If Hillock had thought he was frightening her, or showing her his power over her body and her mind, by violating her, he'd overestimated the impact of his own manhood. She had experienced worse sex while a fully cooperating participant. She had experienced more pain after asking for it.

She was not impressed.

He'd left her, perhaps perplexed at the sudden turnaround. She had completely reversed his expectations. He'd been feeling both sated and gratified; he believed, the old fool, that he was the most virile man alive. His head was probably still filled with visions of her taut curves as he'd exited his car in front of his home across the city.

Deruyter had run him down with the same stolen car she had used to tail him home. She'd backed up and parked the right driver's side tire on his skull, crushing it. And she'd enjoyed very much the sound it made when his brains hit the pavement.

She had hired a professional assassin, a man highly recommended, to deal with Hillock's family. She hadn't cared about the details. She'd only wanted it to look like an accident. But she'd made certain that it was rumored in the right places that Diana Deruyter had personally murdered Benjamin Hillock. Because he had offended her, said some. Because he had failed to please her, whispered others.

After Hillock's death she had gone right back to building her business. Along the way she had developed a lengthy black book of possible customers and interested parties, many of them from the shadier sides of the ledger. She thought of them as collectibles. Among her favorites was a South African warlord, a German politician highly placed in whatever mess passed for their parliament, a couple of American movie actors and a high-powered

German madame whose client list read like a who's who of international finance.

Sapphire Corporation was the result of all her hard work. She provided private armed details to countless wealthy clients. She was also a silent party to multiple small wars across the world, where mercenary proxies funded by Sapphire—and trained by Sapphire personnel—fought for whatever causes people considered worthy of killing and dying. The specifics seldom mattered to her. What mattered was the money. As her bank accounts grew, so did her sense of security. From her earliest days as a slumlord in the worst neighborhoods of Tampa, she had fought and clawed for what was hers, battling always to establish herself and live life on her own terms.

Her latest venture was part of that drive. If you wished to fight international wars by proxy, it was necessary and proper to make international contacts. Cultivating these contacts invariably meant providing them with arms and, more often than not, seeing to it they received something new, something they could get from no one but you. There was no room for a free market, for competition, in such endeavors. Which was why the interests currently competing for the ICBM market opening up in North Korea were a source of irritation for her. As the LED light on the wall began to strobe, indicating that a phone call was coming in on her private line, she suspected that she would not like the news…and that it would, without fail, relate to the North Korean business. Such were the whims of fate. The only constant was the worst-case scenario.

Diana did not believe in hesitating in the face of a challenge. She would rather stare down her competitors, walk with head tall into the jaws of danger, than cower in fear or delay in hope. Hope was never a solution. Fear did nothing to remediate problems.

She grabbed a towel from the rack near the phone, wiped the back of her neck and her face and draped the towel over her bare shoulders. Then she picked up the elaborate wall receiver and put it to her ear.

"Deruyter," she said.

"It's me," said a voice she recognized. Of course it would be him; she had been expecting him to call.

"I'm listening," she said.

"Soong's playing hardball," said the voice. "He says he's going to continue using the competition if we can't meet our obligations and provide the shipment we promised. He hinted around that a discount might be in order, as he sees it."

"Strange," said Deruyter. "We've lost shipments, yes, but we're well within the delivery window. He called to threaten you…by claiming he might keep right on doing what he's already doing."

"He's nervous," said the voice. "And I think I know why."

"You mean, you think you're responsible," said Deruyter. "I know that tone. You're feeling pleased with yourself."

"Possibly," said the voice. "There are agents of the United States government sniffing around. I've put them on the trail of Soong's current contractors. I have it on good authority that those contractors have suffered certain…losses. Significant losses. And it's likely those losses will continue."

"That is a bold move on your part," said Deruyter. "What inspired that?"

"There wasn't realistically much else I could do," said the voice. "These are the government's heaviest hitters, from the look of them. Covert agency stuff. Real black-bag operators. You don't make them go away if they don't want to go. You have to either kill them or give them another target. So I gave them a target I thought would be most beneficial to us."

"At the risk of riling up Soong by damaging his interests."

"He's nervous," said the voice. "Threatening me is his way of asking for reassurance that we can meet his needs, get the ICBM components into the pipeline. We've suffered losses at sea. I'm looking at the reports now, and the government is to blame. But now, with those same government pit bulls snapping at our competitors' heels, Soong will be wondering where to jump. All we have to do is keep holding his hand, make a show of meeting his needs, and we'll 'land the account.'"

"We need to create for Soong the perception of power," Diana said. "If he believes it, he will side with us. Why is the government looking at this now? I am going to have to put my regional offices on alert because of it. Especially the Manila office, given its proximity to the trouble."

"Government investigation was always inevitable. The North Koreans sped up the process by combining the ICBM shipments with their floating drug labs, drawing attention to both because the drug pipeline was already on international law enforcement's radar. That was stupid. But what do you expect? They *are* North Koreans, after all."

"How culturally insensitive of you," Deruyter said.

"Sue me," said the voice. "I believe we are in a good position to use Soong's anxiety to our benefit. But this hinges on us not falling to the same forces that are now chipping away at Soong's hired guns. I've got them knocking down the doors of the competition's factories. Sites we've had on our hit list for a long time now."

"That's actually very clever," Deruyter said.

"I try."

"There are ways to continue using our enemies against each other," she said. "And if it doesn't work, we can always go far, far away."

"I would prefer not to do that," said the voice. "I've become accustomed to a certain lifestyle."

"Let me tell you something about lifestyle," Deruyter said. "I started my career as a slumlord. The worst of the worst. Do you know what it's like to put your mattress on the floor, because that way you'll be lower to avoid stray bullets while you sleep?"

"I can't say I have."

"People who exist in those parts of the world don't care about what you think you're owed," Deruyter said. "They care about *power*. The perception of power is more important than the reality of power."

"I'm listening," said the voice.

"I once had a very large property," Deruyter told him. "Very nice. So nice, in fact, that I decided the tenants living in it, who were behind on the rent, didn't deserve to stay. They were late too many times. I could make some renovations, charge triple what I already wasn't collecting. So I went to the house and pounded on the door until they answered."

"Direct. To the point. You had power and they didn't."

"Wrong," Deruyter said. "They had a different kind of power. The door opened and the man inside punched me in the face. His woman kicked me while I was down. They spit on me. They laughed at me. I was humiliated. I fled to my car."

"That isn't the Diana I know."

"Not now," Deruyter said. "I had a problem. I could kill the two of them, certainly. It would be easy. But I had to humiliate them as they had humiliated me. It was no longer a matter of money. I had to make sure every one of my filthy slum tenants knew that to defy me was to risk my wrath. I had to make that wrath something worth fearing.

"I spent weeks searching the local martial arts schools. It was a different time then. Many of the martial arts clubs were little more than gangs, the students no better than thugs. I watched them for a long time. I needed to find the worst of them. The most brutal thug they could offer me."

"You have an eye for talent."

"You have no idea," Deruyter said, eyeing Andre across the room. He stood, relaxed and ready, as if waiting there were the most natural thing in the world. "I found my thug. He was well built. Solid. But small. The smaller ones always have something to prove. They're forever fighting people who are much larger, so they learn to be vicious. They learn to have no fear. Here was my pit bull. I never asked him his name. I called him Johnny, after the boy from that karate movie. It seemed to amuse him. I think at first he desired me, and thought perhaps that would be part of the deal. He came to listen to my proposal eagerly enough."

"Any man would," said the voice.

Deruyter did not rise to the bait, although it was a compliment. "I explained to him that it was simple. Occasionally I would give him an address. That address would be a property where the tenants owed me money. Once he had the address, he was to go there and take the rent money by force. That rent would be his payment for his services. It was *his* money, and he would be there to collect what the tenants owed *him*. The money didn't matter. It was the power. The show of respect. The tenants had to fear me, had to understand that if they failed to pay me, my dog Johnny would arrive and hurt them until they paid *him*."

"Brilliant," said the voice. "A perfect use of the profit motive."

"Thank you," Deruyter said. "I sent my dog to three locations, total. After that, word got out. No one ever shorted me again. But there was one matter I had set aside. I needed my dog to prove himself first. With my reputation, my power, assured…it was time to settle an open account."

"The tenants who assaulted you."

"Yes," she said. "I took Johnny to a street arms dealer, the sort of person who could sell you anything from a knife to a gold-plated automatic. I told him he could pick anything he wanted. My gift to him, a bonus for good work. He picked out two things. The expensive revolver I bought for him. I guess he liked carrying it. But he never used it for work."

"And the second?"

"The second item he bought with five dollars in his own wallet. An ice pick in a handmade leather sheath. He put it in his waistband, and there it stayed whenever he was working. He said that everyone gets older, and that he would be a fool to rely on his muscle alone. I told him I approved of the sentiment."

"I have to know what happened."

"We went to the house where those two tenants still lived," Deruyter said, "and I told him I wanted to watch him work. Wanted to stand there, be there while he took what was his. I told him I had two more paid men standing by to dispose of the bodies. His reward, for killing them both…after making them suffer first, of course… was the property. For as long as he wanted to live there, free of charge. I was giving him financial independence. A place of his own. The most powerful loyalty money can buy—the loyalty of a man who knows he owes you…a certain lifestyle."

"Touché."

"It was amazing," Deruyter said. "He knocked on the door. Waited while they decided what to do. Then kicked it in as if it were made of paper. The man walked up on him. He was carrying a machete and he thought that made him invulnerable. My dog looked up at him and waited for him to do something more than talk. The machete came up."

"The suspense is killing me."

"Johnny was faster. He had that icepick out of his waistband and pressing against the bastard's crotch before the big man knew what was happening. He dropped the machete. His woman, who had taken so much pleasure in humiliating me, started squawking. 'Get him, get him. Why don't you get him? Teach him who's boss.' That kind of trash. He held up his hand and silenced her without a word. Then she saw what was happening.

"'You tell your woman,' Johnny told them both, 'to drop that knife she's holding, or when I'm done punching holes in you, I will murder her in a fashion your neighbors will only be able to describe as…obscene.'"

"He *said* that?"

"He did. I may be embellishing the language somewhat. But the part about 'obscene,' that he said."

"So?" said the voice.

"He made them pack up all their things," Deruyter said. "Told them to put them on the front lawn by the curb. Told them we had a truck on the way. Cooperate and they wouldn't be hurt."

"He couldn't go through with it?" asked the voice.

"Hardly a problem," Deruyter explained. "It was lies, all of it. The bastard was simply getting them to do the work of cleaning out the place so he wouldn't have to. He was already thinking about moving in."

"Cold."

"Cold was walking the woman to the shower, telling

her she needed to fix her hair and then sticking her with the icepick while he pushed her into the bathtub. He left her like that. Came back, picked up the machete. Caught up with the man down in the basement."

"He fled there?" asked the voice.

"It never made much sense to me," Deruyter said. "Some primal instinct to hide when you know something bad has found you. Over the years I've wondered one thing."

"What's that?"

"If he ever got the basement floor clean."

The voice on the phone said nothing for a long while. Then, finally, it said, "I'll keep that in mind."

"What's that?" Deruyter asked.

"The lengths to which you'll go to assert your power."

Deruyter snapped her fingers. Andre walked over to her, his hands by his sides. Deruyter paused to run her hand inside the fold of his uniform, across his chest. "I'll make arrangements to fly to the United States," she said. "Clearly there are some who could use an object lesson in power. I'll be on a plane immediately."

Andre raised an eyebrow. He reached out, very carefully, and put his hands on her shoulders, massaging the muscles there. When she looked to him, he nodded and, without a word, bent to kiss her neck.

"Well," Deruyter said into the phone. "Perhaps not… *immediately.*"

Then she hung up.

CHAPTER TEN

Outside Mobile, Alabama

"Hey," said Schwarz as Blancanales helped Lyons and Schwarz to their feet. "Those guys look familiar?"

The trio of black SUVs rolled slowly past their position. When they pulled even with Able Team's position, while smoke streamed from the devastated lobby of the ECS building, they poured on the speed.

"Come on!" said Lyons. "I want those bastards."

Able Team's Suburban laid down rubber as the truck roared out of the ECS parking lot. As they were departing, they could hear the sirens of emergency first-response vehicles in the distance. Whether that was the Farm's containment crew coordinating with local emergency departments, or just those local departments responding to reports of the explosion at ECS, it amounted to the same thing. The workers and other personnel who had been forced to evacuate the building would be looked after, and the site policed up.

Lyons, behind the wheel of the Suburban, pushed the pedal to the floor.

"Three by three, gentlemen," Lyons explained. "We neutralize their transportation and leave one team member per vehicle. Pol, you take the first one. Gadgets, you'll take the second. I'll run down the third."

"I hate the part where I jump out of the speeding truck," mumbled Schwarz.

"Everybody does," said Blancanales.

Lyons brought the Suburban up alongside the trailing SUV. "Let's see if we can't really screw up our security deposit," said Schwarz as Lyons opened his mouth to say something.

Lyons glared at him.

"What?" asked Schwarz.

The Able Team leader hauled the wheel over, ramming the rear quarter panel of the SUV. The black truck rocked left, then right, as the driver struggled to reassert control.

Blancanales, in the passenger seat of the Suburban, rolled down his window. As casually as if he were plinking at cans on a shooting range, he extended his Beretta M-9 and put a single 9 mm round through the rear tire of the enemy vehicle. Then, for good measure, he shot the other rear tire as Lyons dropped back to give the wildly swaying truck some room.

"Get ready, Pol," said Lyons.

"Ready," said Blancanales, nodding.

Lyons jammed on the brakes, slowing the truck and allowing Blancanales and his M-16 to leap free of the Suburban. As soon as Blancanales was clear, Lyons stood on the accelerator again, never once taking his eyes off the speeding SUVs ahead.

In the rearview mirror, Lyons could see Blancanales just long enough to know that he had the situation in hand. The soft-spoken Able Team member raked the side of the truck with a long, withering blast from his M-16. An operative tumbled from the driver's side, holding a pistol in his hand. Blancanales shot him in the chest and then began to circle the vehicle. Before the Suburban was out of range and too far away for the other two members of

Able Team to see, Blancanales was hosing down the interior of the SUV from the rear hatch doors. In the rapidly receding image in the rearview mirror, he shot his teammates a thumbs-up.

"Clear," he said through the transceiver link. "It's a mess in here."

"Let's make another," said Lyons. "And, Gadgets?"

"Yeah, Ironman?"

"Try to leave one alive. For questioning."

"Sure, Ironman."

"You're not going to, are you?"

"I said I would try. I'm going to try."

"This is another one of those times I hate you," said Lyons.

"I'm seeing a trend here," said Schwarz.

Lyons accelerated, hard. The nose of the Suburban rocked the rear bumper of the second black SUV. Gunmen on both sides of the truck reached out through their respective windows. One held a pistol and the other a Skorpion submachine gun.

"No good," said Lyons. "We don't want passersby getting tagged by stray bullets." He dropped back a bit, then yanked the wheel to the left, coming up along the driver's side of the SUV. Then he planted the Suburban firmly in the flank of the other truck, pressing the two vehicles together. The scrape of metal on metal made Lyons's teeth ache. The maneuver effectively flattened one truck against the other, presenting the Suburban as the only available target while simultaneously blocking the windows on the same side.

"What if they decide to shoot into—" Schwarz started to say.

"Down!" roared Lyons. He pushed Schwarz's head down, knocking him into the footwell of the passenger side, and slammed his own seat back by yanking on the release lever. Automatic gunfire burned the air above them as rounds poured through their window. The interior door panel on Lyons's side absorbed the burst. The big former LAPD police officer flinched as he was struck by fragments of the plastic molding.

"Is this the part where I get out?" Schwarz asked.

Lyons said nothing. Instead, he reached into the center panel of the Suburban and produced a grenade. This he handed to Schwarz.

"Do it," he said.

"Seriously?" Schwarz asked.

Lyons nodded. Schwarz shrugged, pulled the pin and let the spoon spring free. Then he counted down in his head…and casually tossed the metal egg into the open window of the black SUV.

Lyons tromped the brakes and spun the wheel, putting pavement between the Suburban and the enemy vehicle.

The explosion shattered the front windshield and spread the occupants of the SUV throughout its interior. A plume of black smoke rose from the truck, which rolled to a fiery stop on burning front tires. The engine compartment, at the rear of the hood, was scorched and blackened.

"We could probably still question one of them," said Schwarz, deadpan.

"Shut up, Gadgets," said Lyons. He managed to put the Suburban back on track, bringing the heavy vehicle to the verge of fishtailing before getting it under control. The third SUV was almost out of sight far ahead of them, but Lyons poured on the speed, weaving in and out of traffic, laying on the horn.

"Do you think they know we're following them?" Schwarz asked.

Lyons glared at him but said nothing. The third of the

black SUVs blew through a traffic light at a large inter-section in their path. Lyons never hesitated; he pushed the Suburban through the same light, scraping a passing taxicab.

Under Lyons's heavy foot, they were drawing even with the fleeing vehicle again. Lyons had been searching the landscape for a suitable spot and noticed they were nearing the empty parking lot of a dilapidated car-wash business.

Schwarz took out his Beretta 93-R and checked the 20-round magazine. He looked at Lyons and nodded. "Good to go, Ironman."

"Good," said Lyons. "Let's go."

He rammed the enemy truck.

The perfectly executed PIT maneuver caused the enemy vehicle to slew sideways and into the cinder-block struc-ture of the car wash. Lyons pushed the Suburban on, roll-ing forward to block off the front quarter of the truck, wedging it between the Suburban and the building. Then he piled out of the driver's side with Schwarz following. The two men broke to either side, one taking the front of the truck, the other the back.

"We need at least one!" Lyons shouted.

"Understood!" Schwarz replied. There was no joking now. Both men were deadly serious about the tasks ahead of them.

Lyons had his Colt Python in both hands as he used the engine block of the Suburban for cover. Pistol shots rang out. A black-clad operative in the front seat of the SUV was shooting through the windshield. Starred bullet holes formed in the safety glass. Lyons added one more, rocket-ing a .357 Magnum hollowpoint through the bridge of the man's cheekbone and out the back of his head. The head-rest behind him exploded in a shower of foam padding.

The rear doors of the SUV were thrown open. Lyons

changed course, coming up behind and on Schwarz's flank. The first man out of the back of the SUV was clever, or thought he was. He dumped himself to the ground, rolled and tried to get a shot off from beneath the door at ground level. Schwarz ran a triple burst of 9 mm bullets up his face from chin to crown.

The last man out took off running.

Schwarz and Lyons looked at each other, then back to the fleeing man, who had dropped a Skorpion machine pistol on the pavement and was now sprinting for his life.

"Seriously?" Schwarz asked.

"I'll sweep the truck," said Lyons.

"I thought you'd say that," said Schwarz, sighing. He took off after the running man.

"Don't shoot him too much," called Lyons after him.

Lyons thought he heard Schwarz shout something in reply, but his words were lost as he ran in the other direction. The Able Team leader shook his head, allowing himself a tight grin, and then climbed up into the back of the black SUV, being careful to search for hidden enemies first.

The interior of the truck was awash in gore. The dead man in the driver's seat was now slumped over the steering wheel, where he would remain until somebody moved him. Lyons searched the interior of the truck as best he could, then circled back around to the driver's seat. There he opened the door and searched the corpse's pockets. He was surprised at what he found.

While the dead man carried nothing helpful in identifying him—he carried nothing at all, in fact, except for a few twenty-dollar bills in a cheap gas-station money clip—he did have a device the size of a smartphone in his pocket. Lyons examined the unit carefully, not sure if it might be a detonator. He was *reasonably* sure it was not, but you just never knew. He considered waiting for Schwarz, but decided against it. There was no telling how long it would take Schwarz to return with his quarry.

Lyons found what appeared to be the power switch for the device and clicked it on. Despite himself, he tensed for a distant explosion.

Nothing happened. A glowing green dot appeared on the black screen of the device. Two seconds later, the unit beeped loudly. Then the dot moved. Lyons turned around, and the dot moved again. The beeping grew louder.

"What the hell?" he muttered. Holding the unit in front of his body, he waved it left, then right, following the beeping as it grew louder. The unit turned him in a circle until he was...

...Facing right back at Able Team's somewhat battered Suburban.

"Oh, you have got to be *kidding* me," said Lyons. He marched toward the truck, now holding the device like a divining rod. There was no doubt in his mind: this was a tracking device. Which meant that somebody had planted a bug on Able Team.

The motorcycles, thought Lyons. They got close enough during that initial pass to plant something on us. Had to be.

It didn't take him long to find the bug, not with the tracker in hand. The magnetic box was the size of a hidden-key unit and stuck just within the left driver's side fender. He opened the box and examined the circuit inside. It didn't mean a whole lot to him, but it might to Schwarz.

"Did I miss anything?" Blancanales asked. He looked slightly out of breath. His M-16 was slung over his shoulder. As he jogged up, he paused, leaned against the Suburban and pressed his hands against his thighs, bracing his upper body. "That's a long walk," he said. "I think I might be getting old."

"That'll be the day," said Lyons. He eyed Blancanales. "Nothing?"

"Sadly, no," said Blancanales. "They were definitely uncooperative. I've transmitted ID photos to the Farm for analysis." He glanced at the electronic device in Lyons's hand. "What have you got there?"

"I think our friends had us bugged," said Lyons. "I found a tracking device on the driver that led me to this. Explains how they stuck to us no matter what we did to shake them."

"But they made no attempt to hide the tail," Blancanales said. "Why use the tracker at all?"

"Well, we did try to lose them more than once," said Lyons. "And if these guys are more of those Shining Beanstalk of Dog mercenaries, or whatever they call themselves, that'd be about their speed. They aren't subtle."

"No, they are not," said Blancanales, nodding. He took out his secure satellite phone. "I'll call the Farm," he said, "and arrange for Barb to run interference with the local police. They'll be on top of us before too long."

"I'm surprised we're not hearing sirens already, actually," said Lyons. "Tell her to hurry."

Blancanales made his call. While Lyons listened, he saw Schwarz in the distance. He was prodding along one of the black-clad mercenaries at gunpoint. Blancanales closed his connection to the Farm and said, "Guess who's coming to dinner?"

"Get out the good china," said Schwarz as he pushed his captive roughly toward the SUV. "This is Fred. Fred apparently doesn't speak English."

"Did he introduce himself as Fred?" Blancanales asked.

"No, that's my nickname for him," said Schwarz. The captive mercenary's hands were held together behind his back with a heavy plastic zip-tie. "Fred keeps blurting out what I assume is his idea of name, rank and serial number. But he also seemed real interested when I called the Farm to send them his picture. I'm betting he was listening to see if he could learn anything. And that means he understands English. Don't you, Fred?"

The telltale flicker in the captive's eyes was as clear a giveaway as if he'd nodded. The man slumped to the pavement next to the bloody, shot-up SUV.

"I notice he didn't waste any time mourning over his fallen comrades," said Blancanales.

"They're a stoic bunch," said Lyons. He walked to the Suburban and opened the rear gate, which gave him access to the tool kit in the rear of the vehicle.

"What are you doing?" asked Schwarz.

"Just what you said," Lyons answered. "Getting the good china." He returned with the vehicle's roadside emergency tool kit in hand and dropped it next to the prisoner on the pavement.

In the distance, police sirens echoed.

"You get through to Barb?" asked Lyons, out of earshot of the prisoner. Blancanales nodded.

"She said she would do what she could," Blancanales told him. "But I think we're going to get some grief for this." He jerked his chin toward the tool kit.

"Whatever," said Lyons. He went to the prisoner and squatted next to the man.

"Fred, meet Ironman," said Schwarz. "Ironman, meet Fred."

"Bring me the battery from this truck," said Lyons, smacking the flank of the black SUV.

Schwarz reached into the truck, popped the hood and snapped open the pliers on the multitool he always carried with him. He whistled as he went to the front of the truck and began unhooking the battery.

"Here's how it is, Fred," said Lyons. He pulled a set of jumper cables from the tool kit. "I'm going to hook your frick and frack there up to these cables. That's going to hurt like hell. And you're going to tell me everything you think I want to know either before or after that happens. If I was you, I'd opt for before."

"One battery," said Schwarz, placing the heavy truck battery next to the prisoner on the asphalt.

Police cars were forming a cordon around them. Blancanales, with his Justice Department identification in hand, walked out to meet them. As the team's skilled diplomat, it was always better to let him handle liaison work. Lyons had no patience for it and would rather send Schwarz to banter with the cops than deal with explaining to them, for the millionth time, that they were on government business at a pay grade far exceeding the locals' own.

"Ironman," said Schwarz. He looked aghast. "You don't mean to shock his man-junk with electricity, do you?"

Lyons waited while Schwarz cheerfully connected the jumper cables to the battery. Then he scraped the black-and-red alligator clamps against each other. Sparks flew. "Yes, actually," he said. "That's just what I have in mind."

"But you're completely forgetting about the road flares," Schwarz said. He reached into the tool kit and came up with a pair of flares. "You could be burning him with these while you do it. Save some time."

Lyons smirked. "That's the first good idea you've had in a long time."

The entire display was entirely for the prisoner's benefit. Able Team would no more torture a bound man than they would murder an unarmed prisoner who was no threat to them or anyone else. The captive, however, had no way to know that. The members of Able Team had worked together for long enough that they had no need to plan an interrogation of this type. They were more than capable of taking their cues from each other.

"Which eyeball?" Schwarz asked. He popped one of the flares, which came alive with crimson chemical fire. "Left or right?"

"You right-eye dominant or left-eye dominant?" Lyons asked the prisoner.

"You should probably tell us your real name, Fred," said Schwarz, bringing the flare closer to the man's face. "You know, before you're too overwhelmed with pain to form a coherent thought."

"You are both insane!" screamed the man.

"There he is," said Schwarz.

Lyons waved Schwarz away. "Time to see how much juice he can soak up," he said, menacing the man with his jumper cables. He struck them together again. The captive flinched as sparks struck his black fatigues.

"Name!" Schwarz demanded.

"Omid Attar! I am Omid Attar! Help! Help me!"

"I think he's shouting for the cops," said Schwarz, still holding the dripping, burning flare. He kept it away from his body so that none of the chemical ooze touched his leg.

Lyons looked over at the cordon, where Blancanales seemed to have things well enough in hand. A couple of the officers were looking on with more than casual interest. At least one of them was using a wireless phone to record what was going on.

"Barb's not going to like that," Lyons said quietly to Schwarz. "Hal won't, either."

"Just another video on the internet showing shadowy federal characters roughing up a suspect," Schwarz whispered back. "We can have Barb talk to them through channels, but we'll need to trust Bear's search algorithms to find and kill the fallout."

Lyons nodded. He didn't pretend to understand the black magic Kurtzman and his cybernetics team wielded, but he knew that the Farm routinely routed out and deleted on-line evidence of the Stony Man teams' activities. In an age marked by almost constant surveillance from both closed-circuit cameras and civilian-owned recording equipment, the program was necessary to preserve the secrecy of the Sensitive Operations Group's counterterrorism activities. Lyons rarely dwelled on it, but there were times when he wondered just how many hundreds or thousands of pieces of data the Farm hunted down, hacked into and destroyed every day.

"Shut up, Omid," said Lyons.

"I like 'Fred' better," said Schwarz.

Lyons shook the jumper cables. "Out with it," he ordered. "Why were you following us? Who do you work for?"

"We thought you were working for Clayton," Attar said. "We thought you were Sapphire. He uses the Sapphire Corporation to guard his facilities."

Schwarz and Lyons exchanged glances. "So you stuck this tracker on us…why?"

"We thought you were meeting with Clayton because you serve him," Attar repeated. "We followed you to kill you. To send a message to Clayton. To let Sapphire know they were no match for us, that their people are not safe."

"So you just happened by at the right moment?" Lyons asked.

"We had Clayton's headquarters under surveillance," Attar admitted.

"All right, Omid," began Lyons.

"Fred," insisted Schwarz.

"All right, Fred," said Lyons, without missing a beat. "Let's talk about just who 'we' might be. And then let's get into where 'we' can be found. And let's keep our answers confined to the truth, shall we?"

Omid Attar stared at the Able Team members, pale and shaking. "I will tell you," he said. "I will tell you what you want to know."

Lyons snorted. "I remember when these guys were tougher."

"I know, right?" said Schwarz.

CHAPTER ELEVEN

The Antonov An-24 was old, a relic of sales made to the Democratic People's Republic of Korea by the now defunct Soviet Union. First flown in 1959, the An-24 had been abandoned by much of the world, but a few Antonovs originally fielded during the plane's active service life were still flying. This craft, painstakingly cared for by the Advance Guard's party mechanics, was largely free of malfunction, although Soong il Yun would not want to wager on the strength of the aging airframe should aggressive maneuvers be required.

The plane required a crew of four and had a fifty-person capacity, enough to ferry Soong's elite commando team to their destination. It was powered by two anemic Ivchenko Al-24A turboprops whose specs claimed would produce 2,550 horsepower. The actual power of the craft was considerably diminished by its age and by sometimes improvised repairs. It would, however, get them to their assignment, which was all that mattered. The wretched thing could crash into the ocean, as far as Soong il Yun was concerned, once his men had dropped to the sea for pickup by the lab ship.

As they left North Korean airspace, Soong regarded the engraved Chinese lighter in his hand. It was a polished chrome copy of a much better known American model. It leaked fluid if it was not kept upright, but it usually lighted when he struck its wheel. Engraved on its surface were the words *Chungseong, Daedam, Hyeongje.* Very loosely translated: Loyalty, Fearlessness, Brotherhood. It lost something in that translation, and in the abbreviation necessary to fit the characters on the lighter's surface.

He tapped the dark red pack of Songbong cigarettes on the back of the lighter before opening it. His wife had asked him time and again to quit smoking, and several times he had tried to comply. The stress of operations in the field, and the fact that so many of his men smoked, conspired to ruin him every time he went out on assignment. She worried for him, and for his health, should his smoking begin to take its toll on his body. Medical treatment was sorely lacking in the Democratic People's Republic of Korea. While it might be possible to smuggle him to the South, as so many of the Party elites paid to do when they required quality health care, his ability to pay for that privilege was highly dependent on whether his government was able to pay his salary. Payroll was spotty at best, even among those at the top of the Party hierarchy.

The drastic devaluation of the DPRK's currency had caused much of that hardship. It was forbidden to publicly criticize the policy. Soong himself maintained few savings, if only because he knew he might be killed on a mission at any given moment. This was a reality he held from his wife, who probably understood it on some level, but who preferred to pretend it was not the truth.

He snapped open his lighter, ignited it and fired the powerful Songbong, draggng warm smoke deep into his lungs. To be honest, he preferred the Ch'olijjuks, which were smoother, but the Songbongs were serviceable and had a deep, full flavor. Many of the men preferred foreign cigarettes when they could get them, but Soong took seriously the mantra engraved on his lighter.

The lighter was a gift from the Leader himself, General Secretary of the Worker's Party of North Korea and Chairman of the National Defense Commission. Soong still remembered with pride the day that the Leader had presented that token of his appreciation for all of Soong's efforts. Three days of military parade reviews had culminated in the ceremony, during which the Leader had commissioned the Advance Guard. Being designated the commander of this new commando unit, whose members were among the toughest in the DPRK military, was the greatest honor Soong had or would be granted in life. He would live with the words *Loyalty, Fearlessness, Brotherhood* emblazoned on his heart for his allies and his enemies to see. If he were lucky, he would die in service to his country.

It had taken time, and a life lived well, finally to take the Leader from his people. Soong still had to fight not to tear up when thinking of it. He knew that, in the West, video and still photos of North Korean citizens bemoaning the loss of their beloved ruler were viewed as evidence of their irrational devotion to a man the West called a "dictator." Soong snorted at the thought, blowing strong smoke from his nose. The fools. Much of the world tolerated weakness and arrogance in its leaders. Not so the Democratic People's Republic of Korea, which had installed a man truly worthy to lead and to serve its people, after first honoring the Leader's deceased father as North Korea's "eternal president."

Many times subsequent to the leader's death, Soong had met with the country's new ruler, the Leader's son. Much as it pained him to admit it, if only in his heart of hearts, Soong regretted that he could not think of his new ruler as anything but the son of the man who had served before. When he thought of the Leader, he thought of the man who had handed him that silver lighter and tasked him with the burden of fighting North Korea's most covert battles, defeating its most hated and fearsome enemies.

Fearsome they were. No less than the combined might of most of the world considered North Korea a rogue state. It was the plight of the just, of those who were superior, to be forever condemned by their lessers. The Leader himself had once explained this to Soong. It made so much sense, when one considered it. Of course the South and its many hedonist allies considered the North an enemy. They feared it. They feared what would happen if at any moment the DPRK decided to slip the many leashes they had thrown on it.

He felt his face darkening. Economic sanctions, and the crippling poverty these created, had been responsible for much hardship in the DPRK. The Leader and now his son worked hard every day to combat the negative effects of the Western world's contempt. There were limits to what they could do, limits to the North's resources. While the nation enjoyed limited success trading with partners like Russia, which in some ways remembered its Soviet Communist roots only too well, the day to say suffering of the common Korean people was a knife in Soong's heart.

His wife's brother, a construction worker, had not been paid for so many months that the government ultimately lost track of what his rate of pay was supposed to have been. When last the family had heard from Soong's brother-in-law, he had been provisionally reassigned, which meant he was spending his days selling soap and other goods by the roadside.

The projects on which Soong's brother-in-law had worked were largely what the Leader had termed "projects of hope." Intended to inspire fear and awe among their hated enemies to the South, great skyscrapers and apartment complexes had been erected near the border. They were of the finest materials available and constructed per the most modern new designs.

They stood empty.

There were no businesses to make use of the skyscrapers and their offices. There were no citizens who could afford to live in the gleaming apartment complexes. And so the structures, once erected, stood vacant and hollow, slowly peeling in the baking sun and the driving rain.

Then, of course, there were the famines, again engineered by the economic policies of the uncaring, callous West.

Not since the Arduous March, the famine of the late 1990s, had so many in North Korea suffered without food. At the peak of that earlier famine, in 1997, more than a million people had died of hunger or related sickness. Now famine and blight were moving across the face of North Korea once more, threatening to start the death spiral that had so damaged the DPRK a decade before. In the border villages, the old were dropping dead of malnutrition as if struck by a sniper's bullet. Worse, the accounts of these tragedies were making their way into the propaganda mills of the West's state-controlled media, where they were used to spread rumors of the inadequacy of North Korea's government. Of all the lies perpetrated by America and her allies, the notion that the Leader and his noble son were less than fit to serve was the one that galled Soong most.

How dare they?

Soong dragged on his cigarette, taking the smoke deep into his lungs, then blowing it through his nostrils again. The powerful tobacco still gave him something of a head rush, although this was only a pale shadow of what it might once have been. Soong's habit, assumed again with greater vigor than on previous outings, was verging on a pack a day.

Reminding himself of these petty indignities, the disdain with which the rich and corrupt nations of the world held his people, helped Soong remember why he was here and what he was tasked to accomplish. He was also reminded of the many failures the DPRK and its covert assets had suffered when attempting previous operations against America and its allies. Some of those had involved Soong's relatives, men who had served in the family's proud tradition of loyalty to the North. Soong was ashamed that news of his fellow covert operatives' failures, including those whose failures conferred shame on his own family name, had been brought up, if briefly, by the son of the Leader. He knew this for what it was: a method of motivating him, while also rewarding him with the opportunity to right the wrongs, to redress the failures, of those who had come before him.

Intelligence reports from their spies and paid operatives in America had told him that a disturbing pattern was revealing itself. This he had seen and noted even before the Leader had summoned him to the presidential palace in Pyongyang. Time and again, the North had attempted to execute what the West would invariably consider "terrorist" actions.

America could view no military reprisals taken against it as legitimate. No, any action must be that of a rogue state, one warranting further sanctions, no doubt. Yet the Americans, cowards that they were, and their puppets in the United Nations were afraid to attack the DPRK directly. That might expose the Americans and their allies, the British, for the hypocrites that they were. And so they waged their wars by proxy while condemning the North's justified attempts to seek retribution for past dishonors.

But there was more, an underbelly to the international intelligence actions that the rest of the world was not allowed to see. Soong was aware of it only because covert operations were his stock in trade. The Americans and their allies were illegally diverting agents from their Central Intelligence Agency, or perhaps their National Security Agency, to illegally wage war on foreign soil while thwarting, with military tactics and without regard for their vaunted "rule of law," what they considered terrorist actions within their own borders.

Soong's predecessors had suffered accordingly, especially when they'd underestimated the military might the United States and the rest of the West could bring to bear, secretly, against its enemies. The Americans spoke of human rights and liberty and other nonsense in public, but in private they maintained death squads of cutthroat gunmen whom they dispatched all over the globe.

It was at the hands of these mysterious gunmen that so many of Soong's predecessors had come to dishonor. Each and every time the Advance Guard or other covert units had mounted an attack on the West, the nameless, faceless death squads were there, slaughtering North Korean operatives, mounting assaults on North Korean military elements, even invading North Korean soil. These last were highly classified, held even more secret than the attempts by the North to assassinate the South Korean leader in years past.

That thought brought the flicker of a smile to Soong's lips. The South had been outraged when loyal suicide troops, trained in the North, had penetrated their border and come within a breath of ending their own leader's life. What a glory that would have been had it worked! The avenging soldiers of the North, sweeping across the demilitarized zone, leaving the South helpless in the face of its greater sibling's might. Not since the brave troops of true Koreans had fought back the American invaders half a century ago had such a complete victory been in their grasp. How sweet it must have been, to live during those years, to know the justice that was the humiliation of the United States.

But not so now.

The drug lab ships had not been Soong's business, nor had he held any hand in their creation. He had, however, made an extensive study of the program at the Leader's request, to verify that the revenues from the drug ships were sufficient to offset both the costs of their maintenance and the risks they undertook in plying the drug trade across international waters. It was during this study that he had realized the potential the ships held to act as infrastructure for the creation of a weapons pipeline. If the North had a steady supply of the components needed to build intercontinental ballistic missiles, they could finally reach out and smash their enemies from afar.

North Korea's own missile program had struggled to achieve even distant viability. High-profile failures had made them the laughingstock of other nations. Fortunately the Leader and his son were both adept at using the lies of Western media to their advantage. They had, Soong was told, been instrumental in playing up the rumors, so that the West would underestimate North Korea's military might.

Surprise was an important component of winning any battle, after all.

Finding suppliers for components that had been forbidden North Korea by the self-righteous dictators of the West had proved not at all as difficult as he had thought it would. Soong had forgotten, only briefly, the chief lesson one learned about America and its satellites: they loved nothing but money. Money in sufficient quantity could induce any American to betray any other American. You needed look only to their depraved television shows to see evidence of that. Their people were fat, uneducated, lazy and always seeking money and fame. Their daughters were whores who took off their clothes at the slightest provocation, only to have their dissolute behavior broadcast to their fathers, their brothers and millions of lecherous strangers. Their inability to maintain a family structure was legend and, instead of hiding this shame, they trumpeted even that to anyone who would listen. It was sickening. *They* were sickening. America, the West…they were a wasting disease plaguing the world. Only when their power was smashed, only when their grip on the planet was loosened, could nations like the Democratic People's Republic of Korea truly prosper.

To fulfill our destiny, Soong thought, taking a last drag on his dwindling cigarette, we must force the boot of the West from off our necks.

Initially, Soong's plan had involved paying the hated Americans only indirectly. The Iranians, grasping and desperate though they might be in their own way, were not without their uses. While Soong had little use for religious zealotry, the Iranians were willing to work with him. He was not in a position to be too selective. He needed the components, and the Iranians claimed they could get them, at a level of quality to meet or exceed his specifications. Those specifications were for a caliber of component manufactured only in the West.

It was to his amusement that he had learned of the source of the Iranian ICBM parts, as it was a necessity for him to organize supply lines that mated with the drug ship routes. The Iranians had co-opted American manufacturers and already had in place an extensive network. Using their Revolutionary Path of God foot soldiers to safeguard their interests, the Iranians had bought into or otherwise subverted American manufacturing interests with close ties to the United States Department of Defense.

This would be impossible in North Korea. It seemed in America, even the souls of the Americans themselves were for hire. That was the only conceivable way so many Westerners could look the other way while their weapons were ferried to the enemy from their own soil, in contravention of their own export regulations.

Soong had thrown his lot in with the Iranians early on, and they had started to deliver. Not long after the pipeline was set up, however, they started to experience setbacks. The drug ships had come under attack and Soong had lost all but the largest of the fleet to daring commando raids. These raids were illegal acts of war in international waters. They were carried out with precision and with deadly force. No nation had accepted credit for them, but Soong knew. It was the pattern he had seen before.

It was the Western death squads.

Somehow they had fallen wise to his scheme, and now they were acting with their customary lack of regard for human life. They would hunt Soong's operatives on the seas, they would hunt their own traitors in the United States and they were hunting the Iranians and the Revolutionary Path of God mercenaries defending their American holdings. Already, word of the damage these death squads were wreaking had gotten back to North Korea and to the Leader's son. The threat to the ICBM operation was very palpable.

He was grateful that he had, to now, held the foresight to discuss alternative pipelines with those making inquiries. He did not trust the American businessman with whom he had spoken by phone several times now. How did one trust a traitor, after all? A man willing to betray his nation for money, to endanger the safety of his fellow Americans, his own countrymen, even his own family in a general sense, would betray any ally he adopted subsequently. But the American claimed he could deliver where the Iranians could not. With shipment after shipment falling into the hands of the death squad interdictors, and with more American killers attacking the Iranian-owned manufactories in the United States, it was looking very possible that the American's shipment of components would be the one on which Soong would need to rely.

He regretted this. The Iranians might be zealots, but they were predictable zealots. In theory, a man motivated by love of nothing but money was predictable, as well… unless someone offered him more money to do something else. The Iranians could be relied on to choose a course of action and stick to it for the greater glory of Allah or whomever. None of that mattered to Soong, who was an atheist if he was anything. Most days he did not bother to consider what was beyond. He was too busy focusing on the survival of his nation and of his family.

One was the other. North Korea was his family, as much as were his wife and his infant boy. He would die for his nation as readily as for his own blood.

There were other complications, revealed to him in his intelligence briefings, that demanded his attention and his suspicions. There were possibly more elements in play here than the American death squads, the DPRK and its loyal troops, and the Iranian mercenaries. Evidence in front of him pointed to another paramilitary concern. A private security firm called Sapphire had staged raids abroad on elements of the Iranian mercenaries. It looked to Soong like a proxy war, and that concerned him. Every variable unaccounted for was one that might lead to the failure of the ICBM pipeline.

Worse, Sapphire was in the employ of the American

traitor, which meant the man was playing a dangerous game in the hope of driving business from Soong and to him. But Soong could not afford merely to eliminate the enemy. He might need the American, Sapphire or no, because of the damage already dealt to the Iranian organization by both Sapphire and the Western death squads. The latter had probably only just begun, regardless of whether Sapphire planned further incursions. Soong detested the position in which this left him.

The Leader's son had been very clear: the ICBMs must be completed. The arsenal of North Korea's future supremacy must come to fruition. It was the lynchpin of the nation's future military plans, and would orchestrate the acceleration of the DPRK's status from rogue nation to that which it truly deserved as a world power.

Soong thirsted for that time to come. North Korea deserved to take its place at the table of nations. Respect must be earned, yes, but the respect borne of fear was the truest kind. What was it the philosopher had said? It was better to be feared than loved…if one of the two must be lacking. He would accept fear from the hated nations of the West. He did not need their love.

For his part, Soong loved and feared the Leader and his offspring. He desired nothing but the achievement of his nation. He wished it to *become,* to fulfill itself. And while the Leader's son was as fair and just as his predecessor, there was no room in the DPRK for failures. There was no place for men who were not courageous enough, who were not competent enough, to do what was asked of them…and to succeed at it.

Should his plan fail, should he be unable to make the ICBM pipeline work, his position as commander of the Advance Guard would not be the only thing in jeopardy. Soong's very life would be forfeit.

Hc had considered this possibility. He was resigned to it. He had always known he would die in service to the Leader or his successors.

He did, however, worry about his family. Were he to be executed as a failure by his government, it was likely the wrath of his government would fall on his family, not to mention any members of his unit deemed contributors to his failure. His family would be sent to a labor camp. He did not like to think what would become of them then.

He resolved, then, to do whatever was required to succeed. Should he be unable to achieve victory despite his most superhuman efforts, and if he lived long enough, he would be summoned home to face his punishment. He would be expected to make peace with his family before appearing for an audience with the Leader's son. That would give him the opportunity to kill his wife and son quickly and humanely, on his own terms, preventing them from suffering.

But that was not the way he would face this task. That was thinking for, planning first for, failure and defeat. That was not his way. His way was to fight, and to fight for his nation. His way was to *win*. He decided, then that he would send a message to this Sapphire, while leaving open the path of communication to the American traitor. He would, as they said in the West, have his cake and eat it, too.

He surveyed the ranks of his Advance Guard commandos, who were silently checking their weaponry as they squatted in their jump seats. These were deadly men. These were harsh men. These men were the equal of any enemy they might face. He reached for the satellite phone he kept with him at all times, and began dialing.

They would win.

They would defeat the West.

They would fulfill his nation's destiny and honor the memory of the Leader.

Soong was so pleased at the thought, he did not feel his spent cigarette burning his fingers.

CHAPTER TWELVE

Manila, Philippines

"Reginald St. John-Smythe to see your operations director," David McCarter officiously. He wore an ill-fitting shirt, tie, slacks and blazer, purchased too quickly in a shop in downtown Manila for what was probably a princely sum in the local currency. With him, similarly dressed, were Calvin James and Gary Manning. Manning was particularly conspicuous in his pinstriped polyester getup, for his big frame was simply too out of the norm for Manila. It had been nearly impossible to find something to fit him off the rack. McCarter thought the poor chap might burst the seams of his jacket were he to raise his arms straight over his head.

They were executing a plan that was more casual than McCarter would like, and he was still feeling as if his land legs were slow to return, but when the call had come from the Farm, he'd understood its importance. The links to this Sapphire Corporation that Able Team had only just turned up painted the company as a very likely player in whatever was going on in the industries supplying ICBM components to the North Koreans. It was, frankly speaking, time to get to the bottom of things, and to do that required something that was both a bit less formal and a lot more effective than sending in a team of local investigators from some vaguely affiliated agency.

In other words, Phoenix Force was going to break some laws.

If Sapphire was clean, and its name coming up only a coincidence, then the fact that it had offices very near the part of the world where floating North Korean drug labs were being used to ferry contraindicated ICBM component cargo was an even worse coincidence. All of that seemed too great a storm of happenstance for McCarter's liking. His gut told him that Sapphire was into this up to its eyeballs. When the Farm passed the word that one of the company's major hubs was here in Manila, the team's members had hatched this mad plan to brazen their way into the place and get a good look around.

Given the need for plausible deniability in their raids on the drug lab ships, they could count on neither local cooperation nor a good word from the Farm through channels to nominally friendly intelligence agencies. Word would get back to whomever was interested that a team, possibly traceable to the United States specifically, or to the West generally, had been calling for assistance in conducting an intelligence operation in Manila…all while a series of extralegal raids was conducted in waters not terribly far from that city. If McCarter's gut told him things, and it did, he had no reason to think the Farm's enemies couldn't also see that two and two rarely made five. Even the appearance of impropriety had to be avoided, lest suspicion fall on Western assets and create even worse tensions on the international scene.

So it was that McCarter and his teammates had resorted to the tactics of con men, bluffing their way into the Sapphire building, hoping to provoke a reaction that would expose their potential enemies for what they were. The method was simple enough, if reckless, and a less cohesive unit with less extensive combat experience might not be able to pull it off. It was even, when you thought about it, rather childish: Phoenix Force was going to see who they could make angry in the hope that the resulting explosion would clear away Sapphire's disguise as a reputable private security firm.

It was hard not to feel like a cheap gangster wearing the getup in which he was now dressed, McCarter mused, but that was the point. He was as in character as he was likely to get. At his shoulders, James seemed perfectly at ease playing the heavy. The Briton also had to admit that of the three of them, Calvin James looked the best in the suit he had picked out. Of course, it was easy to look good next to the awkward figure Manning struck. For all that his suit did not fit, however, Manning was still a large, imposing man.

The suit jackets also concealed their weapons nicely.

Hawkins and Encizo, meanwhile, were in their stolen truck in the alley behind the building, ready to back up the rest of the team if the excrement struck the oscillator. McCarter had to admit that stealing the truck from a commercial transport facility's parking lot, in the predawn hours of the morning, had made him feel more like a criminal. It was James who had insisted, if they must steal a vehicle, that it not be some random citizen's ride. It was bad enough dealing an economic setback to one of the local businesses, but there was no way to requisition a vehicle through normal channels without calling suspicion upon themselves. They had to be perfectly deniable. Stealing their transportation during this little tactical layover in Manila was one way to help ensure that.

Some part of him enjoyed being able to play fast and loose with the rules, McCarter admitted. That had not prevented him from transmitting a coded text message to the Farm, with the identification of the SUV they'd "borrowed" and the address of the company from which it had been taken. Price and the cybernetics team at the Farm would see to it that a tax accounting error or some other government windfall compensated the company for the loss. Knowing that did not make McCarter feel less the rogue, though.

It's true what the man said, McCarter thought. Deep within us all lies the urge to hoist the black flag and start slitting throats, or however that old quote goes.

He'd deliberately swept open the double glass doors of the Sapphire facility with more force than was necessary. The doors banged against the wall on either side and almost snapped back on Manning and James. McCarter'd immediately homed in on the shaved-headed tough-guy character behind the "reception" desk, which looked to the former SAS man a lot more like a security checkpoint than an administrative workstation. His suspicions started to rise the second he saw the man's body language change. The "receptionist" had tensed up for the briefest moment before he caught himself. If there wasn't a pistol in a trick under-desk holster waiting behind that workstation, or perhaps even a sawed-off shotgun hanging under the desk, McCarter would be very surprised.

"I want to see whoever's in charge of this affront to God and country," added McCarter, his blustering tone elevated by the exaggerated version of his own accent. "Do you blighters realize how many regulations you're violating? Every inch of this facility screams punitive penalties!"

James turned to Manning and mouthed, "'Punitive penalties'?"

The man behind the desk was no Filipino. When he spoke, he had a slight German accent. He wore a tailored suit that accentuated his broad shoulders and didn't completely hide the bulge of the gun under his arm.

"Just who in the hell do you think you are, now?" asked the man. A placard on the desk identified him as "O. Bader."

"Don't listen very well, do you, Bader?" McCarter said. He marched directly to the desk and poked Bader in the chest, emphasizing each word with another poke. "I. Am. Reginald. St. John-Smythe. And I am empowered by the city government of Manila, not to mention that of the nation on whose soil we both stand, to conduct facility-wide inspections for environmental hazards, be they internal, external or...environmental."

Bader stared at McCarter as if the man had two heads. "Are you daft, man?" he demanded. "I've never heard of you and whatever organization it is you think you represent."

"It doesn't matter if you're aware of the Manila Environmental Element Opposing Pollution. We are governmental and duly authorized. You will step aside and we will conduct this regularly scheduled spot-check of this facility and its neighbors. Unless you would like us to return tomorrow with a police escort?"

A door opened behind Bader's desk, leading to the back rooms of the office. When it did, a cloud of cigarette smoke rushed out to greet the men in the reception area. The two men who stuck their heads out of the doorway were each larger than Bader, who was not exactly small. They wore T-shirts, BDU pants and web gear. When they caught sight of McCarter and the others, the two conferred in hushed tones in what sounded like broken English.

"Well, well," said McCarter. "What have we here? Something of an international workforce, yes? I trust you're compliant with all local environmental standards in addition to applicable labor force laws."

The two hardcases in the doorway looked at Bader,

who shrugged almost imperceptibly. It was obvious he was weighing the pros and cons of simply instructing his two backbreakers—and whoever else might be waiting in the smoky crew room beyond—to come at the visitors with ill intent.

No doubt he's wondering if he can leave us dead in the alley outside, and whether that will bring down any serious law-enforcement heat, McCarter thought. Right now he can't figure out why whatever bribes he's spread around the local government and police aren't keeping us out of his hair. He's probably also curious as to whether or not he can just pay us to go away.

McCarter didn't intend to give Bader that chance. The plan rested on bluffing their way through the building's outer defenses. The key was to get as far into the middle of whatever was going on here at Sapphire before the personnel inside the building thought to oppose them.

"This is bad," sniffed McCarter. "This is very, very bad. Do you have any idea how many smoking regulations you're violating? Why, the secondhand smoke to which your employees are being exposed is itself grounds for a Section 81-74 investigation of these premises." He brushed past Bader, circling the desk, and went straight for the two military-clad stevedores.

"Halt," said one of the two men, another German.

"Holding-uppen-zee yourself," said McCarter in his worst imitation of pidgin German. "Official government business!" He pushed his way into the crew room before the two operators could react. Bader came trailing after, which only allowed James and the awkwardly shuffling Manning to file in behind.

"You cannot simply walk in here and help yourself," said Bader. His voice was a low growl. "There are certain formalities."

"Formalities?" McCarter whirled on him, sweeping his arms wide, deliberately slapping one of the two hardcases. The big man barely flinched, but his eyes went to McCarter's hand and then to McCarter himself. His face began to turn red.

"We have an understanding with the city officials here in Manila," said Bader.

"Ah, well, if it's graft and corruption you like," McCarter said, "you need look no further than this den of iniquity. I believe we'll need to take a good, long hard look through your computer to see if your records are in order."

"I cannot allow that!" Bader protested.

James looked at Manning and mouthed, "'Den of iniquity'?" Manning shook his head.

The crew room contained two more Sapphire operators. One was an enormous black man, while the other was apparently yet another German, judging from the profanities he used. The metal table at which the men sat was covered in money and cards. Evidently, McCarter and Phoenix Force had interrupted a poker game. Glass ashtrays overflowing with cigarette butts and cigars sourced the bluish haze that hung low in the room.

The metal door leading through the back of the crew room was what interested McCarter, however. As if they could read his mind, the two men at the poker table stood and arrayed themselves in front of the door.

"That's enough of your nonsense," said Bader. There was no mistaking the menace in his tone. There was a metallic click. McCarter looked back over his shoulder to see the man holding an out-the-front automatic knife, the kind of high-tech, expensive switchblade that some men found the need to carry. McCarter's own fighting knife was tucked inside his waistband in its sheath, under his suit jacket, opposite the Browning Hi-Power behind his hip.

"Mr. Bader," said McCarter, feigning innocence, "you don't mean to interfere with duly appointed governmental inspections, do you, old chap?"

"What I mean," said Bader, "is to stick you in the belly and watch the expression on your face while you try to hold your guts in. *Old chap.*"

"Then I'm afraid you leave me no choice," said McCarter, lunging between the second pair of operators and hauling open the metal door at the rear of the crew room.

The half-dozen armed men sitting in the locker room beyond were field-stripping automatic weapons. Two or three had cigarettes dangling from their mouths. They stared at the open doorway in frozen surprise. One man, who had been loading magazines for a SIG-Sauer assault rifle, dropped a cartridge on the floor. In the silence, as Phoenix Force, Bader, his men and the operators in the locker room all stared at each other, the sound of the brass-cased round rolling across the concrete floor was astonishingly loud.

Bader took a step toward McCarter. The two men on either side of the Briton reached for him.

"Apocalypse now," said McCarter quietly.

The former SAS commando pulled his fighting knife from his waistband, bringing it first up, then down in a single fluid movement. The blade carved a runnel in Bader's cheek and down his chest, slicing deeply into his knife arm from the inside, cleaving the inside of his wrist. The shriek Bader made was guttural, the abject terror of a man who knows he's been dealt a permanently crippling injury.

McCarter's code phrase was the signal, carried by his earbud transceiver to all of Phoenix Force, that the time for pretending was over. At that signal, Calvin James had drawn two Makarov pistols from his waistband—one his own, the other borrowed from Gary Manning. With his arms wide, he drew down on both the men reaching for McCarter. As their fingers brushed the Briton's suit jacket, James pulled the triggers of his pistols three times, punching both men into the doorjambs behind them. The shots from even the relatively small Makarovs echoed like thunder from within the crew room.

McCarter rammed his knife into the stricken Bader's throat from the side, yanking it back out through the front of the man's neck. He narrowly dodged the crimson spray that resulted. His Hi-Power clone was in his hand as he stepped over the body.

These actions took only fractions of a second to occur. As they happened, the two operators who had first opened the crew room door were scrambling for weapons concealed under their shirts. As they clawed for their guns, Gary Manning was hauling the AK-47 rifle from behind his back, where it had been tucked down one of his pant legs. It was the concealed rifle, as much as his poorly fitting clothes, that had contributed largely to his uncomfortable movements.

Manning positioned himself between the two hardcases. The AK had a heavy wooden stock. He slammed the butt of the rifle into the skull of the man to his right, producing a sickening crunch and a splatter of blood droplets. The man to his left was already bringing up a Glock pistol. Manning swung the rifle like a baseball bat and chopped the man in the neck with it. The operator's head snapped forward. He folded.

The 30-round magazine for his AK was in Manning's back pocket, and as he brought the rifle up to his shoulder, he was slamming the magazine up and back into the weapon's magazine well. He reached over the top of the rifle with his left hand to rack the bolt—the simplified design of the Kalashnikov pattern, which combined the charging handle with the bolt on the side bearing the ejection port, meant it would never be a terribly ergonomic assault rifle—and had time to say just one word:

"Down!" he roared.

McCarter did not hesitate. He hit the floor in the doorway to the locker room. Manning burned the space where he had been standing, filling the doorway with 7.62 mm rounds, spraying out the 30-round magazine in short, measured bursts.

Manning's jacket split in two over his shoulders.

James ducked down, scooped up the fallen Glock and tossed it to Gary Manning, who let his empty AK fall to the floor and caught the Glock with his right hand. He ran the slide back, ejecting an unfired round, and followed McCarter through the doorway with James close behind.

The room was large, with rows of free-standing metal lockers creating a series of fatal kill zones. As bullets struck the lockers, they rang like kettle drums, creating a cacophony that sounded like dissonant church bells. McCarter pointed left and right, directing James and Manning to separate rows, and took cover behind the farthest of these. The gunmen within the locker room had fled to the far end and were using the same lockers for cover, which meant who got shot was really a question of who wanted to make it happen most.

McCarter didn't believe in playing games by the other fellows' rules.

From the pocket of his suit jacket he took the single grenade he had brought with him. The white phosphorous grenade was both an incendiary and an obscurant. It would burn hot where its chemical fire touched an enemy, but it would also produce plenty of smoke to use for cover. McCarter pulled the pin, sent the spoon flying and gently rolled the grenade down the aisle between the lockers.

"Willy Pete," said McCarter softly.

McCarter pitied any man caught by the blast. White phosphorous would burn until it exhausted its available oxygen supply, producing intense heat. It could also poison internal organs, causing kidney failure, heart failure, liver damage and infections in severe cases of exposure. Hypocalcaemia and retardation of the healing process were also possibilities in long-term survivors.

Much as he would hate to be on the catcher's end of a white phosphorous munition, McCarter took a dim view of anyone who tried to murder him and his teammates. This was especially so given that, as far as Bader's Sapphire men knew, Phoenix Force were simply obnoxious bureaucrats.

Not that we all haven't considered burning alive a bureaucrat or two, McCarter thought wryly. The grenade exploded, producing a series of horrific screams from beyond the barrier of the lockers.

McCarter began counting in his head, as he knew James and Manning would be. They would give the grenade's smoke pall enough time to envelope the enemy side of the locker room.

"Calvin, Gary, take the right," said McCarter into his transceiver. "Sweep from right to left. I'll play cleanup from this end, catch any stragglers."

"Roger," said James.

"Affirmative," said Manning.

"Wait for my mark," McCarter ordered. He braced himself against the lockers and aimed for the smoke cloud. There was a man lying on the ground, struggling and twitching, as several hot spots bore into his scorched clothing. Several more operators were still behind cover, but coughing and choking on the fumes.

McCarter put a mercy round through the critically wounded man's head.

The shot brought return fire from the enemy operatives, as it was meant to. McCarter was diverting their attention at a right angle from the alley Manning and James would use to run them down through the smoke.

"Go!" McCarter said.

Manning and James made their play. The light staccato of James's twin Makarovs was easily distinguished from Manning's borrowed Glock. These were followed by the heavy automatic hammer of an assault weapon, possibly one of the SIGs the Sapphire operatives had left behind, no doubt borrowed by either James or Manning on their way to complete their task.

A wounded Sapphire man ran past McCarter. In the smoke, he completely missed the Briton. McCarter simply waited for the distance between to be optimal, then barked, "Hey! Mate!"

The Sapphire gunman swiveled, trying to line up a shot on the fly. McCarter shot him in the throat and then twice more in the chest. The slide of his Hi-Power locked open.

"Clear!" said Manning.

"Clear!" shouted James.

"Clear as day," muttered Manning. "Let's get gone, lads. We don't want to be here when the Manila police show up."

They made a brief circuit of the devastated Sapphire headquarters. McCarter found a single computer, a desktop PC, in a small room off the lobby that he had first taken for a closet. He paused long enough to rip the PC box from the cords connecting it to the wall and to its monitor. He handed the unit to Manning.

"Here, Gary, you carry this," he said. "Your suit is already ruined."

Manning shot him an irate glance but did not comment.

They checked the street beyond from behind the barely cracked door, decided it was as safe as it would likely get and hit the street at a jog.

"Engine's running, y'all," said Hawkins through their transceivers.

"We're going to need to contact the Farm," said Mc-Carter. "Whatever Sapphire's got going, it's more than just a penchant for murdering meddling environmentalists. They didn't get truly serious until I threatened to snoop through their computer. And no legitimate security company is quite so blithe about killing random civilians."

"Do you suppose Barb knew we would burn down the place when she sent us to investigate?" Manning asked.

"Water's wet," James said. "Bears poop in the woods."

"No more poetry," said McCarter. They reached their stolen truck and climbed in. As they were backing their way down the alley with Hawkins behind the wheel, the braying sirens of Manila law-enforcement vehicles were just audible over the sounds of the busy city's traffic.

"This suit is always going to smell like smoke," said James, reloading his Makarov and handing Manning's back to him.

"What, do you have a prom to attend?" Encizo asked.

"David," said James. His face split into a wide grin. "Your made-up organization, Manila Environmental Element Opposing Pollution?"

"What of it?" McCarter asked.

"The Manila Env.El.O.P.?"

"And?" McCarter asked, forcing a completely deadpan expression.

James held his own face in one large palm. Even Manning cracked a smile at that.

CHAPTER THIRTEEN

Outside Mobile, Alabama

Vahid Rahimi backhanded the prostitute. She fell against the edge of the bed and landed on the stained carpet, where she began to whimper pitiably. He raised his hand as if he would strike her again and then decided not to bother.

American whores, he thought, sneering. You cannot tell one from the rest of the inhabitants of this godless land.

His temper had little to do with whether the woman pleased him. Four more of her ilk were here in the rented house, far from where prying eyes or listening ears could detect any sign that something might be amiss. Although how the Americans could detect what was or wasn't amiss was anyone's guess. They lived in filth and misery. They were the epitome of decadence. Nothing about them was free of decay, free of corruption. He would gladly see the entire country destroyed, burned to glass by nuclear weapons. He lived for the day that Iran held the power to be able to achieve that.

Rahimi held no illusions about his nation's own status compared to the West. State control of the economy, and mismanagement of economic policy, had left many in Iran out of work. The private sector was a sham, a joke, confined to small workshops and farms. Subsidies and other price controls squeezed any hope of growth from what little economic activity did occur. All of the government officials, including those responsible for economic monitoring, were corrupt.

Vahid Rahimi had been born with a mottled white birthmark staining his face. His mother had seen it as a mark of his ungodliness, as punishment from Allah. She had been ashamed of him from birth, even abandoning him for a time before finally relenting and agreeing to feed and clothe him. His growth had been affected by that early malnutrition. One of his legs was shorter than the other. He wore an insert in his right boot to compensate.

His early childhood had been horrific. He was aware of this and acknowledged it, but it was not as if he would permit himself to lie awake at night thinking about it. His mother had taken to flogging him every day with a heavy belt, one of his father's old ones. His father, too, would beat him, but with his fists, as if Vahid were a man. Some part of Rahimi appreciated that distinction. It was bad enough to be beaten as a man. It was far worse to be flogged by a woman who held no respect for you, simply because of an accident at birth.

Rahimi had never once thought he was punished by Allah, except to give him the parents he had. A birthmark was a birthmark. His mother was old and stupid, his father a brute who thought only to do as his wife told him. From his early teens Rahimi realized he had no use for either of them.

So he had formed a plan.

He had stolen money whenever possible. He had cached, in an old book bag in the rafters of a nearby abandoned shop, whatever supplies he could. The shop had been damaged in a street bombing and never repaired, something to do with some election or other. Rahimi had never known nor cared. He'd simply needed a place to put away whatever items he could for the future.

The abuse continued. Rahimi was expected to work in the small bakery his father ran, one of few state-sanctioned shops in operation in his decrepit neighborhood. When he was late to arrive, when he was reluctant to leave the bed-roll in which he slept in a corner of his family's kitchen, when he failed to perform as directed in the bakery, his father would punch him in the kidneys. There were days that he could barely move, days that his urine was red with blood.

He would always remember his father's hands. They were large and heavy and soft, the hands of a baker. And he remembered his father's eyes, beady and simple, without a hint of life to them. They were the eyes of a doll, the eyes of a simpleton. Rahimi had never held any emotions for his father except fear and, later, contempt and hatred.

As years passed he became more resigned to his family's abuses. His mother would often hit him with a broomstick or a wooden spoon. He bore the bruises with quiet resignation, learning with each passing day to hate his mother, to hate all women. On the evening of his sixteenth birthday, he went out into the street, found a young girl whom he believed was on her way home and stabbed her with a knife stolen from the bakery. She was still alive when he dragged her into a narrow alley and disemboweled her.

The act had been liberating. He had watched the light, a light he had never seen in his father's eyes and rarely in his mother's, fade from her as her strength failed. The idea that something as simple as a few inches of thin, flimsy metal could throw that switch, could end the existence of a human being…it opened up so many possibilities. Most compelling among these was the idea that he need not accept the beatings, the absolute rule of his parents. The idea had always been there, in the back of his mind, and had prompted him to explore killing...but now he knew the answer. Now he could free himself.

He'd gone home. There he'd found his mother in the kitchen. She'd looked at him angrily when he'd dropped the bloody knife on the counter. The idea that the blood was human occurred to her too late, if at all.

She had reached for her broomstick, ready to strike him. The offense for which she was beating him probably was not even clear in her mind, as Rahimi recalled it. She was simply so accustomed to dealing with him in this way that she'd returned to her habits, as was her way.

It was at that moment that Rahimi realized how physically small a woman his mother was, at least now that he was growing taller and filling out. She'd swung the broomstick and he'd caught it one-handed. The shock on her face, seconds before he killed her, was more pleasurable a memory to him than her death.

He had taken the broomstick in both his hands and struck her in the head with it. She'd fallen to the floor, trying to cover herself. He'd hammered away at her, hacking with the broomstick until he broke it. He would never know how long it took her to die of the beating he inflicted. He'd left her in the kitchen.

His father had been in bed, asleep, and had not heard the commotion. Rahimi had thought to himself, then, that he had never known what it was like to sleep in a bed. On the night table was a heavy clock radio, an ancient thing with a glowing green readout that weighed as much as a cinder block. He'd known that, because he had moved that radio from room to room at his father's request many times. It was the only radio in the family's home.

With great care, he'd removed the power cord from the wall. Then he'd picked up the radio, lifted it high over his head and dropped it on his father's face. There was some struggling as his father, trying to sit up, fought against him, but the injury and the fact that Rahimi's hands were already wrapped around his throat proved to be too much for his father to overcome. Rahimi had crushed the man's throat and listened as the man's labored breathing was finally squeezed off. It was not too much longer after that when his father's body finally relaxed in death.

Rahimi had pushed the corpse onto the floor, then gone to sleep in the bed. In the morning, he'd wakened late, and for a moment regretted that there was no clock to tell him the time. But this feeling passed quickly.

He'd taken the blood-stained pillowcase from the pillow on the bed, packed into it a few things from around the house, including a loaf of bread and a block of cheese from the kitchen, and stopped long enough to select another of his mother's knives.

Before leaving, he'd taken the bottle of kerosene his father kept for their lamps and spread it throughout the home. Then he'd found a box of matches in the kitchen and set the building ablaze.

He liked to think, as he'd walked the streets of Tehran, that the plume of black smoke rising from the house was his mother's and father's spirits. He hadn't cared if they went to Allah. He'd only wanted them away from him.

It had taken a few hours for the afterglow of the killings to leave him. It was then that his thoughts turned to practical matters. He had retrieved his backpack of supplies, and he had the few things he had thought to bring from the house. But he had no prospects for employment, no identification papers, nothing. And it was possible he would be sought in any investigation into his parents' death, unless these were written off as a result of an accidental fire.

He hadn't cared.

What happened, ultimately, was a surprise to him. No

one came looking. No one cared. No news of his parents' death was repeated beyond the most immediate of neighbors. Rahimi was a street child, and nothing more. No one pursued him. He was free.

He'd lived on the streets of Tehran until his eighteenth birthday, with little thought for the future. He'd also managed to remain above suspicion in the string of murders and rapes that occurred in the city. Women of all ages, young and old, were disappearing at night, only to turn up broken, abused and very dead. Never once was Rahimi suspected. He was smart. He understood how to get what he wanted and to go unobserved in so doing. Years living with his miserable parents had taught him the way of it.

At eighteen, he'd realized, on the anniversary of his liberation, that he had no plan for his existence. He had been sitting in a doorway, barely a mile from the house in which he had killed his parents, when members of the Revolutionary Path of God had come through the neighborhood. They'd shouted slogans through bullhorns and waved hand-painted banners. Join the revolution, the banners said. Walk the revolutionary path. Become righteous.

The idea appealed to him. He'd allowed himself to be recruited. When the work of the Revolutionary Path turned to violence, to what others labeled terrorism, he'd accepted this. He was eager for the training he was given, and grateful for the knowledge and skills acquired through it. He'd worked hard. He'd studied well.

Only occasionally did he sneak out at night to murder a woman, and then only when it was completely necessary.

So it was that when the Revolutionary Path of God made its way into the upper echelons of force-for-hire, he was highly placed among it. More training and more independence followed. As Iran's government became more radical, its uses for the Revolutionary Path of God increased.

The two existed in a symbiotic relationship, and Rahimi was allowed to live and do much as he pleased, so long as he served.

Now he was here, in the United States, sleeping with American whores and waiting for news that everything was crashing down around them. Several of his teams, including both the stakeout team at TruTech's headquarters, and the force he had staged at ECS, were now failing to make their regular reports. Agents of the government were involved. The news he was receiving through his monitors on the streets, and from those men still in place at their assignments, was very bad.

He had opted, at least for a time, to try to forget this, at least to whatever degree was possible. He bent over the night table. Licking his index and ring fingers, he dipped them in the pile of crystal methamphetamine he had poured there. Then he snorted the powder from his fingers, enjoying the sharpness, the clarity, that the drug brought him.

His men on the first floor, and in the other bedrooms on the second, were amusing themselves with drugs and more of the paid whores. For his part, he had spent the morning in the upstairs suite of rooms, attempting to distract himself from the realities of the attacks he had suffered, the troops he had lost.

It had taken his government literally years to set up the organizational structure, to smuggle Rahimi and his people into the United States, to set them up for long-term operations. So much money had been spent ensuring that they would not be summarily deported or imprisoned in one of the United States's barbaric rape pens. Of all the indignities his men might suffer if captured while working against the United States, that bothered him the most. You were always at the mercy of perverts and deviants on

American soil. It was endemic to their culture and symptomatic of their lewd corruption.

Things had gone smoothly for quite some time. He and his men had been successfully embedded in America. They had managed to buy off or intimidate most of the management, the employees and the law-enforcement figures in the area. Those who would not cooperate were made to suffer "accidents," some of which even seemed plausible. Rahimi had been proud of the scope of the operation.

He had never particularly liked dealing with the management of ECS, one of the biggest manufacturers into which his people had burrowed. Their shareholders were old, timid men, and all but one of them had been eliminated to make way for the new order. The worst and most scurrilous of these, Lafontaine, had been kept on to maintain the illusion that someone other than Rahimi and his team were in charge.

But open resistance to their operation had started to occur. It had been slow at first. A drive-by shooting here. A break-in and act of obvious industrial espionage there. A few disappearances of employees and even Revolutionary Path of God operators, who were never seen again and were presumed dead.

Counterespionage of their own had revealed their new enemy was Sapphire Corporation, the security company employed by TruTech and Claridge Clayton. This did not surprise Rahimi. He had kept the full knowledge of these matters from the North Koreans because he could not afford to let them know the truth. They had to believe their friends in the Iranian government could deliver the ICBM components after which they lusted. This was important not simply for the money, but because the operation was underwritten by the Iranian government.

Rahimi had been told repeatedly by his superiors that

Iran lacked the technology to build and field ICBMs, but North Korea did not. The Iranians surely could have funneled the results of their illegal and subverted manufacturing to their own nation, yes, but the result would be parts his government was not prepared to use. The North Koreans, on the other hand, had the industrial infrastructure Iran required. And the two nations shared many enemies. It was not at all unlikely that, once it was producing ICBMs on a regular schedule, building up its own armory and then a surplus, North Korea and its military advisors would in turn work with Iran to target enemies the two nations shared in common.

The United States was, of course, foremost among those.

The call from Lafontaine the previous day had come as a surprise, but the content of that conversation was even more disturbing. Lafontaine, in his circumspect way, was begging for permission to negotiate with what were apparently agents of the United States government. Dealing with attacks and harassment by Sapphire was one thing. Being exposed by the American government, and by its armed agencies, was quite another. Rahimi had warned Lafontaine of the dire consequences for disobeying Iranian orders. He had not heard from the little man again. Apart from stopping automatic payments to Lafontaine's accounts, this meant little to Rahimi…except for the implications regarding their manufacturing operation at ECS.

His satellite phone began to ring.

The prostitute whimpered and tried to cover her tanned, naked body as he stepped over her. Snatching up the phone, he put it to his ear and said, "I am here."

"Tell me what you know about Sapphire."

Rahimi paled. It was Soong, his North Korean contact. It was as if the man were reading his thoughts from hundreds of miles away and had just decided to call on him, confront him with his deceit. He could not risk angering Soong, not without earning himself a death sentence from the Iranian government. Revolutionary Path of God was expected to kill and die rather than admit defeat.

"Sapphire is a security company employed by TruTech," Rahimi said carefully. "Armed mercenaries."

"And you did not think to mention it when elements of Sapphire began attacking both our interests abroad."

"To my knowledge," Rahimi said, still choosing his words with utmost care, "Sapphire has struck only Iranian holdings abroad, chipping away at the manufacturing pipeline we are setting up in the South Philippine Sea. I did not mention this because it seemed trivial. We are fully capable of handling…competition."

"You claim this," said Soong. "Yet my informants tell me you have suffered significant setbacks thanks to Sapphire interference. And this was before the American CIA, or whatever agency it is, became involved."

"We are committed to establishing the component pipeline," said Rahimi. "You know as well as I do that my government stands to gain greatly from both the sales of the merchandise and the subsequent alteration in the global power balance."

"You speak like an educated man," said Soong. "But you seem to take me for a fool."

Rahimi paused. He dared not anger Soong. If he alienated the man, those to whom he answered in the Iranian government would do more than refuse to pay him for his services. They would make him pay for ruining the deal and their prospects for future power.

"I do not take you for a fool," Rahimi said. "If there is fault, the fault lies with my sincere belief that we ought not trouble you with our internal problems. You are the buyer. We are the supplier. Our responsibility is to supply you with product."

"But we are linked by the nature of the arrangement we are attempting to make," said Soong. "I can no more fail to establish the pipeline than can you, given our respective masters. This has been understood since our two countries first began negotiating the possible parameters of the component shipments. If your ability to feed that pipeline is jeopardized, then the entire plan is at risk. Your interests are my interests in this regard."

Rahimi sighed. "The security company, Sapphire, works for TruTech. We believe it is TruTech with whom we are now competing for your business. Sapphire has mounted certain operations intended to cause difficulties for us, to include armed action against us abroad."

"I thought as much," said Soong. "It explains a great deal. But there is more you have not yet told me."

"How can you possibly know that?" Rahimi asked.

"Because our operation is under attack from this side, as well," said Soong, "and not merely from some private security firm. Western governmental entities have fielded what they would call 'counterterror' operations. They have attacked our ships. I have seen operations like these before. Members of my family…" Soong paused, then began again. "Members of my government have encountered these Western operatives, these death squads, previously. They are adept at coordinated and overwhelming attacks. If you have not been attacked by them by now, I am indeed a fool."

It was Rahimi's turn to pause. "You are correct. We have suffered significant losses at their hands. It is much worse than the Sapphire incursions. But we can handle both. The pipeline will not, I must repeat to you, will not be broken. We can meet our obligations."

"You will forgive me if I do not put much faith in those promises," said Soong. "I need results, not assertions. Already I am forced to consider using this 'competition' of which you speak."

"You would insult me so?" Rahimi asked, unable to contain himself.

"Do not be ridiculous," said Soong. "The death squads have targeted you. Do you have any idea how many of my own people have fallen to them in the past? How many operations they have… Forgive me. I have spoken too freely."

"The offense was mine," said Rahimi. He was now only too aware of what Soong, in his agitation, had revealed: he was on the precipice of taking his business elsewhere. Rahimi was very close to the point of no return, and down that road lay torture and execution. If he were lucky.

"You speak of death squads," Rahimi said. "The Americans do not employ such tactics. They are corrupt and weak, yes. They use their military to bomb the innocent and to occupy nations that possess resources they desire. But they lack the resolve to field a death unit."

"You are wrong," said Soong. "Our intelligence network is more extensive than yours. For years, we have heard rumors of tactics employed by the West worldwide. There were even rumors that such operatives may have had a hand in your own elections, a regime or two ago."

"I have heard nothing of the kind," said Rahimi. "Governments change quickly in my country."

"Not so much in mine," said Soong. "And perhaps that explains some of the difference."

Rahimi was uncertain how to respond to that. If Soong intended an insult, he dared not rise to it. "You were saying," he prodded.

"The rumors are that the American CIA, or perhaps the NSA…we are not sure. But some government agency sends highly trained special forces operatives to safeguard key American and Western interests around the globe."

"I have heard of this," Rahimi said. "It is called their military."

"No," said Soong. "Not the military. Allied with it, certainly. Supported by it, almost necessarily. But not bound by their military's rules of engagement. Not crippled by international sensibilities. A ruthless unit of armed troubleshooters who appear where most needed to murder the enemies of the West."

"Hiding under my bed, no doubt," Rahimi said. He spared a glance for the weeping prostitute, who fled to the bathroom. "You tell stories to frighten children."

"I speak the truth," said Soong. "Whom do you think is now the cause of your troubles? If you wish our deal to remain in force, you will have to find a way to neutralize them. It will not be easy. You will lose many men. You may face death yourself. And when you realize you face these killers, it may be too late for you."

"That is ridiculous," Rahimi scoffed. "What would you have me do? Losses are part of the business. We will cope with them. We can still supply you."

"Not if you are dead," said Soong.

"It is if you think the murderers are at my very door, ready to put a bullet through my head!" Rahimi said, suddenly outraged. "I will not sit here and listen to your ghost stories—"

A grenade, accompanied by the sound of broken glass, rolled across the floor to rest at Vahid Rahimi's feet.

CHAPTER FOURTEEN

The stun grenades detonated. The concussions made Carl Lyons's teeth vibrate. He planted the sole of one combat boot against the door and kicked it in, splintering the jamb and causing the door to bounce off the wall inside. The snout of his Daewoo shotgun led the way as he entered the Alabama safe house.

Omid Attar, known member of the Revolutionary Path of God, had given up the goods relatively easily. The Iranians had been renting this safe house outside Mobile for some time. If his superiors had been sufficiently alarmed by the attacks on ECS and the stake-out teams, Attar claimed, they would withdraw to this safe house and remain there until the danger had passed.

They hadn't counted on the danger passing right over *them*.

Setting up the raid had been relatively simple, although Attar had confessed there were likely to be civilians there—specifically, working girls brought in for the entertainment of the Iranian operatives.

As he stepped over the threshold of the safe house, Lyons leveled his automatic shotgun and put a single 12-gauge slug through the chest of the Iranian gunman waiting there. The man had been sitting on the couch in front of a coffee table covered in what looked like cocaine. The woman on the couch next to him, clearly a prostitute, was half-dressed and screaming, squeezing her eyes shut and holding her hands over her ears. The stun grenades had not harmed her; she would be all right in a moment. For now, she did not see the dead man sharing the couch with her. Lyons had put the slug in him before he could grab the Skorpion machine pistol that was waiting on the table.

Lyons let his shotgun fall to the end of its sling. He picked up the Skorpion, unloaded it and removed its bolt, throwing the pieces of the weapon behind the couch.

"Must have been a sale on those dumb things," he muttered.

The safe house was a large one, probably originally set up as a multifamily dwelling. Right now, Schwarz and Blancanales were working their way through the rear of the safe house. Whichever members of the team reached the stairs first would take the second floor. This entailed a certain amount of increased risk, because by the time the Stony Man commandos reached the second story, any Iranian Revolutionary Path of God mercenaries waiting there would be tipped off and ready, dug in to fight.

Lyons was reaching for his shotgun when he was tackled.

Wearing the same black battle utilities the rest of the mercenaries wore, the man who body-checked Lyons was big even compared to the Able Team leader. He snarled something that Lyons assumed was Persian as the two went down. Fetid breath hit Lyons's face. The man was trying to get position on him, hold him on the ground, so he could stab and kill him. The kitchen knife in the man's hand was as long as a fighting knife. Its triangular blade tapered to a needle point. Lyons grabbed the man's knife arm with his left hand, struggling to reach inside his bomber jacket with his right. The Iranian used both hands to try to force his blade down onto Lyon's face.

"American dog," the man snarled in English. "I will enjoy gouging out your eyes."

"Less talk," said Lyons. "More bang."

"Bang?" breathed the Iranian.

Lyons's Python boomed. He had drawn the weapon and jammed it against his attacker's ribs. He pulled the trigger twice more, causing the big Iranian mercenary to jolt each time. Finally he rolled the man off. He could hear the mercenary's labored breathing.

"Do not…let me die like this," begged the man as he struggled to breathe. "I deserve…a warrior's…death."

Lyons stood. "No," he said. "You don't." He paused to reload the Python before holstering it. Shouldering his shotgun, he grabbed the hooker with his left hand, helped her up off the couch and pushed her through the open door onto the front lawn. "Get lost, honey," he told her. "And stay low while you do it."

The prostitute fled. Lyons moved to leave the room, the automatic USAS-12 once more leading the way.

"Wait…" said the wounded Iranian. Whatever else he might have said was lost in a choked gurgle that became a death rattle.

Lyons stalked on.

He entered the dining room. Beyond this was the kitchen, and past that, a corridor leading to the back bedrooms on the first floor, as well as a back porch. Schwarz and Blancanales were actively clearing those bedrooms. He heard gunfire, screams and the explosion of another stun grenade, which at this distance made his ears ring.

"Status," he said quietly.

"Enemy contact." Schwarz's voice came back to him through the transceiver link. "We are neutralizing." The normally flippant Schwarz was all business when it was time to get down to real combat. Lyons had never doubted that.

He heard movement from within the kitchen.

A half-height wall, like a window island, separated the dining room from the kitchen. Lyons threw himself to the floor and pressed up against it. The Daewoo was of no use to him in this posture, so he withdrew his Colt Python again.

"Come on out," said Lyons from his position on the floor. "It's over. We've got this place surrounded." He felt silly even as he said it, but you never gave up a chance to psych out the enemy if one came your way.

There was more movement. Lyons wondered if perhaps he wasn't trying to smoke out another prostitute. That's when a single, ancient, World War II era pineapple grenade landed with a thump on the carpet next to him. He reached for it—

"Complaint department," read a metal tag attached to the grenade's pin, which was still in place. "Take a number."

The grenade was a dud, an office decoration. Lyons realized, too late, that he had been scammed.

There were two of them, not one, and they tried to come at him from two angles. The first Iranian dived through the entrance connecting the kitchen to the dining room. He carried yet another of the Skorpion machine pistols and did his best to line up the impossible shot as he threw his body through the air. The spray of small-caliber bullets stitched the drywall above Lyons's head, showering him with plaster dust and forcing him to flatten himself to the carpet.

The second man tried to dive through the hole above the half-height island window. The problem was that he and his partner had misjudged the drop...and how badly it would hurt. The man hit the floor with a sickening crunch as his head was jarred at an unnatural angle.

The man with the Skorpion had landed heavily on his side. He extended his arm, pointed the Skorpion and pulled the trigger.

Nothing happened.

"Please," said Lyons. "The way you were spraying and praying? That little magazine doesn't hold all that many rounds, and your rate of fire is ridiculous." He stood, dusting himself off. His shotgun hung on its sling, while his Python was still in his hand.

"You okay back there, Ironman?" Blancanales asked in his ear.

"Fine," said Lyons. To the Iranian, he said, "I don't think Einstein there's going to make it." He jerked his chin at the man with the twisted neck. "Looks like he snapped his own neck going down. They teach you jokers not to land with your face in terrorist school?"

The Iranian looked down at his empty weapon. He raised his arm as if he was going to throw it at the Able Team leader.

Lyons shot him in the face.

"Always with the empty-gun thing," muttered Lyons. "If he'd grown up in this country I would say it was too many Saturday-morning cowboy shows."

Schwarz and Blancanales appeared at the end of the corridor at the opposite end of the kitchen. Blancanales was covering behind Schwarz with his M-16, while Schwarz held his 93-R machine pistol in a two-handed grip.

"Everything under control, Ironman?" Schwarz asked.

"Didn't you hear? I said I was fine."

"But that was followed by a flying 'crunch,'" said Schwarz. "And that's almost never good." He pointed to the dead man with the broken neck. "You didn't even shoot that one, did you?"

"Would you believe he took a header off the kitchen-counter-wall thing over there?"

"Reminds me of an old joke," said Schwarz. "How many gangsters does it take to push a stool pigeon down the stairs?"

"None," said Blancanales from behind Schwarz. "He fell." Over Schwarz's shoulder he said, "First floor is clear. Second floor, I have hostile contact."

Lyons looked up. All three of them could hear the heavy footsteps of men running around on the second floor. The squealing of heavy furniture being moved was all the proof they needed of barricades being erected.

"Yeah," said Lyons. "Right. Let's go. Pol, cover the rear. Gadgets, watch my back. I'm going up."

"Affirmative," said Schwarz.

"In position," said Blancanales. He dropped to one knee with his rifle, making sure all avenues of entrance and exit were covered from the bottom of the stairs.

Lyons took the stairs two at a time, slowing as he reached the top, careful not to expose his head should someone be waiting at the top of the stairs. What he discovered was an enclosed entrance, however, and not an open, railed area that might have provided the enemy with a shooting gallery.

It was a fact that all of their weapons, especially Lyons's shotgun and Colt Python, could penetrate those walls. They could simply fire blindly into the drywall—Lyons brushed more dust from his shoulder—and probably take out most of the Iranian mercenaries with very little effort. But that would result in dead civilians if there were more prostitutes present. And firing blindly had never been Able Team's way.

He tried the doorknob. It was locked, which was actually a good sign. Had it been open, inviting them to come blundering in, it would probably have been a trap. It probably still *was* a trap, but Lyons hated being predictable.

He paused for a moment to jack a buckshot round into the chamber of his USAS-12. Then he put the barrel over the lock area, raised his off hand to shield his face and pulled the trigger.

The doorjamb exploded. Lyons used his boot to kick open what was left and hit the floor in a hard roll, twisting as he went, bringing the barrel of his shotgun up to cover his body. Bullets struck the wall and the floor near his head, his shoulders, his legs. He paid them no mind, focusing instead on lining up the kill shot.

The Iranian had a lever-action rifle, of all things, possibly purchased locally to bolster the team's firepower. Some part of his mind analyzed the thunderous noise of the heavy rounds. Probably a 30.06, if Lyons was any judge, and he had spent enough time getting shot at to develop a keen sense for these things.

The gunman had taken up a position too close to the door. His misses were purely a function of adrenaline and the weapon's slow rate of fire, coupled with the fact that running the lever on the gun caused him to jar his rifle as he tried to shoot quickly. Lyons's leg shot out like a cobra and smashed into the Iranian's ankle. The bone snapped. Screaming, the Iranian struck the floor. Lyons smashed him in the temple with the butt of the USAS-12. The man's eyes rolled into the back of his head and he went limp.

Lyons bent, jacked out the remaining rounds in the rifle and tossed the weapon down the stairs. It landed at Schwarz's feet.

There was a good chance the guard on the floor would not get back up again from a blow like that, but it didn't matter either way. He was out for the duration, and once the house was clear, Able Team would summon appropriate medical attention for him.

Three closed doors awaited him.

These led to the upstairs rooms of the house, and now Lyons was playing a deadly game show. Would it be door number one, door number two or door number three? Any or all of them could contain deadly surprises, and at least one of them probably held an innocent or two.

Well. "Innocent" in this case was a civilian designation. But no working girl deserved to get shot for being in the wrong place at the wrong time.

Schwarz emerged from the stairwell as carefully as had Lyons. He took up a position on his team leader's flank with this Beretta at the ready. "What do you want to do?"

"Left to right," Lyons whispered, so quietly that only his transceiver's pickup made him audible to Schwarz. If there were enemy shooters behind the doors, they might be listening close to the barriers. "Watch for shadows under the door cracks. I'll stay as far left as I can get. Going in."

"Roger," said Schwarz.

Lyons moved as close to the far wall as he could get. There was about eighteen inches of clearance between the wall and the edge of the first door. He reached out and tried the knob. It moved.

There it was. The trap he had been expecting. He turned the knob and threw the door open, yanking his left hand back as fast as he could.

There were three of them, kneeling on the floor, all of them holding the ubiquitous Skorpion automatic weapons. A wave of hot lead scorched the space where Lyons's arm had been. Schwarz was forced to roll to his right to avoid the spray. Lyons simply held his position, counting in his mind, as one by one the Skorpions ran empty.

"Stagger your reloads, amateurs!" Lyons called. He shoved the snout of the USAS-12 through the doorway. In the fraction of a second that he had seen the interior of the room, he had assessed the targets within. There were no civilians, at least none within sight or behind his enemies. There were only the three gunmen.

Lyons walked the Daewoo across the doorway, spraying out its box magazine of 12-gauge slugs. The heavy rounds turned the men inside the room to hamburger, painting the walls crimson.

The far door, the one Lyons thought of as door number three, burst open. Lyons and Schwarz both held their fire as a naked woman ran screaming from the room. She did not even glance at them as she bounded over the railing and down the stairs, never stumbling once.

"Wow," said Schwarz. "She was…athletic."

"I want to negotiate!" called a voice from inside the third room. The man who stuck his head out held a Colt 1911 pistol. He was pointing it at his own head.

"Oh, you've got to be kidding me," said Carl Lyons.

"I want to negotiate," said the Iranian. His accent was light; he had obviously been in the country awhile. He had probably seen too many television shows in that time, too.

"We don't negotiate," Lyons lied. "I'll guess you'll have to kill the hostage."

"You're a credit to the service, Ironman," said Schwarz through the transceiver.

"Shaddap, Gadgets," Lyons returned.

The Iranian's features hardened. He knew he was being mocked. "You make fun of me?" he demanded. "I know valuable information. Things you can use. You will want to interrogate me. I am no good to you dead."

"That's a risk I'm willing to take," Lyons said blandly. He put his hand to his mouth and feigned a yawn.

The Iranian turned bright red. "You will be sorry—"

Lyons whipped his arm forward. The object he had palmed, then brought up in front of his face, whistled through the air and rapped the Iranian in the forehead. He yowled and his head snapped back. Lyons lunged forward, grabbed the gun and stripped it from the man's grasp, breaking his trigger finger in the process. He screamed.

On the floor was the little tactical folding knife Lyons had recovered earlier.

"Hey," said Schwarz. "You forgot to open that knife before you threw it."

"What am I, a circus act?" Lyons asked. "All I needed was the weight. I'm not going to throw a blade that small at a target and hope to stick it unless I've got all day…and a magic genie in a lamp to wish on for luck."

The Iranian was screeching in pain. Lyons looked down at the pistol he had taken from the man, then pistol-whipped the Iranian across the temple. He collapsed, unconscious.

"We'll question him when he wakes up, then?"

Lyons glared at Schwarz but said nothing. He went to the middle door, stood well to the side and motioned for Schwarz to do the same. Then he rapped on the door.

Immediately bullet holes formed in the hollow-core wood, blowing splinters across the landing space by the stairwell. Lyons looked at the ceiling and whistled as if waiting impatiently. Eventually the gunner inside stopped shooting.

"My name is Abraham Lincoln," said Lyons. He shot a preemptive, angry look at Schwarz before the other man could comment. "I am an agent of the United States Justice Department. Come out with your hands up and you will not be harmed. Resistance will be met with deadly force, as will any attempt to harm—"

"I have a hostage!" screamed the shooter. "I am Vahid Rahimi of the Revolutionary Path of God. You will grant me safe passage from this place! I will not die here, not like this, not for the likes of you! Do as I say or the floor will run red with the blood of this harlot!"

"Harlot," said Schwarz. "That's a ten-dollar word right there."

"Let's stop him before he can make change," Lyons said quietly. He tried the knob, but this one didn't move. "On my go, give me a burst to take out the lock, but keep your rounds angled toward the empty bedroom. We don't want to risk hitting his hostage."

"You got it, Ironman."

"One," said Lyons. "Two. Three. Go!"

Schwarz blew apart the locking mechanism. Lyons was right behind the electronics specialist's bullets, kicking the door in and throwing himself through the opening. The maneuver had the desired effect. Rahimi took the gun he had been holding on his captive prostitute and fired three times at the doorway, missing all three times.

Lyons dumped a .357 Magnum round from his Colt Python, spearing Rahimi through the bridge of his nose, blowing his last thoughts out the back of his head. He collapsed, his finger clenching on the trigger. His weapon loosed a round harmlessly into the floor.

The prostitute fainted. Lyons rushed forward to catch her before she could strike her head.

Schwarz stuck his head in the doorway. "Clear?" he asked.

"Clear," Lyons breathed. "Give me a hand here. And if you say anything smart you'll be wearing my boot for a hat."

"Somebody shot a bullet through the floor at me," said Blancanales through the transceiver link.

CHAPTER FIFTEEN

The Philippine Sea

The container ship sat in calm seas under clear skies. Only the occasional sound of gulls broke the silence. Soong il Yun of the Advance Guard of the Democratic People's Republic stood in the bow of the smaller attack craft. He had watched as the freighter bearing Sapphire and its personnel—and its cargo of TruTech ICBM components—pulled alongside the drug ship and offloaded its cargo. Now the Sapphire men were aboard, probably haggling with the drug ship's captain over the price.

It was time.

He signaled to his lieutenant, Han. The man nodded and raised a two-way radio. He clicked the send button three times in succession, waited, then clicked it three times more. Soong watched the deck of the drug ship carefully. He was rewarded with a flash of light from a railside signal lamp.

"That is the signal," said Soong. "Go."

They moved in. His pilot was careful to keep their craft on the opposite side of the freighter, well out of sight of any lookouts the Sapphire personnel might have posted. It was important that this portion of the operation go smoothly. He needed to get his Advance Guard in position before he could get on with the business of sending messages...

messages to those who dared interfere with the DPRK's business.

Soong was no rear guard commander. He let two of his men take the skeleton gangway to the main deck once their craft was docked, but he followed directly after. Were it not procedure and simply good sense, he would have gone first…but in the event of an unforeseen attack, he would be risking too much to put himself in the line of fire. Thus he tolerated a pair of point guards, but no more. It was important that his men know he was as strong as they were. In truth, he believed himself to be stronger and, more important, so did they.

Soong believed in maintaining that belief. It was part of his command. It was how he commanded respect. And it was how he defined himself as a man. You could not lead men into battle if you did not understand who you were. You could not order others to their deaths, righteously kill the enemies of the Democratic People's Republic of Korea, if you did not stand strong and sure in the face of ill winds.

Soong was proud of his ability to withstand the storm that was his life. It was out of this pride that he had recommended his own adult son, Dae Kim, for the Advance Guard. Dae was not his biological son, of course—the difference in age between the two men was not great enough—but Dae was his orphaned nephew. Thus it had fallen to Soong to care for the boy, to raise him, to teach him to be a man. Most critically, he taught Dae to be useful to the DPRK.

With Soong pulling the strings, Dae was admitted to the officer's corps and given accelerated training. He was to become Advance Guard…and to do so meant surviving for ninety days at what was called, simply, the Island.

The Island was a training facility ninety kilometers off the cost of Donggang. It was a crucible, a place where young men were forged into the reliable, loyal, capable machinery of the DPRK's elite armed forces. It was, as Lieutenant Han had once called it, "the incubator of the Advance Guard."

Soong had personally designed the brutal training regimen that was used at the Island. Troops were subjected to extended periods of sleep deprivation, cold and lack of food. They were beaten with sticks continually. Pain became their only constant, endurance their only option. Division was encouraged and cultivated by the trainers, all of whom were North Korean Special Forces, many times decorated. Any hint of weakness, any deviation from the myriad rules set in front of them, was punished severely, even cruelly. Every attempt was made to drive the trainees to the breaking point and beyond. They had to learn that divided, they would fail. They had to be made to see it. They had to come to the realization as if through epiphany. They had to learn to be a unit, to live and die as one, to know that their only hope lay in fighting together against common foes.

It was a difficult game and one that did not always go as planned. Trainees sometimes snapped only too readily, whereupon they attempted to murder their trainers. At times they succeeded. At other times, they were put down as enraged animals. Attrition was high, as it was meant to be, among both the trainees and those instructing them. Whenever possible, whenever duty allowed, Soong served at the Island to oversee this difficult process. He enjoyed seeing soldiers born.

Those who survived the training became Advance Guard. They were the most vicious soldiers the DPRK could train and field. They were utterly loyal, utterly ruthless.

Loyalty. Fearlessness. Brotherhood. Every Advance

Guard bore the scar of a hot branding iron on his chest.
The mark was the Korean lettering for these principles.
The pain of receiving the mark was as nothing compared
to the joy of being worthy of what those principles con-
veyed, what they implied, what they *demanded*.

Advance Guard trainees were pushed and pushed until
they valued the brotherhood of unit more than they valued
anything else. They bonded. They came to respect and to
trust each other. They lived close, closer than brothers,
and in knowing each other's minds, they became a single,
living organism. That organism had but one purpose: to
follow the orders of their commanders and to acquit themselves with honor in service to the DPRK.

It was with pride that Soong had recommended Dae for
the program. He had hopes his adopted son might one day
command the Advance Guard. He could see no more worthy candidate, no more honorable soul. He had invited Dae
to participate, giving him a choice few men were offered.
Most of the trainees sent to the Island were ordered to go,
culled from the ranks of the regular army or recruited from
the streets for strength and ferocity. Dae was allowed to
choose what he wished for his destiny.

Soong, to this day, could not fathom what he might have
done or said had Dae refused.

But Dae had not refused. He had agreed to serve with
honor. He had agreed to travel to the Island and to participate in the training. He wished to be what his adopted
father was. He wished to follow in his father's footsteps
and to bring honor to his family.

Soong deliberately forced himself to stay away from the
Island during the many weeks that his adopted son trained
there. The appearance of impropriety must be avoided,
always, and he could not be expected to be impartial in
matters of honor and family. No man, not even the Leader,

could expect that. And so Soong waited out the long weeks of Dae's training, knowing only too well the pain and the hardship his son must suffer.

He would be a better man for it, Soong knew. Dae would be Advance Guard.

When the notice came that Dae had passed, that he had completed the training, that he was to be commissioned an officer in the Advance Guard, Soong had locked himself in his office, smoked a cigarette, held his head in his hands and silently wept. He'd wept with joy. He'd wept with relief. He'd wept for the pain he knew his son must have undergone.

That pain, that fire, had forged his adopted son, had made him an instrument, a weapon of the DPRK. Soong knew in his heart that the Island was not an incubator at all. Incubators provided gentle warmth. They provided comfort. The Island was instead a furnace, burning with a cleansing, destroying fire, a fire that burned away all impurities, ate away all that was not desirable, removed from the man all that was *not* the man.

Dae was assigned an apartment in the officers' facility in Pyongyang, not far from Soong's own. Soong called in many favors and spent much of the money he had hoarded for the occasion. He'd rented a fine hall, one used only by the members of the Party to entertain guests for special occasions. While Soong was not the match for a Party official in terms of power, he did have the ear of the Leader. He was no man to be trifled with. This was a very special occasion. They would permit him this indulgence.

He'd arranged for all the pleasures his son had been denied in training. There was rich food. There was entertainment. Jugglers and comedians and actors had been brought in from the outlying provinces. Fine women, the best the Party officials enjoyed, were brought in as well, told to give Han whatever he desired.

The time of the party arrived. Soong, dressed in his finest formal uniform, bearing a box of cigars rumored to be the favorite of the Leader himself, had seated himself in the hall with the other guests. The guests were a mixture of party officials and even some of Dae's fellow graduates. It was always the way to mix pleasure with currying favor. Dae would do well to learn that lesson early. It was knowledge that had served Soong over the years.

The hours passed. Dae did not arrive. At first Soong had tried to tell himself that his son was attempting to be "fashionable," though he knew this to be a lie. Dae would never be late for anything. He was born to military precision. His training would only have made him more so.

Honor, saving face, demanded that Soong continue to entertain his guests. He could not end the gathering. He could not risk the ire of the party officials assembled there. And he dared not bring attention to Dae's unusual behavior.

It was possible, he'd told himself as he rushed to Dae's apartment late that night, that his son was merely feeling unworthy. Perhaps the training had taken better than even Soong knew possible. Perhaps Dae was uncomfortable with the thought of so elaborate an honor bestowed on him. After all, he had spent week after week suffering deprivation. To be thrust into luxury, into relative opulence, into what he might well define as hedonism…he might reject that. He could scarcely do otherwise.

I have been a fool, Soong had thought. Of course. He will be waiting for me in his apartment. He will apologize for not coming to the party. He will ask me if I enjoyed it, and implore me not to make a fuss over him in the future. And I will promise him as much, because that is a reasonable request.

He'd knocked on Dae's door. There was no answer. He'd knocked again, more loudly, and still more loudly, until finally he was forced to kick in the door with a single, well-placed blow. He remembered vividly the polished black toe of his boot as he crashed into Dae's dwelling.

Dae was waiting for him.

Soong's son wore his formal uniform. His boots bore a mirror shine, just as his father's did. On the floor just within the doorway was the chromed pistol Dae had been issued shortly after graduation.

His son had placed the barrel of the pistol in his mouth and pulled the trigger.

Soong paused. Later, he would remember giving himself thirty seconds in which to grieve.

Thirty seconds of weakness, no more.

When he'd raised his head once more, he saw no longer his son Dae. He saw only a failure, a man who had not, in fact, successfully passed the training. This man was not Advance Guard.

This man was a washout. He was better off dead.

Soong had left the room and never looked back. He would never speak Dae's name again. When asked on rare occasion in the future whether he had family, he would say that, yes, he had a wife and son. His son was but a child yet. Soong had come late to marriage. Such were the rigors of placing a military career first.

He had no other family, he would say.

As he walked the deck of the drug ship, the last and the largest of the North Korean fleet, Soong was not sure why thoughts of Dae had returned to trouble him. They darkened his already bleak mood.

In an open space on the deck, convenient to the larg-

est of the cargo elevators, the Sapphire personnel stood
with their weapons slung over their shoulders. Interspersed
among them, as they had been ordered to insinuate themselves, were members of the drug ship's North Korean
military contingent. At the moment Soong and his men
rounded the nearest cargo containers, the Sapphire men
tensed and then reached for their guns.

Soong nodded once.

The boat's military crew immediately put their pistols
and Kalashnikovs to the necks of the Sapphire men. The
first of his messages this day was clear enough: move
and die.

"I," said Soong as he neared, "am Commander Soong of
the Advance Guard. Who is in charge of your company?"

The Sapphire men looked at each other. They wore mottled blue camouflage fatigues, web gear and other paramilitary trappings. Soong took one look at them and knew
them for the undisciplined pretenders they were, compared
to his own troops. They were little better than armed rab-
ble, civilians in costume, mercenaries and pirates.

Pirates The idea came to him, suddenly, and he knew
he could do something more to safeguard his nation's in
terests, to endear him to his Leader's son.

On the deck in front of the Sapphire men were several
crates. The man who stepped forward, as if to insert himself between the cargo and Soong, had the bearing of a
leader, indeed.

"Helmut Kohn," said the man in the blue fatigues. "We
are here as requested. We are escorts on behalf of our employer. We were told the employer was known to you. We
were told we were expected. We are here to fulfill the shipment your Iranian suppliers could not."

"In the spirit of amity and capitalism, no doubt," said
Soong. He took a Songbong from the pack in his pocket

and fired it to life with his lighter, reading the engraving once more before pocketing the treasured heirloom. He looked Kohn up and down. "You are their leader. You take responsibility for them. For their actions. And ultimately for the actions of your company."

"Yes," said Kohn. "What of it?"

"You will have a lieutenant, a second in command," Soong said. "Point him out to me."

Another of the Sapphire men stepped forward. "Manuel Avery," he said. "What is the meaning of this? Are we doing this deal or not?"

"Oh, we are most certainly doing the deal," said Soong. "My government needs these components. And they require the pipeline. We accept the materials that you have been sent to safeguard. Consider your task accomplished." He took a long drag from his cigarette and then blew the smoke at Kohn's face. "Now turn over your weapons."

Kohn looked at Avery. The rest of the Sapphire troops looked among themselves. Fingers tensed on trigger guards. It was obvious they were thinking of resisting.

"Wait just one moment," Kohn began.

"Do as I say," said Soong, "or I will have all of your bodies dumped in the sea when my men finish killing you. Unless you believe you can bring up your weapon in the time it takes each of them to pull a trigger already half-squeezed."

Kohn paled. He placed his MP-5 submachine gun very carefully on the deck. His men, with equal reluctance, did the same. The weapons were immediately appropriated by Soong's men, who by now had formed a ring of Advance Guard around the Sapphire personnel.

"In some ways I am not unsympathetic to your plight, Mr. Kohn," said Soong. "You are not privy to all of the actions of your employer, not at the highest levels. You follow orders, as do I. You are but a tool, to some extent. While you are a crude and soft tool, compared to my men, we are not altogether dissimilar. It is a question of degree."

Kohn was looking around now, perhaps understanding where this was leading. "I answer to powerful people—"

"No," said Soong. "You answer to people who merely think they are powerful. As I am about to demonstrate." He snapped his fingers. "Han. The video camera."

Lieutenant Han was at his side in less time than it took for him to wish it. Han held a compact digital videocam. He switched it on. A red LED blinked above its lens.

"Sapphire has mounted certain attacks abroad and in the United States," said Soong. "Minor attacks. Nuisances, for the most part. But depredations that have harmed the business interests of your competitors. You are competing for the ICBM component business. You believe that if you damage your rivals, you can have this business for yourselves. But you have forgotten something important."

Kohn started to speak. "But—"

"Be silent," Soong said. "I am not finished. In the future, your employer will not interfere in any way with anyone who seeks to serve our needs. We will make our commercial decisions based on who offers us the best value. If you take any actions that can be considered harmful to North Korea's wishes, to the fulfillment of the component pipeline, you will be punished. That punishment will take the form of the…retribution…that I administer now. Han."

Han took a combat knife from his belt. The weapon was double-edged, a dagger with serrations near its base. Its handle was of textured rubber. The Advance Guard lieutenant tossed the weapon to the deck between Kohn and Avery.

"We possess an extensive intelligence network," Soong

said. "We know what Sapphire has been doing. We know that it possesses sufficient resources to make further problems for us. We will not tolerate this. The two of you will fight to the death. The one who survives may leave this ship alive."

Kohn and Avery stared at each other once more. Neither moved.

Soong took the Type 68 pistol from his belt. He racked the slide and pointed it at Kohn. "One of you kills the other," he said. "Or I will kill you both." When the two men still did not move, Soong swiveled and shot one of the Sapphire men standing under guard. Then he shot a second one. The remainder began to howl in outrage, but the Advance Guard held them at bay with their Kalashnikovs.

"Shall I keep going until your entire crew is dead?" Soong asked.

Avery, wild-eyed and looking desperate, lunged for the knife. He picked it up and ran at his commander. He slashed wildly. Kohn's instincts and training took over. He was able to avoid the worst of Avery's blows, but it was clear he was not as comfortable facing a blade, unarmed, as he might have been wielding a gun. Then again, thought Soong, one never knew. It was possible the Sapphire fools were not terribly well trained. Few men were, compared to the standards of Soong's people.

Kohn tried to use the backs of his arms to guard his body. This simply gave Avery a target to slash. He carved away on Kohn's arms with the sharp knife, drawing lines of blood that spattered the deck.

"This is not necessary!" Kohn shrieked. "We can make a deal! We can come to an arrangement!"

"We are making a deal," said Soong. "We are coming to an arrangement."

Avery slashed high, a feint. Then he cut low, slicing

deeply into Kohn's thigh. From the resulting flow, he had struck an artery. Kohn struck the deck, clutching at himself, pallor creeping across his face like a wave.

Avery stood over his former leader. He looked up and dropped the knife to the deck, placing his hands behind his neck.

"Very well," said Soong. "Han. Be certain to capture in detail what follows." Very deliberately, he raised his hand and let it fall.

A cloud of gunsmoke and the concussive wave produced by multiple automatic weapons washed over the deck. The Advance Guard fired their guns and killed every last one of the Sapphire troops standing on the deck. Bodies fell this way and that. The carnage was total.

When it was over, the only man standing who was not Korean was Manuel Avery.

"Get one of the inflatable lifeboats," said Soong. He went to the stunned Avery, grabbed the man by the collar and dragged him to the railing.

"Please," said Avery. "I did as you asked. Please don't kill me. I was only following orders. I am a soldier like you."

Soong backhanded him, breaking open Avery's lip. The man squalled in pain and held his face.

"Never compare one such as yourself to my troops," he warned. "You are no more a soldier than the Iranian trash you contend with. All of you are merely a means to an end. The sooner you realize that, the sooner you will treat us with the respect you owe us. And the sooner *that* happens, the greater your lifespans will become."

His troops brought a small inflatable raft. Soong motioned over the side. The Advance Guard soldiers threw the boat over the rail.

"Give him the knife," said Soong. "He has earned it."

One of the regular Korean military soldiers assigned to the drug boat brought the bloody combat knife. He extended it to Avery, but the man shook his head. "No," said Avery. "I don't want it."

"A wise decision," said Soong. "As the boat is made of rubber." He chopped Avery across the throat, although he was careful not to hit the man hard enough to kill him. The Sapphire operative went over the rail and into the ocean. Soong took the knife from his soldier and threw it over the side, too.

He turned and looked into the camera that Han held. "See to it the video is delivered to one of Sapphire's corporate offices," he ordered. "In case brave Mr. Avery does not survive to deliver them the message I am sending." He drew his finger across his throat. Han nodded, shutting off the camera.

"Is the payload of explosives on board?" Soong asked.

"We are loading it from our boat now," said Han.

"Wire the ship," said Soong. "Use the minimum necessary. We have need of the Semtex for other parts of the operation. Take the Sapphire craft with the men you will require. Locate a suitable passenger craft or freighter, something with a civilian crew. Pirates will seize that ship, do you hear me?"

"I understand, sir," said Han.

"And make sure they get out a distress call with accurate coordinates," said Soong.

Soong was not done sending messages. To keep the government death squads at bay, he was going to take the fight to them.

He would not fail his country. Not now.

Not ever.

CHAPTER SIXTEEN

"You're sure the intelligence said 'pirates'?" McCarter asked Barbara Price. "It seems a little random, doesn't it?" They were once more being ferried aboard their loaned CH-46 Sea Knight, while Grimaldi flew air support in the chopper. Normally a report of pirates would be something to be handled by local navies, but there was nothing in the Philippines or nearby that could be brought to bear. The radio message, intercepted by the algorithms used to parse local hot-spot chatter, had been flagged in the Farm's computers and relayed automatically.

McCarter didn't like it. It smacked of a trap, and he wasn't sure how or why that could even be possible.

Intelligence updates from the Farm had carried other interesting news. The computer Able Team had recovered from Sapphire's headquarters in Manila verified that Sapphire was working for Claridge Clayton, providing him with muscle both at home and abroad. More significantly, Sapphire had been involved in several low-level attacks on the Revolutionary Path of God's operations, in what was described as an attempt to interdict competing ICBM components. Sapphire and the Iranians were engaged in a dirty bidding war. TruTech was involved somehow, even if Clayton wasn't actively involved. It wouldn't be the first time a well-meaning idiot had found his company hijacked out from under him by smarter and more nefarious people.

As Price reported, blacksuit teams domestically and

various allied law enforcement and intelligence agencies abroad were being mobilized to knock on the doors of Sapphire facilities in nine different countries. McCarter was genuinely curious how that might turn out. It was entirely possible that Claridge Clayton knew more about the counterfeiting of his components than he had told Able Team. The computer had revealed a series of money transfers from holding companies owned by Clayton to Sapphire. Was Clayton using Sapphire to run interference, to try to stamp out the counterfeiting on his own? It would explain a great deal. It was not unheard of, after all—a wealthy man taking the attitude that something would not get done if he did not do it himself.

Price reported further that the government of Iran, in response to postmortem identifications run on the Revolutionary Path of God mercenaries Able Team had killed, was issuing firm denials of any operations on U.S. soil. They were washing their hands of their personnel in the United States.

Brognola had been in conference with the President all morning. It was beginning to look as if a huge portion of the American defense industry had been compromised by external enemies, working covertly on U.S. soil. Taken at its face, it was an act of war…McCarter knew it could never be that simple, especially since most of the information establishing these connections had been dug up by Stony Man Farm in the course of what was supposed to be a deniable operation. They could hardly pressure the Iranians to come clean on the basis of intelligence the United States was not supposed to have, obtained through means it denied using officially.

McCarter could feel the operation coming to a head. Something was about to give, something that both Able

Team and Phoenix Force were taking big bites out of from either end.

"We're in range of your target," said the pilot over the helicopter's communications system. This was once again patched into the team's two-way earbuds. Off their flank, Grimaldi in his Cobra chopper was a welcome presence. The Stony Man pilot had saved their collective posteriors more than a few times, McCarter knew.

More than a score of few times, thought McCarter. Multiplied by years.

He surveyed the target far below. A launch was visible tied up to the small cruise ship, which was part of the *Anabelle* line out of the Philippines. The launch squared with the pirate report. Pirates preferred small, mobile vehicles, which they used to get in and out quickly.

Their target was still there.

The plan was as simple as their earlier drug ship busts had been. They would rappel to the deck, sweep it for hostiles and work their way from bow and stern until they met in the middle, where they would take the superstructure and the decks below.

"All in, mates!" McCarter said. "Time to make the high seas safe."

They descended. The deck rushed up to meet McCarter and James, who would take the bow section. Encizo, Hawkins and Manning would take the stern. McCarter brought his Kalashnikov copy to his shoulder and lined up its iron sights. He and James were mirror images of each other as they crept down the deck, glide-walking in an operator's semicrouch.

Ordinarily, McCarter would not have anticipated much in the way of organized resistance. Pirates were cowards. Certainly the Somali lot had proved to be less than effective, capable of being scared off by the slightest aggression.

Some of the more politically correct cruise lines employed sonic cannons to drive off pirates, which worked many times. The slightly more traditional among cruise line and freighter captains resorted to a variety of more direct options, such as arming their crew with privately purchased weapons. And then there were the men who simply turned their much larger vessels on the pirate craft and ran them down, sometimes with devastating results.

Then, too, occasionally the pirates carried rocket-propelled grenades and other heavy weapons. It was a gamble. Most of the time, driving them off was the smartest and most likely course. Once they were on your ship, once they had boarded you, their small arms and machetes were enough to turn any seagoing vessel into a hostage-crisis bloodbath.

Phoenix Force would not permit that to happen.

He had not gone far on the deck when some sixth sense, some combat intuition, kicked in again. Something was wrong. Something didn't feel right.

Automatic weapons opened up from the superstructure. McCarter had enough time to shove James toward the left and break to the right, where he encountered the deck rail. Suddenly he was over the rail, the water far below looming, his own death hurtling toward him with sudden clarity.

This is it, he thought. This is the moment. Falling off a boat into the bloody sea.

It hardly seemed fair—

"I got you, man." Calvin James's hand was on his web gear, hauling him over the rail, returning fire one-handed with his AK.

"Drop me!" McCarter ordered. "They'll shoot us both!"

"You belay that, man," James said. Amid the gunfire he dragged McCarter back across the deck, to the cover of a large ventilator.

"Everyone's a mutinous sailor all of a sudden," McCarter said. "Thanks, mate."

"De nada," said James. "What do you figure that's all about? That was no Somali pirate shooting with his rifle sideways and up in the air."

"No, it was not," said McCarter. The gunfire had stopped, but that meant their enemy was moving or waiting. Either was bad. If the shooter was on the move, he would have to reacquire the target. If the shooter was waiting, it meant that he was patient, and patient gunmen were few and far between. It implied a level of discipline.

"Element One," said Hawkins through his transceiver. "This is Element Two. We are under heavy fire." The bursts of automatic weapons were audible from their position. As McCarter tried to edge away from the cover of the ventilator to see farther down the deck, a line of bullets walked up past him. It stopped quickly. The gunners were using well-aimed bursts and employing tight trigger discipline.

"On my signal," McCarter said, "head farther down and cut into the superstructure at the first opening. Try to come in behind the blighter. I'll cover you."

"You don't know what you're shooting at, David."

"I'll make do," said McCarter. "When in doubt, just close your eyes and pull the trigger."

"Right," said James. He reloaded his AK. "Don't be afraid to go mobile if it gets nasty."

"Again with the mutiny," said McCarter. He grinned. "Appreciate the concern, mate, but I'll manage. Now come on, let's do this up right."

"Set," said James.

"Three…two…one…mark!" McCarter raised his AK and started firing in short bursts, shooting, swiveling and moving in turn to some rhythm only he could hear. There was return fire, but McCarter's shots were having the desired effect. James took off, headed away from the bow, doing his best to stay out of the line of fire.

A grenade bounced across the deck. Before McCarter could react, the bomb slid under the deck rail and out to sea. The explosion showered him with droplets of water.

The Briton didn't wait for more explosive surprises to find their way to him. He continued down the deck. As enemy fire came his way, he returned it, doing his best to target the muzzle-blasts when he could see them and the sounds when he could not. The latter was trickier, for the water had a way of distorting sound and there were many echoes in and around the superstructure of the ship.

His weapon ran dry. He took another magazine from his web gear, slapped the paddle release of the AK with the magazine and let the old one fall away as he locked in the new one. The Kalashnikov pattern was not ergonomic, but it was built for heavy use and abuse. If you beat the bloody hell out of it, it would respond favorably to the rough treatment. He kicked the empty magazine across the deck as he went, dodging bullets, unconcerned with recovering the spent mag.

"Element One, Element Two is mobile again, headed your way," said Hawkins.

"Understood," said McCarter. "Meet me amidships. We need to get belowdecks and see what's going on here."

"We have encountered heavy resistance so far," said Encizo. "They appear to be Koreans in battle dress utility. Special forces."

"Understood," said McCarter. "Rendezvous as soon as you can reach us."

The team members reconnected amidships and found the break in the superstructure they needed. The choice was go up or down, but it was unlikely any high-value assets would be kept anywhere but belowdecks. Belowdecks enabled greater control and protection. It was the logical place for any hostages to be kept.

McCarter was beginning to think that piracy was not the point of this ship's capture, however. This smelled, felt and tasted like a trap. It was a trap intended to catch Phoenix Force, or whoever came after the hijacked cruise ship.

"All right, lads," said McCarter. "Let's—"

The two Korean commandos who rappelled from the superstructure started firing at them while still inverted. The men of Phoenix Force scattered, returning fire. Manning managed to blow one of the men over the side of the deck, while James burned down the other, who collapsed on the deck almost on top of them.

"I'll be damned," said McCarter, examining the subdued uniform insignia on the dead man's collar. "These men are Advance Guard."

"They're what?" James asked.

"It's a North Korean special operations outfit," McCarter explained. "Very elite. The top of the top. I heard about them in the SAS. They don't spend much time anywhere the light can hit them. Truly dangerous men."

"Wonderful," said Hawkins. "So what on earth are they doing *here?*"

"I would say that's obvious, lads," McCarter said. "The North Koreans got tired of us knocking over their drug business one floating lab at a time, to say nothing of the ICBM operation they're trying to build. So they called in the heaviest hitters they have. It's possible the Advance Guard has been involved the entire time. They're the sort of chaps I would put in charge of an operation this critical from the outset. We're digging well past the surface here now. This is true black ops."

"Well, let's get going," said James.

"Right you are," said McCarter. He threw open the hatch. "Inward and onward."

They worked their way down the gangways, then split up, first by element, and then again deck by deck. McCarter was alone before they were done separating, but their transceivers had more than enough range and strength even among all that metal.

McCarter found himself in some kind of tool room. It seemed deserted until he found the overhead light switches. When he turned them on, he heard movement.

"Come out," he called. "You're outnumbered."

"Your grasp of mathematics is…interesting," said a voice.

McCarter froze. He let his AK fall to its sling and took out his Hi-Power clone. He was in close quarters now; the pistol would avail him better than the rifle.

"Show yourself," he ordered.

"I will," said the voice, "if you will."

McCarter edged toward the center of the tool room, where the light was brightest. His counterpart stepped forward, as well. The man was dressed in the battle fatigues of the Advance Guard and held a Type 68 pistol in his fist. He moved with the grace of a cat.

This one, thought McCarter, is muscle on muscle. Very dangerous.

All of the stories he had heard about the Advance Guard had indicated that these men were, to a man, some of the deadliest killers on the planet.

"I will give you credit, mate," said McCarter. "You run a disciplined crew. Perhaps you should tell me why we're talking." He held the Browning clone dead level with the Korean's chest. The Advance Guard man did the same.

"I see we are both men of rather established tastes."

He gestured, ever so slightly, with the Type 68. "Yours is a fine weapon."

"As is yours," said McCarter. "Are we through with the small talk yet?"

"I am Han," said the Korean. "Lieutenant to the Advance Guard. I was assigned to kill you."

"You're awfully up front about it, mate."

"Yes, well, that is the other part of my assignment. I was told that if I could not kill you, I should explain to you that continuing to interfere in the operations of the Democratic People's Republic of Korea will result in the deaths of a great many innocent men and women."

"You don't say," said McCarter. "Please explain. And might I say that your grasp of the queen's English is superb. Oxford?"

"Hardly," said Han. "My people prefer to keep to themselves."

"Seeing as how you have no choice, living in a prison state, that makes sense," said McCarter.

"Please," said Han. "You are being rude. You have not given me your name."

"Call me Renfield."

Han smiled. "Indeed? Very well. My men made a trip away from this craft before returning to it. They carried with them hand-selected hostages from among the crew. These hostages are now human shields, being held aboard... Well. Perhaps you know where they are being held and perhaps you do not. But I assure you that if you attack our interests, these innocent people, all of them Americans, will die. You are with the American death squad, yes?"

"Death squad?" McCarter snorted. "Mate, do I *sound* American to you?"

"Britain and the United States enjoy a strong relationship as allies," said Han. "It makes perfect sense that you would work together on this death squad, this means you have of keeping the West's thumb on the rest of the world."

"You're daft, man," said McCarter. "Where did you hear this nonsense?"

"My commanding officer," said Han. "We have an extensive intelligence network. You men of the West believe you are the only ones with technology, with resources. You are incorrect."

"All right, then," said McCarter. "We've had our little *High Noon* moment. You've given me your threats and your ultimatums. We've traded expressions of mutual respect. Your trap didn't work. My men are still alive. Now you have a choice to make, Lieutenant Han. Will you free the remaining people on this vessel?"

Han looked at the watch on his wrist.

"David," said Jack Grimaldi's voice in McCarter's ear. "The launch is leaving. I count uniformed troops but no one in civilian dress. Do you want me to target it?"

"Negative," said McCarter. When Han looked up, McCarter added, "That's some seriously negative energy you're bringing to this interaction, Han."

Han smiled. He was not fooled. McCarter could read that much in his eyes. "My men have been given orders to leave the ship. The honor of the final act of our little drama has fallen to me." He removed a black plastic box from his pocket. It bore a bright green LED. His finger was pressing down on a button inset in the unit.

"This is a detonator," said Han. "I am holding a dead man's switch. But the switch has a delay. When I let go, a timer begins. Should the button be pressed a second time, the explosives will deactivate. If it is not pressed, the explosives will shatter this vessel and send it to the bottom of the sea. With it will die every member of the crew and the passengers who are not serving aboard...another vessel."

"Where are they?" McCarter demanded.

"There is a ballroom," said Han. "You can find it on any of the lurid deck maps in the corridors. We have locked them inside. They will be fine. That is, unless this ship explodes."

"You blow this ship and you'll go down with it," said McCarter.

"Do you believe for a moment that I am not prepared to die in service to my country?" Han asked. "Why do you think I have permitted myself this conversation with you? Do you know, in all the years I learned English, I never had the pleasure of speaking it to someone who was a native speaker of the language. You have made what will likely be my last moments...very satisfying. I thank you."

"There's no need for that," said McCarter. "No one else has to die."

"Do you know what Advance Guard training is like?" Han asked. He backed to the far bulkhead and let go of the detonator. McCarter sucked in a breath. Han placed the detonator on the floor and returned to his position closer to the Briton. "They strip us down to our bones. They hurt us. They hurt us a great deal. You reach a point during the training where you wish to die. But then you move past that. You no longer pray for death."

McCarter's pistol never moved an inch. "I'm listening," he said. His eyes flickered to the detonator on the floor. How much time was left?

"There comes a moment where you realize you no longer long to die," said Han, "because you are already dead. You are a ghost walking among men."

Han bent and placed his pistol on the floor. He stepped away from it.

The dagger that appeared in his hand was suddenly just there, as if by sleight of hand. He lunged at McCarter.

The Briton got off a single shot, but Han was already colliding with him, dropping McCarter to the deck with a body blow that belied his smaller stature. McCarter managed to block the knife with his pistol but the weapon was wrenched from his hand. Both knife and pistol clattered to the deck. Both men circled around and back to their feet, moving to face each other. Han adopted a tight fighting stance, ready to kick or punch. McCarter knew instantly that he was in great danger.

Probably an expert in tae kwon do, he thought. *And not the watered-down version they teach to kids in American strip malls. This man is accustomed to killing with his hands and feet—*

The kick scythed in almost faster than he could track it. McCarter ducked under it but caught another in the chest that sent him reeling. He fired back with blows of his own, using the edge of his hands and short, stomping side kicks for close-range power. Han danced away each time. The expression on his face seemed more amused than anything else.

He's toying with me, McCarter realized. He wants his last moments on this world to be as interesting as possible. He knew, then, that he would have to try one of the strangest plays he had ever managed. He held up a hand.

"Wait," he said. "Just…wait."

Han paused. "Your time is running out," he said. "Please do not spoil it. Soon we will all be at the bottom of the ocean."

McCarter removed a grenade from his web gear. He put his finger in the pin. "I'm going to make this terribly boring for you, Han," he said. "I'm not keen on drowning to death. I'd rather go out my own way. I'm going to blow us both up."

"You would not," Han said. He sounded almost peevish. "Please. This is not the—"

McCarter beaned him in face with the grenade. He threw the bomb for all it was worth. It struck Han between the eyes and knocked him cold. McCarter immediately dived for the detonator.

The LED was red, but when McCarter pushed the button, it turned green again. He hoped and prayed that meant the explosion had been averted.

McCarter put the detonator on the deck again. He went to the grenade and picked it up, making sure the pin was still in place. Then he looked down at Han. The man was smiling.

"You are clever," said Han. He never tried to move from the floor. His hand went quickly to his mouth. "But you will not take from me this moment. I have...what is the expression? My heart set on it." He bit down on whatever he had put between his teeth.

Cyanide, thought McCarter. He backed off a pace so as not to inhale the fumes. Han died quickly, but not well. Cyanide was fast, but it did not leave a smile on the victim's face.

"David here," he said to his transceiver. "Mates, we've got problems. The drug lab is protected by human shields. Hostages taken from this vessel. We need intel on the current location of the drug lab vessel now. And we need to free the crew and passengers remaining on this liner."

"Here we go again," said James.

"Bloody hell," said McCarter quietly.

CHAPTER SEVENTEEN

Winston-Salem, North Carolina

"RegiCorp," said Lyons. "This is the place our helpful little Iranian mercenary gave up. Supposedly this is the last of the Iranian's domestic holdings." He drove past the building. It was large, with a high chain-link fence around it. The modern steel-beam construction meant it was really just a glorified warehouse, with a high ceiling and a faux brick facade.

"You mean, we might be getting close to the completion of the mission?" Blancanales asked.

"You know how that goes," said Schwarz.

Lyons rolled up to the intercom station at the automatic locking gate. There were no guards outside the building that they could see, but chances were good the place would be thick with Iranian mercenaries. If this facility had been in communication with the other Iranian elements, the men inside would be armed and very nervous. This was especially so now that the Farm had confirmed Vahid Rahimi was the leader of the North American contingent of the Revolutionary Path of God. In eliminating him they had cut off the head of the snake. The tail was still twitching, but they were about to put an end to that.

Lyons reached out and pressed the intercom. There was a pause. Finally a voice laced with static replied, "Yes?"

"Misters Curly, Moe and Larry to see your plant manager," said Lyons. "We have an OSHA inspection to run."

"We don't have anything on the schedule."

"ISO audit?" Lyons tried.

"No."

"Change the floor mats?"

"That's a good one," said Schwarz. "No one ever thinks to check the floor mat guy. Maybe we should have led with that."

"Plant's closed," said the voice on the intercom. The burst of static that punctuated that remark was very final.

"I am so sick and tired of playing games," said Lyons. "Everyone knows what's going on. Nobody wants to admit it. Let's stop screwing around. Let's just do what we do."

"Anybody think we're getting our rental deposit back on this truck?" Blancanales asked.

"Technically, this is not a rental," Schwarz pointed out.

Lyons actually smiled. Then he threw the big Suburban into Reverse, slamming his foot down on the accelerator to send the big vehicle burning rubber backward.

"This is going to be the cool part," said Schwarz.

Lyons hit the brakes, then popped the truck into low gear. He floored the accelerator once more and drove the Suburban through the gate, smashing it. Then he stopped, backed up and ran down the intercom box.

"We need to talk about your repressed-anger issues," said Schwarz.

Lyons kept on driving. The Suburban picked up speed. It was headed straight for the double doors at the front of the building. A large professionally lettered sign bearing the logo of RegiCorp was hanging over the doors.

Schwarz rolled down his window. Lyons shot him a quizzical glance.

"Candygram!" Schwarz shouted out the window as the

Suburban burst through the double doors of the building. Shattered glass filled the lobby. Lyons brought the truck to a halt, leaving black tire marks across the polished floor.

"Let's wreck this joint," said Carl Lyons.

Able Team piled out of the Suburban. Blancanales had his M-16, and for this operation, Schwarz had opted for one, as well. Lyons had his USAS-12, as ever. He gave the shotgun a workout, emptying one of its box magazines into the fire doors leading into the RegiCorp building. He lowered his shoulder and pushed through them.

A corridor filled with offices greeted them. Lyons paused just long enough to take a pair of Claymore mines from his gear bag and arrange them in front of the doors. He carried a remote detonator with him.

"Gadgets," said Lyons into his transceiver, "take the left. Pol, take the right. If you find anything interesting, shout out."

A beautiful blonde appeared in the closest doorway.

"Shouting out," said Schwarz. He took her by the arm and began to lead her out of the office area. "You'll have to come with me, miss," he said. "Working conditions in this building are about to become untenable."

"Good word," said Blancanales. "'Untenable.'" The second and third offices were empty. Lyons ducked into them anyway. He searched through some of the desks until he came up with something useful. The sheaf of papers he held were in Persian. He snapped a picture with his smartphone and sent it to the Farm.

A moment later his phone began to vibrate.

"Lyons," he said, answering it.

"Ironman," said Price, "we're running the document you just scanned through translation. It's component lists, relating to export regulations and how to circumvent them."

"So, smoking gun, in other words," Lyons said.

"Yes," said Barb. "Consider it a license to break heads."

"That's good," said Lyons. "I was going to need that."

"You've already started inflicting damage on the place, haven't you?" Price asked suspiciously.

"I'm not the most patient guy, Barb," Lyons told her. "Maybe you've heard that about me."

"Good hunting, Ironman."

"Thanks. Able out." He put his phone back in its pouch on his web gear.

Carl Lyons dropped the box magazine of slugs in his USAS-12 and loaded a magazine full of double-aught buck. Holding the Daewoo shotgun at hip level, he held the trigger back and swung the barrel in an arc across the office.

The shotgun pellets, each a sizable projectile on its own, demolished the office space. They shredded papers and desktops, punched holes in desk drawers and reduced lamps and computers to shards of plastic and metal. Fragments of electronic equipment covered the floor.

Lyons grinned. He moved on to the adjacent office and gave it a similar treatment, spraying out the rest of his magazine, churning the equipment and furniture inside to confetti.

"Down the corridor," said Lyons. It was labeled; the manufacturing area was beyond the doors at the end. "They'll have heard that. They'll be coming."

"They're already here," said Schwarz.

The doors swung open. The men who came through were wearing black fatigues and carrying Skorpion machine pistols.

"Well, now they're not even trying to hide," said Schwarz. He drew a bead with his M-16.

"Wait!" screamed the Iranian in the lead. "Wait! Do not fire!"

The men of Able Team were ready to shoot with the slightest of additional pressure on their triggers.

"Identify yourself," said Lyons. "Or I'll kill you where you stand."

"Farouk," said the man. "Please! Hold your fire!"

"Weapons down," ordered Lyons. "Unless you want to find out what's on the other side of the white light."

The three Iranians put their guns on the floor. Farouk stepped forward. "I wish to negotiate," he said.

"That's far enough," said Lyons. He let his shotgun rest on its sling and withdrew his Colt Python, which he aimed at the spot between Farouk's eyes. "Talk fast."

"Our leadership is gone," said Farouk. "We have...we have tasted life here. We wish to remain."

"Are you...are you trying to cut a *deal?*" Schwarz asked.

"We will show you the manufacturing facility," said Farouk. "The components are useless if we have no organization through which to deal them. We want immunity. We want witness protection."

"You want more than we can offer you," said Blancanales. "Cooperation is good. Cooperation helps us to help you. But you've got to set your goals more reasonably or we won't be able to come to an agreement."

Farouk and his men traded glances. "Which of you is the leader?" he asked finally.

Lyons stepped forward. "I am. I'm the team leader."

"These men will abide by your wishes?" asked Farouk.

"Within reason," Lyons said. He wasn't sure he liked Farouk's tone.

"Then there is nothing more to discuss," said Farouk. "We will surrender."

"That's excellent," said Blancanales. "Then all we have to do is—"

Farouk screamed. The blade of a knife appeared in his chest, thrust through from behind.

"Down!" roared Lyons.

Gunshots rang out. The three men who had sought to negotiate a surrender, Farouk included, collapsed. Behind them, a horde of Iranian mercenaries had gathered and was now swarming down the corridor.

The enemy swamped them.

Lyons found himself at the bottom of a dog pile of writhing human beings. He did what he could, firing elbow shots at his opponents while trying to dig his way clear of the morass. With each maneuver, though, he felt like he was losing ground. There were simply too many of the enemy.

"Weapons!" shouted Lyons. "Shoot your way clear!" His Python was in his fist, then, and he began shooting into the mass of enemy bodies. As long as he did not accidentally target Schwarz or Blancanales, he could neither miss nor fail to hit an assailant. There were no innocents here. There was only the crush of mercenary operatives now fleeing through the corridor.

Suddenly they were through the doors and into the manufacturing space.

"Use the machines," Lyons ordered. "Take cover behind the machines." The Iranian mercenaries were now headed for the exits. It was time to close the escape route.

Lyons removed the detonator from his web gear and squeezed its paddle switch three times in quick succession.

From where they waited, they could hear the explosions...and the screams of the Iranian mercenaries caught in the Claymore's vicious blasts. The shaped charges released swarms of round shrapnel when fired. The payload was directed in a cone of fire that was tightly controlled by the shaped charge. Have a set of Claymores guarding a narrow space was almost as good as having an armed man there.

In a facility this large, having just three men did tend to feel a little on the light side...

"Guys," said Schwarz. He stuck his head up over the industrial press behind which they had sought cover. "Look at this."

At the center of the manufacturing space, a fully automated pick-and-place machine was whirring away. The machine, about the size of a Volkswagen sedan, contained a pair of machine tool clusters that ran on opposed rails. As tool heads moved back and forth or up and down, components were plucked from a bank of machines inserted in the pick-and-place station. A conveyor belt carried partially assembled circuit boards from one end of the manufacturing space into the pick-and-place machine and then out again, whereupon the circuits created were readied for inspection or more part placement.

Schwarz quickly scanned the area. Then he checked his smartphone. Meanwhile, Iranian mercenaries from both the corridor outside and hidden behind workstations around the perimeter of the manufactory were boiling forth like angry ants, firing small arms in their direction.

"There's no pretense here," Schwarz said. "They're manufacturing critical missile components here, without a thought to security or concealment. This is brazen. How did we let this happen under our collective noses?"

"No time to worry about that now," said Lyons, returning fire with his Python. He was being as restrained with his return fire as he could afford to be. There were still some civilians in and around the manufacturing area, most of them huddled behind their workstations and as close to the floor as they could get.

"We've got to clear these people out of here," said Lyons

into his transceiver. "And control some variables. Gadgets, circle around and flank the shooters in the middle perimeter of the manufacturing area. Pol, get back to that corridor and mop up as many armed Iranians as you can. We'll rotate around, see if we can tighten the noose as we go. The lives of innocents come first."

"Got it," said Blancanales.

"Always," said Schwarz.

Lyons began a search-and-destroy circuit around the manufacturing floor. There was ample cover. All he had to do was to glide, heel-to-toe, in a semicrouch, keeping his shotgun's stock tucked against his shoulder, letting the weapon guide him from one target to the next.

Lyons knew that in combat, motion was life. There were stories, frequently repeated, of American soldiers fighting in Afghanistan and Iraq in built-up urban areas. More than once, those stories had ended in good news for the Western troops, who had significantly more combat training than the enemies they faced. This was not to say their enemies weren't experienced. In Afghanistan especially, the fighters Americans faced were battle-hardened troops who already knew what to expect from combat. They had already tried what they thought might work and discarded what did not. They made fewer mistakes than, say, their younger adult counterparts.

What these veteran enemy soldiers lacked was modern combat doctrine and tactics. Weapons evolved, and while some battlefield principles remained unchanged, many specific tactics were altered and updated. The soldier of today knew that if presented by a cluster of enemy shooters across a block or street, he could drastically alter the outcome if he simply got up and moved, angling to flank his enemies or simply coming up behind them. These were lessons to which the older dogs among the savage enemy warriors were less receptive. Theirs was a powerfully tribal culture, with all the tribal biases and reluctance that went with it.

All of these thoughts raced through Lyons's mind as he cut through the enemy. He shot those he could and battered down with the stock of the shotgun those who came too close. He made an ever-tightening spiral, working his way toward the center of the manufacturing floor, where the pick-and-place machine hummed like a giant mechanical spider.

And then he had reached it.

Lyons, breathing heavily, his clothes flecked with blood, the barrel of his shotgun burning hot and trailing smoke, stood at the center of the factory. The pick-and-place machinery kept right on running, producing circuit boards that would find their way into…Lyons wasn't sure, but Schwarz had identified it as ICBM parts. Probably guidance systems or related electronics, Lyons thought.

"Emergency stop," muttered Lyons. He pumped a 12-gauge slug into the body of the machine, then another, then another, smashing the arms and the tool head with precisely placed blasts. At this range, he could not miss.

Then it was over. He was out of targets.

"Gadgets," he said. "Pol. Report."

"Clear," said Blancanales.

"Clear," said Schwarz. "No more enemy contacts. Hostiles have been neutralized."

Lyons realized he was breathing heavily. He focused on controlling his respiration as he had learned while training in karate years ago, pulling air in through his nose and blowing it out through his mouth. Soon, both his respiration and his heart rate were under control.

"We need to walk the perimeter of this building," said Lyons. "Look for stragglers, and especially any holed-up

civilians. I want to make sure the Iranian presence is neutralized. We'll contact the Farm for a mop-up presence if
we have any prisoners to transport."

"What sort of prison does a plausibly deniable Iranian
black-bag operator end up in?" asked Schwarz.

"Someplace awful," said Blancanales. "The kind of
pit where they dump you when they want to forget about
you…because you're inconvenient. A political liability. In
this case, acknowledging their agents on our soil would
be tantamount to a declaration of war. And it makes our
own government look bad if we admit they were here in
the first place."

"They can't just sweep this under the rug," said Lyons.
"Look around. Look at the scope of this place. It's too big
for everyone just to avert their eyes and pretend it wasn't
here."

"You'd be surprised what the proverbial 'they' can make
disappear," said Schwarz.

"No, I wouldn't," said Lyons, suddenly cross. "I've seen
it all before. We've all seen it. It's how these missions end
up resolved to everyone's satisfaction, more often than not.
Everyone's satisfaction but ours."

"We need to get containment on this," said Schwarz,
knowing that focusing on routine, on duty, would help snap
Lyons out of his grim mood. "Barb has to know how badly
we need a clean-up team."

"On it," said Lyons. He dialed the secure line to the
Farm.

"Ironman," said Price, "what is your status?"

"We're all still in one piece," said Lyons. "Although
Gadgets has been annoying the hell out of me."

"I can still hear you," Schwarz put in from where he
was frisking a prisoner. The plastic zip-tie cuffs the team
carried would go a long way toward securing their new

charges until the blacksuit team scrambled from the Farm could take possession of the captured Iranian operatives. Then it would be time to drop them into one of those black-hole prisons, Lyons supposed.

He did not envy them that.

On the many battlefields they walked, that type of cold-war mentality, secrets layered on secrets, men "disappeared" by their leaders or their enemies into places reminiscent of French Revolution era prison fortresses... that was all incredibly distasteful to Lyons. He preferred a stand-up fight to espionage and intrigue.

"Multiple teams are inbound," Price told Lyons. "You should be...Carl. Wait. Wait, I'm getting some new telemetry here. Ironman, we have reports that the TruTech headquarters is under assault."

Schwarz had returned to Lyons's side. "You think it's more Iranians?" he asked.

"This was supposed to be the last of them," said Lyons. "And you heard them yourself. Their leadership is gone, or they think it is. Who does that leave? What secret reserves could they be drawing from?"

"Maybe our informant didn't know everything," said Blancanales. "It isn't unusual to keep the lower ranks less informed."

"It doesn't feel right," said Lyons. "We're missing something."

"Uh, Barb," said Lyons. "Any chance of getting a replacement vehicle?"

"Was your sport utility badly damaged?"

"A bit," said Lyons. "It's probably going to get worse when we drive back out of the lobby."

"Back out of the lobby...?" Price repeated.

"It's a long story," said Lyons.

"We were practicing the direct route," said Schwarz.

"I'll make arrangements," said Price. "In the meantime, we need to get you to TruTech. You're the most qualified unit we can send, and of course this is precisely the type of scenario for which Able Team was created."

"And I thought it was just my boyish charm that got the ball rolling," said Lyons.

"There's something else," said Price. "Aaron and his people are working overtime with their internet search-and-delete programs," she said, referring to the algorithms the Farm used to remove sensitive material from the internet. The definition of "sensitive," in this case, was anything that might bring too much scrutiny on areas of the United States's covert and intelligence communities, as well as anything to do with the Sensitive Operations Group.

"Regarding what?" Lyons asked.

Price hesitated. "Have…have any of you been throwing around the term 'death squad'?"

Lyons tensed. "No," he said. "Why would we do that? We don't even 'throw around' the term Able Team in the field, depending on how sensitive the operation is. Why?"

"Chatter," said Barb. "Culled from phone and web traffic. While Stony Man Farm and the Sensitive Operations Group remain uncompromised, it's a fact that more people every week are using the term to refer to the type of counterterror op we run. Our work is getting noticed, even if we aren't. That's good on a moral level, but frustrating on a security level. You know how Hal gets."

"I do know how Hal gets," Lyons echoed. "We'll lock things down here as best we can and wait for transport."

"Be on your best behavior," Price warned. "Federal departments will be crawling all over the place with representatives from the Department of Defense, trying to figure out just how badly exposed we are as a nation on this."

Schwarz got serious. "I can tell you that it's bad, Barb."

"I know," said Price. "Keep me advised. Farm, out."

CHAPTER EIGHTEEN

The Philippine Sea

"Thar she blows, lads," said McCarter. The cargo chopper swooped in low and fast, carrying them to the rappelling points with more velocity than most human beings knew was possible. To fly a helicopter was more than sitting at the edge of your seat. It was flying at the very brink of losing control, a constant process of nearly-crashing-and-recovery.

To learn to fly a helicopter was to squeeze an amount of information comparable to medical school into your brain—and in much less time than medical students had to absorb the information for which they were responsible. That was how Grimaldi had once described it, and his colorful elaboration on the concept had always stuck in McCarter's mind.

With Grimaldi once more maintaining station well above the ship, ready to provide necessary air support, McCarter and his men would rappel in…but not before they softened up the target. That was where Grimaldi's Cobra came in.

"G-Force," said McCarter, "you are go for your run."

"That is a roger," Grimaldi said. "Commencing run… now."

The Cobra dipped out of the clouds like an armed boulder, hurtling seaward with impressive velocity. Just when it seemed Grimaldi might collide with the massive drug ship, he applied thrust and fired up his electric cannon and Hydra rockets. The Cobra unleashed an airborne fury that seemed to shake the helicopter in the sky.

Thermal imaging of the drug ship had shown there were no hostages on the upper decks. The only men moving around where Grimaldi's weapons could reach, without sinking the ship, were armed members of the Advance Guard. Image enhancement showed a mixed contingent of both Advance Guard soldiers and regular Korean military, in fact. That meant that, once the Phoenix Force operatives rappelled into the storm, the enemies facing them would be a mixed bag of dangers. While the regular Korean military was not as ferocious as their elite forces, they were still dedicated, persistent and very dangerous, willing to take their own lives rather than admit failure.

No sooner had his boots hit the deck than McCarter was dodging gunfire from soldiers positioned in and around the large cargo containers on the ship's deck. The size of this ship, the biggest and the youngest in the North Korean drug fleet, could prove to be a problem, especially when it came to searching for hostages. McCarter weighed his options carefully. Somewhere belowdecks were human shields used to protect the Advance Guard. It was like rescuing hostages from rabid wolves, if the fight Han had offered him was any indication.

"Calvin, T.J., take the bow," said McCarter. "Gary, Rafe, take the stern with me."

His team acknowledged his orders.

At the first deck junction, he went flat on his belly, firing the AK with the ejection port pointing skyward and the magazine nearly flat against the deck. The weapon performed admirably. He killed one, then a second opponent, realizing only after he stepped over their bodies that they were regular Korean military. That was fine with Mc-Carter, who was not eager to come to blows with a carbon copy of Lieutenant Han.

"Elements, report in," McCarter said. "I am penetrating more deeply into the—"

A squeal of static unlike any he had heard the transceivers make suddenly struck his ears. He thought he heard his teammates trying to report in, but their voices were drowned out by the interference.

"Can you hear me?" said the lilting, educated voice. It bore the unmistakable hint of a Korean accent.

"I can hear you," said McCarter.

"Am I addressing the death squad leader?" asked the voice.

"We are no death squad," said McCarter, bristling at the thought.

"Nonsense," said the voice. "You are sent throughout the globe to kill the enemies of the West. Are you not?"

McCarter had no response for that. It ignored the spirit of what Stony Man Farm did, but not the technical letter of its charter, so to speak. He continued to move and shoot through the superstructure, knowing that his teammates would continue to do so, as well. He needed to get to the lower decks to locate and free the human shields being kept onboard.

He would have to be careful speaking directly to whoever was on the line. It would not do to give the enemy too much direct knowledge of the operation being mounted against him.

"How are you on this transmission?" McCarter said. In truth, it was supposed to be impossible, and he knew Schwarz right now would be going out of his mind trying to figure out how it was done. Schwarz had even had a hand in developing the transceivers. He would not take kindly to their being compromised.

"First let us get the formalities out of the way," said the voice. "I am Commander Soong of the People's Democratic Republic of Korea. I am master of the contingent of Advance Guard who are now arrayed before you. To answer the question you *did* ask, I am seated behind a rather sophisticated array of jamming and interference equipment, which incorporates the very latest in smart decryption technology."

"North Korea doesn't have technology like that, mate," said McCarter, wondering to what degree the voice was shamming him.

"I regret that it does not," said Soong. "But our traitorous cousins in the South possess such technology, and the infrastructure to manufacture it. Imagine what we could accomplish if only the Democratic People's Republic had access to the manufacturing facilities in the South. It is one of the many reasons I look forward to invading that whelp of a nation. We will execute its whelp of a president, finishing a job we attempted to start too long ago. Messages will be sent. Messages that cannot be ignored. I am very fond of communicating in that way."

"Oh, I can imagine that you just can't wait to put on your junior Hitler outfit and goose-step around the plazas after the mighty conquest of your neighbors," said McCarter. "Why are you wasting my time?"

"I am not wasting your time," insisted Soong. "I am not a brute who thinks only in terms of one way, one method. How is the saying in your countries? When one's only tool is a hammer, every problem becomes a nail?"

"More or less," said McCarter. He paused to shoot a Korean military man through the face as the gunner leaped from behind the corner of a corridor juncture.

"I know, if you are here, that your intelligence is good," said Soong. "You know much about our operation, as I would expect you to. I honestly thought these ships, so far in international waters and so far from the West, would be a relatively safe means of transporting our component shipments. You Americans are a troublesome lot."

"Not American," said McCarter. "Mate."

"Indeed," said Soong, actually chuckling. "Forgive me. Tell me your name, not-American mate."

"Roosevelt," said McCarter. "Theodore Roosevelt."

"Very well, Roosevelt," said Soong. "You are the commander of your contingent?"

"I am."

"Then listen to me well, Roosevelt. Did you think I drew your attention to the hijacked cruise liner by accident? I set that trap. I did it deliberately."

"We sprang your trap and defeated your men. I will give Lieutenant Han credit. For a man with a death wish he held his own."

"You do not even begin to understand what it is we think, or how," said Soong. "The ship was filled with video cameras transmitting wirelessly to a relay buoy. I watched your team operate. I understand your tactics. I know how it is you work."

"Yet here I am, moving around the ship, pretty much doing what I want to do," said McCarter.

"Have you found the hostages yet?" asked Soong.

McCarter didn't answer. You always gave a cracked nut like this one enough time to expose his own dirty laundry. Most of these fruitcakes were only too eager to tell you what they thought, and why. It was if they spent so much time plotting and scheming that the opportunity to unload on someone who wasn't one of their minions was too great to resist.

The bastard was clever, though. He might be trying to keep McCarter occupied, get his brain engaged in speaking and answering questions, driving that portion of the mind into overdrive that led to distraction, to lack of focus at critical moments. McCarter stopped at another junction of intersecting corridors, taking the time to fire out a quarter of his AK's magazine in all four directions. Then he slapped the magazine out with another fresh one and fitted that home.

"I set up the ambush at the cruise liner hoping you would be killed," said Soong. "I did not wish to lose Lieutenant Dae."

"Who?" McCarter asked.

"Lieutenant Han, I said," Soong said. He seemed rattled all of a sudden, as if he had given something away that he had not meant to reveal.

"All you wacky villain-types gloat about what you meant to do," said McCarter. He was climbing down a dimly lighted gangway now. He was deep enough in the ship that he thought he might be getting close to where the hostages were kept.

"Please," said Soong. "I sense you are a worthy opponent. My evaluation of you in watching you operate bears that out. We are men of action. Unnecessary hostility does not become us."

"Are you quoting—?" McCarter began.

"Han had instructions to wire the ship with explosives," said Soong. "He made…interesting use of the detonator. It is possible I missed some subtle cues in his psychological makeup in the last. But you need to know that he also wired this vessel."

"Not surprising," said McCarter. "Let me guess. You have your finger on the button of another dead man's switch, and we're going to have to have some sort of climactic duel before I pluck it from your fingers and kill you."

"Not apparently," said Soong. "Instead, Han wired the bombs after bringing me his hand-selected hostages from the cruise ship. Most of them are women. Han had an eye for female flesh. Many of them are very pretty. Sometimes I think he waited to collect them until he was certain he had the most beautiful ones. Your culture may be fat, lazy and decadent, but many among the whores you call women are quite lovely. If we look to the exterior only."

"Not American," McCarter insisted.

"No, of course not," said Soong. "You are British. Such fun, the British. Shall I tell you what you face?"

"Do your worst, mate," said McCarter. He was growing tired of Soong's game. The man was obviously trying to buy time by jamming their transmissions, engaging in this ridiculous conversation to distract him. Why were so many of the enemy so long-winded? Perhaps being a bloated windbag made you want to turn to a life of crime and unpleasantness.

He was so busy thinking about his conversation with Soong that he almost died for it. The Advance Guard trooper who attacked him from the shadows tried to blind him with a tactical light. McCarter blinked the afterimages away and went straight for the man, ramming the barrel of his AK into the Korean's gut, using the weapon as a blunt spear. As the Korean recoiled, McCarter pulled the trigger, spraying the man's guts all over the bulkhead.

Clever bastard, thought McCarter. He nearly got me.

"Roosevelt?" asked Soong. "Are you still there?"

"What's in it for you, Soong?" McCarter countered. If he could get the man focused on something other than his game, some unanticipated question, perhaps he could seize the initiative in this little verbal sparring match.

"I should think that is obvious," said Soong. "I seek superiority for North Korea. You and your men are attempting to disrupt the component pipeline I am establishing. That is why you will die. That is why I tricked you into attacking the cruise liner."

"And here I thought you attacked that liner to kidnap human shields we would actually consider innocent," said the Briton. "After all, random freighters are often crewed by unsavory characters. And they have a real lack of pretty girls."

Soong paused. When his voice came back on the link, he said, "Well played, Roosevelt. I will bet you believe you have me and my men all figured out. You men of the West are so often smug in your sense of superiority."

"I've seen your kind before, mate," McCarter said. "A ruddy genius, you take yourself for. If you ask me, your kind has cornered the market on smug." His voice turned cold. "Let the hostages go. Your country is committing an act of war."

"My nation will disavow me," said Soong. "At least as far as you and your government will ever know. North Korea commands no respect from the United Nations now. It is laughed at. It is not seen as a power. But my work will make it impossible for you to ignore us."

"What you're doing isn't going to work," said McCarter. He had found a cargo compartment guarded by two Korean military men. He took a moment to pop the magazine from his AK, strip a round from it and then reinsert the mag. Then he threw the loose round down the corridor in the opposite direction, where it rattled against the bulkhead.

One of the two Korean soldiers went running toward the sound. McCarter let him go. "Manifest Destiny!" he shouted out. "Monroe Doctrine!" Belowdecks, his voice echoed from the many steel surfaces.

The guard at the door pointed his AK into the darkness, eyes wide, clearly terrified. McCarter shot him, almost casually, through the throat, watching him fall to the deck clutching his neck. His partner came running back and made the mistake of checking his comrade first before turning to survey the threat that had taken the man down. McCarter shook his head. The Advance Guard might be crack soldiers, but the rest of these Korean military operatives were just so much filler. He walked a short automatic burst up the man's chest, folding him back.

Whatever was beyond that hatch had been worth guarding. The most likely reason was that there were hostages beyond.

"Are you still there, Roosevelt?" asked Soong.

It was time to give Soong something to think about. Given where these hostages were located, McCarter was more certain than ever that the area above decks would be a free-fire zone if it was anything. He said aloud, "G-Force, I don't know if you can hear me. But if you can, I want you to expend your payload wrecking this ship from bow to stern. Keep it above the deck line."

"Oh, very good," said Soong. "In your position I might do much the same."

"What *is* my position?" McCarter asked. It was his turn to keep Soong talking, while he waited to see if Grimaldi's attack would make a difference.

"You are the defender of a corrupt regime," said Soong. "You cling to a discredited ideology. Yours is a system that cannot perpetuate itself. It is doomed to fail."

"Funny," said McCarter. "I could say the same thing about you." He spun the wheel on the hatch in front of him. It opened, squeaking loudly. He brought his AK up as soon as the hatch afforded him a line of sight.

There was a guard inside, too.

The bullet the man fired from his Type 68 pistol very nearly took McCarter's head off. It ricocheted from the bulkhead and whined past the Briton's ear, uncomfortably close and very loud. The former SAS commando's ears were ringing when he made the matter worse by squeezing a three-round burst from his Kalashnikov clone.

The Advance Guard trooper hit the deck. McCarter moved into the cargo compartment and put a mercy round through the man's head. He wished he could communicate with his men. Whatever jamming gear Soong had aboard the ship was very powerful.

We should have anticipated that move, he thought. Well, live and learn.

What confronted McCarter in the middle of the room was the strangest thing he had yet seen on a mission.

Four attractive women and two men, all dressed in civilian clothing, all wearing canvas backpacks, were chained by wrists and ankles to D-rings in the deck in the middle of the cargo compartment. They were arrayed in some kind of bizarre pretzel formation, either standing or holding themselves up by their palms on round metal buttons inset in an electronic control pad beneath them.

The civilians were alive and seemed unharmed. They had all been gagged with silver adhesive tape. Sweat poured from their skin. Their arms and legs shook. How long they had been holding these awkward positions, he couldn't say. As he watched, one of them moved a leg, forcing the woman next to him to slap her palm on the button he had previously been covering with his foot.

"You twisted bastard," said McCarter. "What have you done?"

"Oh," said Soong, sounding very pleased with himself. "You have found my little creation? You should be impressed. I had it designed after the inspiration of your insipid Western entertainment."

"You might just as well have forced them to fight to the death," muttered McCarter.

"I grew bored with sport of that type," said Soong.

McCarter felt his face flush. Soong was a madman. It was far worse than he had originally believed. It wasn't merely that Soong was a dangerous, well-trained military commander. He was also mad as a hatter. That made him especially dangerous. The man was getting his jollies from the predicament in which he had put those people.

"The principle is simple," explained Soong. "The prisoners each wear on their backs an explosive device. Those devices, should they detonate, will detonate the rest of the ship, killing both the hostages here and the ones I have on the deck below in a more conventional cell. Many innocent lives will be lost if the bombs go off."

"What are you doing to them?" McCarter demanded.

"That is the best part," said Soong. He sounded so engrossed in the hostages' plight that McCarter started examining the darkened corners of the cargo space more carefully. It was then that he saw the tiny red LED of the camera mounted to the bulkhead. Soong was watching them and enjoying the show.

The entire vessel shook then. The vibrations felt like thunder, which grew in intensity. Grimaldi was making his strafing run. He *had* heard the transmission.

For the moment, Soong acted as if he did not notice. "The electronic platform on which the hostages are arrayed contains a complicated system of weights and magnets. The prisoners must maintain at least three points of contact with the board at all times. But the pads pop up after a preset interval, becoming no-play zones, forcing them to change position. And there are not enough pads for all of them. It is fascinating to see them divine how the game is played as they fight to survive. If too many pads are free, the bombs explode."

The ship rumbled again. Grimaldi was dealing death and destruction above decks.

"You hear that, you nutter?" McCarter said, unable to help himself. "That's an attack helicopter taking apart your precious gunboat. We're going to disassemble this thing to the component pieces, and I'm going to start by disassembling your sick bomb. You're torturing these people! For nothing!"

"Not for nothing," Soong insisted. "I am a student of human nature. Every good commander is. Would you not agree? You do not strike me as a stupid man."

"I'm not a pervert with a voyeur's sensibilities!" McCarter shouted. "I don't enjoy seeing people in pain!"

"Well," said Soong, sounding disappointed. "That is of course your choice and your preference. I am sad that you cannot see things more in keeping with my own worldview. It is borne of harsh experience."

"I'll bloody well enjoy killing you, you son of a bitch," said McCarter.

"I take that as a compliment," said Soong. "Whenever I can inspire a worthy enemy to hate me, I know I have acquitted myself well for the DPRK. I have enjoyed our conversation, Roosevelt."

"I don't suppose now that it's finished you'll consider killing yourself," said McCarter. "That's what Han seemed bent on doing."

"Dae would not have done that," said Soong. "I mean... my men would not do that. Han was not suicidal."

"He was a clown short of the circus and you know it," said McCarter. "He was as daft as you are."

"There really is no need to insult me," said Soong

through the transceiver. "Not after I've gone to so much trouble in combatting you. Is not a worthy opponent preferable to the refuse you deal with the rest of the time? And now you have put me out of sorts and made me forget. I wished to compliment you before, and you have derailed my train of thought more than once. That is unusual. Rarely do I forget a plan."

"What is that?" McCarter asked. "What was it you had to compliment me on?" He was utterly disgusted. As he surveyed the people suffering for Soong's torture machine, he wished he could wrap his fingers around Soong's throat.

"Your skillful use of the attack helicopter for support is what made your last raid so successful," said Soong. "I anticipated this. It's why I have surface-to-air wire-guided missiles emplaced on this ship. They're quite impervious to most countermeasures."

The interference faded. Suddenly, McCarter could hear the voices of his other team members, demanding to know what was going on, what was happening.

"Mayday!" shouted Jack Grimaldi. "Mayday! I'm hit! I'm going down!"

CHAPTER NINETEEN

Atlanta, Georgia

"I've had it up to here with these Sapphire pussies," growled Carl Lyons. He kicked in the door to the TruTech headquarters. The same pretty blonde sat behind the reception counter. When she saw Able Team marching into the lobby of TruTech with their weapons in hand, she screamed. The Sapphire security men guarding the lobby immediately raised their TP-9 pistols.

"Federal agents!" bellowed Lyons. "Lower your weapons or you will be killed."

The Sapphire men continued to point their weapons. One of them opened his mouth to speak, no doubt to give them some order, some ultimatum.

Carl Lyons hated it when second-rate thugs tried to get pushy.

As the man opened his mouth, Lyons put a .357 Magnum bullet through it. It exited through his cheek and hit the man next to him before he could pull his trigger. His shot went into the floor.

Lyons dropped to the ground, pushing the shotgun ahead of his body. He rolled across the floor as if he was trying to fold up a carpet, and as he did so, he triggered a full automatic blast from the USAS-12. The result was an ankle-level spread of slugs that chopped down several of the guards before they knew what hit them.

Lyons gave each of them a mercy round. The alternative was to let them bleed out, which seemed needlessly cruel.

The elevator doors opened and more guards piled out. Lyons shot one and then the USAS-12 ran dry. He swapped magazines and continued shooting, very nearly breaking some of the attackers in two. He knew it was an optical illusion, but he still held tremendous respect for the power of the weapon.

Able Team broke into a jog in different directions, routing their target profile to make it harder for the security guards to get them all at once. The guards fired wildly. High-tech weapons did not make up for their lack of discipline. The men of Able Team dropped them easily.

The girl behind the reception desk was still screaming.

"Hey," said Schwarz. "Know what I don't see?"

"What?" asked Lyons.

"Iranians. I see no Iranians here. Only Sapphire men in uniform."

"Funny how that works," said Lyons. He walked to the reception desk. The girl screamed at him until she was red in the face. Lyons reached out with one large hand and covered her mouth.

"Do me a favor," said Lyons, "and *shut up*. And while you're at it, maybe you could tell me why we got a report that this building has been taken over by terrorists, that your boss has been taken hostage, or whatever."

The woman looked up with tears in her eyes. Lyons took his hand from over her face.

"They made me call 9-1-1," she said. "They told me I would get fired if I didn't."

"Who's 'they'?" Blancanales asked.

"The security team," she said. "Richards, the man who's in charge of the Sapphire people, told me to put out the call. I didn't want to. I was worried I could get arrested for, you know, making a false report? It's not my fault. They had guns."

"Well, now all they've got are bullets," said Lyons. He helped the receptionist out from behind her desk. "Where can we find this Richards?"

"He'd be somewhere on the upper floors on the way to Mr. Clayton's office," she said. "He moves around all the time."

"Wonderful," said Lyons. He propelled her toward the other two Able Team men. "Grab her," he told Schwarz, "and throw her out the front door."

"Roger," said Schwarz. He did as he was told. The woman looked quite indignant by the time she reached the parking lot.

"Come on," said Lyons. "No death-box elevator. We'll take the stairs up, collect this Richards on the way and then see what Clayton has to say for himself."

"I'm not going to lie, Ironman," said Schwarz. "You seem genuinely crabby."

"That's because I am," Lyons said. "We let Clayton jerk us around. I think he's dirty. I think he's into this up to his eyeballs. And I think he employs a security team that was only too happy to kill us. Drawing down on federal agents is one of those things that sets you apart from the law-abiding citizens and the squares."

"I love that you actually still say 'squares,' Ironman," said Schwarz. "I bet your inner dialogue is like a hard-boiled detective novel."

They opened the door to the stairwell. A Sapphire hard-man was waiting there for them. Lyons slammed the butt of his shotgun into the man's face. He collapsed.

"That looks *really* painful," said Schwarz. "I think that every time you do it."

"Come on," said Lyons. "Landing by landing. It's a long way up, with Clayton waiting for us at the top."

They began to climb. They had not gone more than a flight and a half when Schwarz put his hand on Lyons's chest and said, "Stop! Nobody move!"

"What the hell?" Lyons said.

A silver tripwire extended across the landing. It was connected to a shaped charge that resembled a small Claymore.

"This is a nice piece of hardware," Schwarz said as he knelt over the tripwire and used his multitool's wire-cutter jaws to snip the line. "Very expensive."

"I'm glad you appreciate their taste in things that will blow us up," said Lyons.

"Little things, Carl," said Schwarz. "Little things."

A voice echoed down the stairwell. "Hey! You down there! Stay back! You keep coming and Clayton gets a bullet through the head!"

"Go ahead!" Lyons shouted back up. He motioned for Schwarz and Blancanales to move so that, should someone target them from above on the stairs, they would not be in the direct line of fire. "Honestly, I'm not sure I like the guy that much!"

"We have Clayton!" shouted the man. His accent was typical Midwestern; this was not one of the Iranian stooges. Lyons had his money on Sapphire again, unless this was a direct employee.

"Keep him!" Lyons shouted back.

"I'm not sure Barb would appreciate that kind of hostage negotiation," whispered Blancanales.

"I'm following a hunch," Lyons told him. "And really. He was a jerk. You could tell. He just had that vibe."

"We should probably really try to keep Clayton present-tense instead of past-tense," said Blancanales.

"You used to be fun," said Schwarz.

"All right," Lyons shouted. "I'll bite. What do you want?"

There was a pause. When the voice came back, it was an angry shout: "I want you to die!" This was followed by gunfire that rattled against the stairwell below but did not come close to where Able Team was standing.

"He's got us gauged wrong," said Blancanales quietly, pitching his voice low so that the stairwell could not convey his words to those above or below.

"Yeah, let's encourage that impression," Lyons whispered back. "Hang back against the wall. Get down real low." To the center area of the stairwell, he shouted, "Oh, my God. I'm hit. I can't see. I can't see!" The pitch of his voice rose at the very end in what Lyons hoped was a suitably pathetic plea.

A few more shots echoed down, but they fell well wide of the mark. Lyons did nothing and signaled for the men of Able Team to follow his lead.

They waited barely two minutes before the man above came marching down the steps. He didn't even try to crouch to show him more from the angle as he stood at the top of the landing; he just wandered blithely down. Lyons looked disgusted. The man in the Sapphire uniform was wearing a shoulder holster for his TP-9.

When the man was in range, and just before the rest of Able Team was visible, Lyons pulled back the hammer of his Python. "Drop the gun," said Lyons.

The guard tried to bring up his TP-9.

Lyons smacked him across the face with the heavy barrel of the Python. The guard screeched and hit the floor heavily on his rump. Lyons plucked the TP-9 from his fingers.

"What the hell is wrong with you guys?" Lyons demanded. "We are federal agents. What, did you think the government would run out? Killing a Fed is like shooting the first guy out of a clown car. There's lots more coming and they're never going to run out, even though you know it's got to be a finite number."

Schwarz and Blancanales exchanged glances.

"I want to know how many people you've got up there," said Lyons. "And I'm deliberately doing this loudly so your fellow jerks at the top of the stairwell will know we're coming for them and that we don't care."

"Don't care about what?" the young man in the blue uniform asked.

"About your rights," said Lyons. "About due process. About red tape. I'll tell you, kid, I have had one *long* day. And I'm out of patience. I mean, completely out of patience. I'm right at the straight-to-pistol-whipping part of the program. You tell me what I want to know or you're going to be spitting teeth and I'm going to carve another notch on this barrel."

"I have rights!" squealed the Sapphire guard.

"You tried to murder us," said Lyons. "So now comes the question-and-answer part of the program. How many people are up there? How many Sapphire goons do you have?"

"I don't know," said the guard.

"Ah-hh," said Lyons. He opened his mouth and stuck out his tongue.

The guard looked at him curiously. He wiped blood from his split lip. "Ah-hh?" he said, imitating Lyons.

Lyons stuck the barrel of the Python in his mouth. "Wow," said the former LAPD cop. "They really didn't give you much in the way of brains on the assembly line, did they?"

"Mmpphh," said the guard.

"You do that so often," said Schwarz casually. "Do you have, like, a special bore brush for the brains and stuff that you get in that barrel? Because I would think that it would really clog it up, and I know you keep your pistol really clean. So is it a lot of work?"

By now the guard had responded to this curious form of "bad cop, worse cop" by trying to shriek something around the barrel of the Python. Lyons took the barrel out of his mouth and then backhanded him. The guard hit the floor coughing.

"You're going to knock out whatever brains he does have," said Schwarz.

"I'm okay with that," said Lyons.

Another bullet struck the wall nearby. Blancanales took careful aim with his M-16 and fired a short burst. A screaming man in a blue Sapphire security uniform plummeted down the stairwell opening and crashed to the floor below. He would never get up again.

"Jerk," said Lyons.

The blade of a throwing knife clattered to the floor nearby.

"What was that?" asked Schwarz.

"What the hell?" said Lyons. He reached down and picked up the triangular throwing blade. It had a ring in its pommel. "Who up there is using ninja throwing darts?"

"What now?"

"Come on," said Lyons. "This I have to see."

They began to move up the stairwell again. Occasionally, whoever was above would toss yet another throwing knife, never accurately. Most of the time, the knife would land with the flat of the blade on the hard concrete of the stairwell. When one finally stuck in the wall briefly before falling to the floor, Schwarz and Blancanales cheered.

"Don't encourage that stupidity," said Lyons.

They reached the top of the stairs. A single Sapphire man stood there in front of the coded, locking doors that led to Claridge Clayton's suite. While the stairwell was not as opulent as the elevator entrance had been, the doors were still of heavy hardwood and gilded for appearance. Lyons assumed that the supposedly "wooden" doors actually had steel cores, given how security-conscious Clayton had been to this point.

The Sapphire guard was wearing some kind of shoulder harness across his chest. It bore what just had to have been a good ten or twelve slots for the throwing knives. Only one of these was still full. The rest of the knives had been thrown at them in the stairwell.

"Honestly?" Lyons demanded. He reached out, grabbed the ballistic nylon shoulder holster and shook the security guard like a rag doll. The last of the throwing knives fell out of the shoulder harness and struck the floor. Schwarz kicked it down the stairs.

The Sapphire guard tried to protest. "I am a duly authorized employee of—"

"Oh, can it," said Lyons. "You expect me to take you seriously as a duly authorized anything after you use these… these toys to try to take us out? I'll tell you something, kid, I'm kind of insulted by that. I think I'm more insulted by that than if you'd just kept taking shots at us."

"My pistol is empty," complained the guard.

"I don't believe this," Lyons said. "You give me one good reason not to pitch you down these stairs right now."

"Please don't, sir," said the guard. Tears formed in his eyes. These crocodile tears soon became great, racking sobs. Lyons dropped the man in disgust.

"Either he's a brilliant assassin with masterful acting skills," said Blancanales, "or he's just what he appears to be."

"Voting for 'appears to be,'" said Schwarz. He stared up at the double doors and then examined the lock. The lock was an unusual one. It bore musical notes instead of letters or numbers.

"Oh, this is rich," said Schwarz. "This is like something out of a survival-horror game. We've got to solve a puzzle if we want to get in."

"No," said Lyons. "We've just got to get laughing boy here to tell us the combination."

"Just tell him," urged Schwarz to the guard. "He loves shoving that big revolver where nobody wants it. Trust me, kid, nothing good is coming."

"But I don't know it!" protested the guard. "I really don't! They don't trust me with that information. That's why we're posted out here, in the stairwell, and at the base of the elevator. I'm not supposed to even face front when I guard the elevator at the bottom."

"The more I learn about Claridge Clayton," said Lyons, "the more there isn't to like. What a gem."

"Is there anything you can tell us?" asked Schwarz. "A musical pattern? A series of letters we can turn into notes?"

"I don't read music," said the guard.

"You don't have to," said Lyons. "'Every good boy deserves firepower,' or however the saying goes. All we have to do is sketch it out."

"But I really don't know," complained the kid. "I'm just a low-level employee. They don't trust me with Mr. Clayton's security codes. Please don't kill me! There's nothing I can give you!"

"You know something," Lyons insisted. "Think, kid. Think real hard. Or I just might get cranky. And while we're on the topic, why aren't there any hijackers or terrorists or kidnappers or whatever up here?"

"What?" asked the guard. "I haven't heard anything like that."

Lyons shot Blancanales and Schwarz a meaningful look. "Figures," he said.

"Let's just throw him down the stairs," said Lyons. "Maybe he'll roll fast enough to pick up some of those knives as he goes." The big former cop wasn't serious, as usual, but anything that elicited something useful from the captured guard was worth a try.

"Wait!" said the man. "I think…I think I remember him saying it was a patriotic song."

"Of course," said Lyons. "That's exactly the kind of self-absorbed thing this guy would do."

"Which one?" asked Schwarz. "Do you remember?"

The guard stared at them in horror. "I…I don't. I'm sorry. Please don't kill me."

Lyons pushed the guard down, yanked his arms behind his back and secured them with a plastic zip-tie. Then he took a strip of duct tape, peeled it from the flattened roll he kept with his web gear and wrapped it around the man's mouth.

"Blessed silence," said Blancanales.

"Yeah, that," said Lyons, looking at him. "Cover the stairwell. I don't want anyone sneaking up our tailpipes while we're dealing with this dumb thing." He went to the musical lock panel and told Schwarz, "Get on this. Any ideas?"

"How about the national anthem?" Schwarz said.

"Worth a try."

Schwarz punched in the anthem. Nothing happened. The door did not budge, nor did they receive a signal that they were in error.

"'Battle Hymn of the Republic'?" said Lyons.

"Down here in Georgia?" Schwarz said. "Probably not." He tried it anyway, to the same result.

"'When Johnny Comes Marching Home Again'?" suggested Blancanales.

"Try that," said Lyons.

Schwarz flubbed the notes twice before finally getting the pattern right. There was a buzzing noise. The double doors popped open on pneumatic hinges. Schwarz pulled the door back the rest of the way while Lyons covered the widening gap.

"I'll be damned," said Lyons. "I never thought that would work."

The three men entered Clayton's office. Each had his weapon at the ready. They were prepared to douse the office in bullets and, Lyons had to admit to himself, he wouldn't mind doing that just to break up some of the arrogance to the room.

But the room was empty.

"So where the hell is he?" Lyons growled. "We've got a supposed hostage situation with no hostage, and these Sapphire goons throughout the building."

"Were we too quick to let the receptionist go?" Blancanales asked. "Maybe there's something we didn't think to ask her."

"Doubt it," said Lyons. He sat at Clayton's desk, took out his secure satellite phone and dialed the Farm.

"Price, go," said Barbara Price.

"Ironman here," said Lyons. "We've got a problem. We responded to the hostage situation at TruTech. We capped some Sapphire goons, and generally made a mess of the place. Some kid with a box of throwing stars tried to chuck them at us."

"Throwing knives," Schwarz corrected.

"Whatever," said Lyons. "We're boned here, Barb. I

don't know what our next step is going to be. We've run down all the Sapphire leads and I think we've exhausted our supply of Iranians."

"Let me consult Hal," said Price. "I'll conference him in. Hold on."

Lyons put the back of the chair back and put his stained combat boots on top of Clayton's desk.

"Make yourself at home, Ironman," said Schwarz.

"Wow," said Lyons. "This is a really comfortable chair."

"Can I try?" asked Schwarz.

Lyons waved him off. Brognola came on the line. "There's more you don't know, Able," he told them. "Justice just received the message through channels. It was actually a ransom demand in the form of a video. Clayton's been kidnapped, all right. The kidnappers are demanding fifty million in cash."

"Fifty million?" Lyons asked. "Whew. Tall order. Is there anyone from Clayton's estate who cares to entertain negotiations on that score?"

"Apparently," said Brognola. "He has an accountant somewhere in Atlanta who maintains separate offices. It was that man who brought this to the local FBI."

"So what does this mean?" Lyons asked. "Is Clayton dirty or is he a victim?"

"Judging from the video," said Brognola, "the man's been beaten up. He appeared well enough apart from that. Clayton's bookkeeper claims he can get the cash together for us to ferry it to a drop."

"We going to take him up on that?" Lyons asked. "Clayton might never see that money again. He'd probably have to go through his couch cushions to replace it."

"We have told him we will facilitate the transfer," said Brognola. "Overtly, that is. Covertly, we will use the transfer as bait."

"What are the details?" Lyons asked.

"I am asking Barb to transfer them to your phones now," said Brognola. "They are quite specific. Even the denominations of the bills in the payoff have been specified."

"This feels like a trap," said Blancanales. "In fact, it feels like a backup trap."

"Meaning we just tripped and walked out of the first trap, and the ransom trap is the trap meant to collect us if the first one doesn't."

"Yeah," said Lyons. "Which means our best bet is to do just what we did here."

"And that is?" Brognola asked.

"Walk right into the trap to see where this goes," said Lyons.

CHAPTER TWENTY

New Orleans

The manor house on the outskirts of New Orleans was a large, sprawling structure. It had seen better days. The bottom had fallen out of the real-estate market some years before and had not returned. In some ways, the city had never recovered from the hurricane that had dealt it so much damage. The thought would have been depressing had Claridge Clayton allowed himself to dwell on it. He found the decor in this room just as depressing. Someone had once used this place as a boarding house. There was a box of dusty old toys in the corner of the room. One of these was a rusted metal fire truck.

Is there anything, he thought, more depressing than a discarded toy?

Fortunately he had a marvelous distraction in the person of Diana Deruyter. The owner of Sapphire was stretching languidly in the center of the master bedroom. She wore a pair of tight-fitting yoga pants and a sports bra. Her curves, and the firm play of her muscles, were on full display. She had tied her hair back with a length of black silk. She was absolutely beautiful.

There was a danger to her as well, as sweet as the perfume she wore. As she finished her stretching regimen and ran through a series of martial arts exercises, he found himself hypnotized by the way she moved her body.

"You look thoughtful," said Deruyter. "Or you're just thinking about my body."

Clayton eyed her with open lust. "Both," he said. "I'm thoughtful about your body."

She laughed. She had a musical, lyrical laugh, the kind of laugh one associated with so beautiful a woman. As if they had not spoken, she continued executing the moves of the martial arts form, graceful and lethal as she kicked, punched and chopped her way through an elaborate series.

Clayton wondered what his father might say, if the evil old bastard could see him now.

Claridge Clayton had been a bookish, uncoordinated child. This had always been a disappointment to his father, who had been a star football player in high school. The man had even entertained the thought of a football scholarship before finally studying law at Yale. Perhaps, Clayton thought, his father would not have been so miserable had he pursued his football dreams. It was possible the thoughts of what might have been had contributed to Norman Clayton's profound sense that he was missing out… and that his son was failing to make up for this by proxy.

His father had never been an easy man to please. "Impossible" was probably a more accurate word. Deep down, Norman Clayton was not happy, and thus nothing his only son did was likely to make him so. Norman's inability to live vicariously through Claridge only made everything worse.

Growing up, Claridge excelled in few things except academics. His father, disappointed in Claridge's many failures at sports, eventually came to understand this. Though he detested Claridge for his lack of athletic ability, he knew that his son could still be prodded to acquit himself well in the one arena where he had any skill. Thus Claridge Clayton was told that he was to maintain an A average.

He was to become valedictorian, if he could manage it, and if he could not, then—Norman grudgingly allowed— a slot among the graduating class's top ten students would be considered adequate.

High school and college were thus a living hell for Claridge Clayton, whose father would punish him if he dared to get so much as a B+. His college average was expected to be 3.9 or higher and, if it was not, Clayton would be given no spending money while away at school. His car privileges would also be revoked.

Claridge Clayton had tried many times to "bond" with his father. He had tried going hunting with the man, only to discover that he lacked the facility to remain still for long periods of time. He had tried attending his father's favorite sports, but these, too, bored him. Norman Clayton was keenly aware of his son's moods. If Claridge was bored, it meant that Claridge was doing something wrong, failing to appreciate the opportunities afforded him. Such a failure was yet another punishable act.

It was while in college that Claridge Clayton, once more poverty-stricken after receiving a B in macroeconomics, had decided he must achieve financial independence.

He spent considerable time mulling over his situation. Claridge Clayton's problem was not that he was stupid. He was not. But he also was not the smartest. He was comfortably above average, which made him more intelligent than was comfortable for the lowest common denominator on campus—the jocks and the self-important art students— but not smart enough to excel in the business classes his father had insisted he take. Wandering the campus late at night, with no girlfriend and nothing to do, he had contemplated dropping out, taking some menial job somewhere.

Then came his epiphany.

He had been watching other, happier people move

around campus, when he found himself downtown. The college town in which he lived was small, but even it had its seedier elements. This was especially true after midnight. Walking downtown at two in the morning that fateful night, Claridge Clayton encountered a prostitute.

He knew about hookers, of course, and he understood the concept. But for some reason the reality of the transaction had never really occurred to him before. Confronted with a not altogether unattractive woman, he was told that for twenty dollars, certain pleasures could be his. He had twenty dollars in his wallet, saved at great pains over the previous few weeks. And he had, he decided, nothing better to spend it on.

When he woke up the next day, he understood something that had eluded him previously: money was power. Power was success. Therefore, money was success. The equation was that simple. He did not have to be the smartest, the fastest, the most coordinated. He did not even have to be the most successful, as that quality was gauged by others.

He merely had to make money.

Making money he could do. Claridge Clayton took his first job delivering pizzas for the local pizza shop. He disliked the work, but he liked the money. He was good at saving money when he earned it…and, as it turned out, he was exceptionally good at investing it.

He financed several budding businesses on campus, some of them legal, some of them not. He invested in his roommate's marijuana trade and made a healthy profit. He invested in a budding artist's paintings, mostly because he found the girl attractive, only to lose money on the deal. He learned that people would pay to have their homework assignments completed for them, and these assignments did not even have to earn A grades. They only had to receive passing scores. To pass without being forced to do the work was all his customers really demanded.

In so doing he learned his second valuable lesson: you need do only enough work to satisfy the customer. You never apologized if a customer did not complain first. You did the absolute minimum required of you to get their money. If they did complain about poor quality, you cut them a deal for even poorer quality at greater quantity and the same price.

The third lesson Claridge Clayton learned, therefore, was that people were lazy and stupid. That meant they could be controlled with relatively little effort, simply if you were sufficiently smarter by comparison.

That he could do.

As he entered adulthood he took night classes in engineering, eventually starting his own engineering, consulting and fabrication shop.

Meanwhile, his father, Norman, grew older and experienced his midlife crisis late, leaving Claridge Clayton's mother for some stripper he'd met during a night on the town. Clayton worked his way up into the defense industry, mostly by hiring the right engineers and giving them free rein to design useful things. Once he found himself poised for success in the field, it was relatively easy to stay there. Just as having money enabled one to make money, producing a successful, government-subsidized product led to further opportunities for subsidized products.

While the money was decent, it was not truly marvelous. To make that kind of cash, Claridge Clayton realized, he would have to return to the lessons of his younger days. His marijuana business had always far outperformed any of his legitimate ventures. So it was that he discovered the superior money to be made in illegal ventures.

Export restrictions were his friend. How did you command truly astonishing prices for a given commodity? You offered it to people who could not possibly get it otherwise. You held them over a barrel. You made deals they could not refuse because you were the only game in town.

The United States put severe export restrictions on a variety of technology. There were countless "rogue" nations that weren't supposed to have these contraindicated goods…and so it was these nations that would pay most handsomely for them. It took him a few years to build up his business in illegal exports, but once he did, he had made quite a fortune from them.

Complications arose, as they did in all businesses. Investigations by government agencies had forced him to invent the fiction that his goods were being counterfeited. There were also actual counterfeits that cut into his profit margins, the irony of which was not lost on him. Worst of all were the threats from competing "firms," for in the world of illegal business, everyone was a criminal by definition. "Muscle" was commonly used and abused.

After his employees and management teams were threatened, Clayton had gone looking for appropriate muscle of his own. He had found Sapphire Corporation and Diana Deruyter. While Deruyter was incredibly sexy and extremely good-looking, that was not his primary interest in her. It was her almost obsessive ruthlessness that he admired most. It was a quality he knew he did not fully possess, for few people did. It was therefore necessary that he hire the services of someone who did.

Clayton and TruTech were Deruyter's biggest customers. As such, he received certain…customer service…that not everyone received. The promise of Deruyter to share his bed for the duration of her stay here was one of those benefits. As he watched her work out, he experienced a moment of doubt, wondering if he was still up to the task.

It was not as if he were getting any younger.

Thinking about his security concerns caused him to frown. The Iranians had proved to be a tremendous thorn in his side. Try as he might, even with Sapphire's resources, he had not been able to run them off or out of business. The more he tried, the more keenly aware he became of the extensive Iranian-backed presence in key Department of Defense industries. He wouldn't have believed it possible if he were not already in the business of exporting forbidden military technology. Still, the sheer number of Iranian mercenaries living and working in the United States was staggering to him. He had never realized the American border was that porous.

You grew wiser as you aged, he supposed. Well, all except for his father. His father's complete collapse, as a man and as a citizen, had given him an abject lesson in what to avoid. Over the years he had watched as his father went from the overbearing, controlling, unpleasant man of Claridge Clayton's childhood, to an irresponsible lout who'd abandoned his family for the sake of his own fleeting pleasures, to a helpless man-child who could neither pay his own bills nor manage to cope with the vicissitudes of life.

As a wealthy man, Claridge Clayton was used to people asking him for money. Investors regularly called on him, and if he liked their ideas, he would listen to their pitches and their business plans. Sometimes he even chose to invest, for such were still his talents.

He had also seen, over the years of his success, a steady stream of family members, distant and otherwise, who showed up on his doorstep with their hands out. For the most part he had turned them all away, although he provided for his mother completely and saw to it that she had anything she wanted. His mother, after all, had never participated in the choice to destroy his family. She was as much a victim as was he when Norman Clayton abandoned the family for an obnoxious, vapid whore.

Norman Clayton could not even stick to his vices in his new incarnation as helplessly immature and a self-centered failure. He'd left the stripper for some other floozy perhaps two years after they'd taken up together. These days, though he did not keep track, Claridge thought his father was on girlfriend eight or nine. Each one was more useless than the previous.

Then there came the day that Claridge Clayton would later look back on as the proudest of his life.

He had been in his office when his secretary reported that he had an unscheduled visitor. His schedule was tightly controlled and he seldom deviated from it, but he permitted it this time. He allowed it precisely because the girl had told him Norman Clayton wanted to see him.

Norman had looked small, used up, old. He'd sat in the chair opposite Claridge Clayton's desk, staring at the wall of Clayton's achievements, probably comparing his own life and his utter lack of success to the achievements of his son. He'd seen, also, in his father's eyes, a mixture of hope and greed: hope that Claridge Clayton had enough money that he would not miss some spent on his father, and greed over precisely what amount that might be.

"Norman," Claridge had said, refusing to call his father by "Father" or, even worse, "Dad." "I understand you're having some financial difficulties."

"It's just until I get back on my feet," Norman said. "I don't need that much. I just need—"

Claridge Clayton held up his hand. "I'd like to know one thing, Norman," he said. "I'd like to know what I ever did as a boy to make you proud. What is your proudest memory of me?"

He could tell as the words escaped his lips that Norman had been unprepared for the query. The elder Claridge's face fell. He'd looked to the desk, then back to his son and then to the ceiling. He'd wrung his hands together. He'd stammered.

"Well," said Norman. "I… Uh… I mean, you were such a successful boy, and I…"

Clayton put up his hand again. "That's all right. I did not mean to be cruel. I know, as well as you do," he said, "that you were never proud of me for a moment in your life. That's all right, Norman. We can't all be the sons… or the fathers…we would like to be. Don't give it another thought."

"But I need money. You can give me money, right?"

"Oh, yes, Norman," said Claridge Clayton. "I can give you every penny that you are owed." He reached into his desk and removed a printed sheet of paper. He placed it on his desk and slid it across the surface. "Do you remember that when I was in college, you used to present me with invoices that represented my portion of the phone bill?"

"I…guess so," said Norman.

"I found a box of the invoices and receipts in storage," said Claridge. "A habit of mine, never throwing away financial documents. And you know, I found an invoice that I never paid. It got lost in the shuffle." He pointed to the printed sheet of paper. "That is an email you sent me some years ago. In it, you indicated that I owed you a great deal of money. For raising me, caring for me, feeding me as an infant. That sort of thing. You seemed quite adamant that it was I, your son, who owed his father money simply for existing."

Norman looked uncomfortably at the desktop. "I don't see…"

"Of course you don't see," said Claridge. "You never did. You were an insufferable, controlling, intolerant man when I was a child. You browbeat me and criticized me and left me feeling like I would never amount to anything. I grew up believing my father never loved me. Do you recall the moment that you confided in me that your marriage to mother began to fall apart after I was born? Congratulations, Norman. You managed to tell a young man that the failure of his parents' marriage was his fault. For existing."

"Please, son," Norman said.

"Don't ever call me that," said Claridge. "It's time you learned, Norman, that actions have consequences. You are never to contact me again. You are not my father. I do not have a father. I don't believe I *ever* had one. If you present yourself on any property belonging to me for the rest of your miserable life, I will have you arrested and taken to jail. I can make things very difficult for you if I choose, Norman. You would do well to leave me be."

"But I need money," Norman whined.

"Ah, yes, the money you are owed," said Claridge. "You're in luck, Norman. I've done some math. Taking as a baseline your own figures for the money I owe you for being born, I subtracted from it the free labor I supplied to you in the form of chores, gardening and other manual labor over the years. To it I added the phone bill that was missed, all those years ago. From it I subtracted certain expenses relative to other assistance I rendered you while I was growing up. There was that summer you were on vacation in Europe, for example, that I opened, sorted, scanned and emailed you your vital correspondence and bills. I've billed you at a competitive concierge rate for those services."

"Please," Norman Clayton begged. Tears rolled down his cheeks.

"You'll be pleased to know," announced Claridge Clayton, "that the difference of all those figures amounts to exactly six dollars and eighty-one cents. I am prepared to pay you this amount in cash." He'd taken the bills from his wallet and the change from his desk drawer. Then he'd recounted them carefully, subtracted an extra penny that had been miscounted earlier and slid the money across the desk to Norman. "I have to admit, Norman," he'd said, "that some part of me wonders if you have so little dignity that you will take this six dollars and change."

To Claridge's complete lack of surprise, his father indeed took the money and stuffed it into his pocket.

"Oh," Claridge said as his father—stooped, broken and miserable—turned to leave. "One more thing. You've never been particularly good with hints. I meant what I said. Set foot on any of my properties and I will have you forcibly removed and charged with trespassing. Also, there is something I've never said to you in so many words that I would like to. Turn around."

Norman turned to face his son. Tears formed twin runnels of water in his cheeks.

"You were a miserable excuse for a father," Claridge told him. "My life will be better without you in it. When you die, I will not mourn you. When I eventually find out about it, I will know a quiet sense of satisfaction and relief. And that is all. Now get out, you pathetic sack of garbage."

That was the last time he had ever seen his father. The memory was intertwined with the feeling of satisfaction he experienced whenever he earned money. To his knowledge, his pathetic father was still alive. That surprised him some days, but he did not spend much time dwelling on it.

"You were far away just now," Deruyter said, breaking him out of his reverie. She walked over to him. The intensity, the femininity of her presence was intoxicating. "Did you know you are quite an attractive man? But it's your ambition that I appreciate most."

Claridge Clayton smiled. "My ambition could yet get us both killed or imprisoned," he said. "Moving to eliminate the Iranians, risking making the North Koreans angry... you know that's why you're getting the reports you are about your own business. What if Sapphire is crippled in the fallout from all this?"

"What does it matter?" Deruyter asked. "It would be an inconvenience, yes. But businesses rise and fall. I have a great deal of money put away in Swiss accounts. It is anonymous. I have the account numbers memorized. I would imagine you have made similar arrangements."

"Of course," said Clayton. "Anyone of means would do the same."

"Just so," said Deruyter. She pushed Clayton down on the bed and straddled him, running a finger over the lapel of his suit jacket. "And with money comes the means to start over. If we cannot eliminate these government interlopers, we will have to set ourselves up in a country that has no extradition to the United States."

"Just so long as it isn't North Korea," said Clayton. "Do you believe this plan will work?"

"I wouldn't have pretended to kidnap you if I thought otherwise," she said. "My troops protect this building and will repel any attack by your government commandos, if they ignore their instructions. Should they manage to make payment through your company, your insurance policies will cover the loss, essentially doubling your money. You've never made a quick-turn investment that was so easy."

"So we wait," said Clayton. "You gave them days to put together the ransom money."

"We wait," she said, nodding. Reaching down, she pulled her sports bra up over her head and threw it across the room. "Perhaps," she said, reaching down to tug at his belt, "we can think of something to keep ourselves entertained in the meantime."

CHAPTER TWENTY-ONE

The Philippine Sea

"Well, this was clearly a trap," said T. J. Hawkins.

McCarter spared him a baleful glare and returned to what he was doing.

"Please," said one of the hostages. "Please help us out of this. I don't want to die like this." The pads on which the captives were standing suddenly popped and shifted. They moved accordingly. McCarter felt his teeth clench as he waited for the explosion that might come. It didn't.

"You're not going to die, miss," said McCarter. "That I promise you." To Encizo, he said, "Do we have eyes on G-Force?"

"We did," said Encizo from the hatchway. "The other pilot ran him out to one of the support boats to get him checked over. He wasn't too happy about that—he wants to be helping us. But it looks like he ditched his Cobra in time. Apparently the only hurt was his dignity. The Sea Knight pilot extended his apologies already. He couldn't pursue Soong's launch, for obvious reasons. We don't want to lose *both* our rides."

"Indeed we don't," said McCarter.

"We've got company," said Manning, behind Encizo. "It looks like the Koreans left behind some personnel. And I don't think they have any intention of trying to get back home again."

"Suicide troops?" McCarter asked.

"Looks that way," said Manning. "We ran a patrol from stern to bow and took fire once we got amidships. They're close, and on the move."

McCarter said to T.J., "I'm going to stay here and help these nice people." He slapped one of the pads on the electronic base as the one adjacent to it shifted. The pad beeped, then synced with the one next to it. The men and women on the pad continued to mutter, cry or call out in distress as was their wont. McCarter was apparently doing his best to ignore that, putting on a good show of confidence in the face of one of the most insane schemes Hawkins had ever seen.

"Whatever you need," said Hawkins.

"Get up into the superstructure," McCarter said. "We need a sniper. It's time to cull those madmen. And…leave one alive if you can. A live captive could be very useful. You have GPS tracking locators in your kit, yes?"

"Standard gear," said Hawkins, nodding. "Why, what are you thinking?"

"This barge has a couple of emergency launches of its own," said McCarter. "They've got sufficient range. A man, a desperate man, might take one back to his comrades, if he were to be captured and then slip his leash. You know, with a tracking device planted somewhere on his person. Perhaps another in the boat for backup."

"I follow you," said Hawkins. "I think I'm going to need to get more perspective on this than the superstructure affords. Sort of a death-from-above thing."

McCarter nodded. "Good idea. Do it."

"On it," said Hawkins.

Hawkins took his Kalashnikov clone, racked the bolt partially back to check the chamber and set the safety. He slung the weapon and then took the nearest gangway up onto the deck. When he was at the railing, he put the call through to the pilot of the Sea Knight.

"Hey, y'all," he said when the pilot acknowledged him. "I wonder if I could get a lift down here. Be careful, though. We're getting sporadic small arms fire. The Koreans left us behind some surprises."

"Roger that," said the Sea Knight's pilot.

The big helicopter came in low over the superstructure of the drug boat. The rope ladder that dangled from it was all the leverage Hawkins needed. He grabbed it and hoisted himself up. Then, in the open payload area of the chopper, he hooked himself to a safety harness and took up a prone position on the deck of the chopper, shoving the Kalashnikov out in front of him.

"You're going to play sniper from the air with that?" asked the pilot. His flight suit tagged him as Chapman, K. He was on loan through official military channels, but to this point the Stony Man team had not asked too many questions of him, nor had the pilot inquired too much into their activities beyond where to take them and how to drop them.

This was the dance the intelligence community played. No one knew of the existence of Stony Man Farm except Hal Brognola, head of the Sensitive Operations Group, and perhaps a handful of other people in the world. Whenever the warriors of Stony Man Farm availed themselves of military support and logistical backup through either international intelligence agencies or the United States military, it was always under the guise of some other agency. Folks always seemed to assume that was the CIA or the NSA, two agencies invariably grouped under the "spookery and skullduggery" category. Enemies the teams faced always seemed to think, when up against Western troops, that the Central Intelligence Agency was somehow to blame. Stony

Man did not disabuse them of these notions. The first rule of covert ops was that if your enemy made incorrect assumptions, you sure didn't correct them.

"Chapman, I want you to circle that ship," said Hawkins. "Give me as stable a platform as you can. We've got some barflies who refuse to listen to last call. Got to root them out before they can do any damage."

"You'll need to be in close with that Kalashnikov," said the pilot. "I'll skim that deck if I need to."

"Much obliged," said Hawkins.

Hawkins would have given a lot for a dedicated sniper rifle right about then, but there wasn't time to make arrangements and, truthfully, he did not need to do so. Sure, the weapon he was using was not ideal. But it was sufficient for the task. That was the key to flexibility in combat operations. You adapted when you needed to adapt.

Hawkins, for his part, was looking forward to punching some holes in the enemy. He was sick and tired of these rogue nations and their tin-plated dictators sending crack suicide squads, or whatever they wanted to call themselves, out into the world to wreak terror and destruction.

There was always some cause, always some lofty explanation for why they were doing what they were doing. The team had been forced to listen to the Advance Guard leader, Soong, gloat over their jammed transceiver line. Hawkins knew the kind of man they were up against because Phoenix Force had seen this type of character over and over again. He was undoubtedly well trained, he was ruthless and he was completely comfortable with hurting innocent people to get what he and his crazy government wanted.

Hawkins took a bandanna from his pocket, folded it several times to make it thick and put it between the stock of the Kalashnikov clone and his shoulder. Then he tucked the rifle to himself, getting a good cheek weld. The stock of the AK was a little small for someone with a standard Western frame. The weapon had been designed to be handy, and especially during the bad old days of the Cold War, the type of folks who used it tended to be on the small side. During Vietnam, for example, a rifle this size was perfect for the opposition because they were physically shorter, with a shorter reach.

The pilot's question was understandable. Most civilians didn't understand the concept, thinking of assault rifles as overpowered artillery, but any military man would know right away that the weapon was not ideal for distance shots. The concept behind the assault weapon, pioneered by the Germans during World War II and epitomized by both the AK-47 and the AR-15/M-16 platforms, was that in past wars, troops had carried very powerful rifles whose rounds had very long range. Compared to the actual ranges at which combat happened in warfare, these weapons were too powerful. The cartridges they fired were therefore heavier than they needed to be.

Shorten the distance at which the rifle was effective, give it a select-fire capability and increase the magazine capacity to twenty, thirty, even forty rounds, and you had a relatively light rifle that many people would hesitate to use to shoot deer. It was hell on wheels at putting down men, though, and the lighter weight of the ammunition it carried meant the soldier could carry more rounds overall. That made him better equipped for the modern battlefield. Just like that, the assault rifle was a standard of conventional warfare…and all the while, it was just what it had started out being: an underpowered long gun firing what was, relatively speaking, an anemic cartridge.

The thought made Hawkins smile.

He liked the Kalashnikov. It was heavier than it truly

needed to be, which meant you could use it to deliver a pretty good beating and not worry about breaking it. The gas-piston system it used drove the bolt reliably. The sloppy tolerances, in conjunction with that design, meant you could run the AK dirty and expect it to continue functioning. In an M-16, propellant gases from the fired cartridges, which were what was bled off to push the bolt back, operated directly on the rifle's bolt. This meant the M-16 had to be kept relatively clean if you expected it to keep working. Not so with the AK.

There was an old joke. To clean an AK, you ran the bolt to make sure there were no rocks in the bore. Then you kept on shooting it until the next time someone mentioned it to you.

One of the reasons that even Third World child soldiers could run the AK without training was because of the robust design. The weapons designer had deliberately consolidated components, making them heavy and overbuilt in the process. For example, the cocking handle was on the right-hand side of the weapon, not an ergonomic layout at all. But it had to be on that side because that's where the ejection port was. The bolt and cocking handle were all the same piece of heavy metal.

And the atrocious safety lever on the AK was loud. It clacked when you ran it. It was enormous. It would give away your position every time. But it was all part of the simplified design.

Well, that was the old Soviet Union for you, Hawkins thought. The Soviets had always taken a low-budget approach to warfare. They fielded simple, overbuilt equipment that was durable but not terribly complex. Their air force was the same way. The first time one of the Soviets' new fighter craft was captured by the West, analysis of the plane had shown it really wasn't all that advanced in terms of its hardware. But the Soviets had plenty of people. They considered their troops an expendable commodity. The resulting philosophy of combat was that you threw men and simple machines at your objective, expecting to break a lot of them before you came out on top. And, hey, none of the individual items you'd just expended were all that expensive. There were plenty more where those came from.

He reached over the top of the AK and ran the bolt from habit, ejecting a live round that rattled across the deck of the Sea Knight. The action was a practiced one, nearly identical to the movements he made when operating just about any other assault rifle. Commonality of your training, as it applied to your manual of arms, was essential to a well-honed fighting man. You couldn't afford to do things differently every time. You had to be able to do them in your sleep, backward, while walking a tightrope in a snowstorm uphill. Both ways.

Hawkins smiled. That had been a favorite expression of one of his drill instructors, a million years ago.

Hawkins watched the superstructure go by as the Sea Knight pilot brought them in slow, almost lazy circles around the ship. His eyes scanned every corner, every crevice. The Korean suicide commandos were down there somewhere, probably eyeing the Sea Knight and wondering what they might be able to do to bring it down. Unless they had another guided rocket, Hawkins doubted they could do anything quickly enough that Chapman couldn't handle in time to preserve the aircraft.

That was another of those secrets of modern warfare most people didn't grasp. Helicopters were fragile things. Hawkins, who had spent more of his life than he liked to think about being inserted into combat zones or picked up from hot LZs by chopper, had a healthy fear and respect for the machines. A helicopter was basically a shell of aluminum always a fraction of a second from turning to wreckage, held in the air by spinning knives that could be blasted apart easily by small-arms fire. The rotors of the chopper would always be its weak link, and every man who had ever set foot aboard a helicopter, from the pilots to the men the chopper transported, knew their lives rested on those tiny slivers of metal.

During the infamous events surrounding the battle of Mogadishu in the 1990s, the locals had found a way to use rocket-propelled grenades to bring down choppers. It wasn't supposed to be possible. An RPG was a versatile weapon, yes, but it was no antiaircraft gun. In Mogadishu, the hostiles had dug pits in the ground to accommodate the back-blast from the weapon, which made it possible for them to elevate the RPGs and use them to shoot upward. That was the technique with which they'd brought down that Blackhawk in Somalia.

The fact was, though, that you didn't need to get nearly that fancy to punch a helicopter out of the sky. Concentrated small-arms fire would do it, and do it every time. All you had to do was instruct your squad to focus on the rotors, on those delicate little joints where the rotors spun. The main rotor held the chopper aloft, yes, but the tail rotor was even more vulnerable. You shot that out, you owned the chopper, because without the tail rotor the pilot had no control.

"Seven o'clock," said Chapman.

Hawkins tracked the bearing with his eyes and was rewarded with the sight of one of the Advance Guard troops trying to cross the superstructure. He drew a bead on the man and held his breath. Then he let out half that breath, paused and let the rifle go off when it had a mind to do so.

The AK clone bucked slightly. Its recoil was not great, not compared to "real" hunting or sniping rifles.

For a second Hawkins had thought he'd missed. Then his target hit the deck.

Hawkins put another round in the prone man, just to be sure.

"Nice shooting, Tex," said Chapman.

"Thank you kindly," said Hawkins, exaggerating his own drawl.

They circled for a few minutes more. When nothing presented itself, Hawkins decided he needed to tempt the opposition. "You mind indulging me in something a little reckless?" he asked.

"I can probably get behind that," said Chapman. "What are you thinking?"

"This big chopper sure makes a tempting target," said Hawkins. "If I was a Korean suicide commando, I'd like to take a whack at it. But I'd need it to be a lot closer, because I wouldn't want to give my position away unless I thought I could do some real damage."

"Man," said Chapman, "you weren't kidding about reckless."

"I get it if you don't want to try."

"You kidding?" said Chapman. "I'll try anything once."

Chapmen brought the chopper so close to the drug boat's superstructure that Hawkins thought the belly of the helicopter must be scraping the deck. They made passes at the ship for ten minutes before the maneuver finally had the desired effect.

A bullet sang out, nearly taking Hawkins's face off.

Chapmen bobbed the chopper and then immediately leveled out, allowing Hawkins to take the shot. The North Korean commando was just fleeing for better cover in the superstructure when Hawkins put a single 7.62 mm bullet between his shoulder blades.

A third man ran across the deck.

"We flushed another!" shouted Chapman.

Hawkins realized that now was his opportunity. "Put me down over the deck!" he shouted. "I need to drop in on that guy."

Chapman nodded. Despite the looming superstructure, he put the chopper practically on top of the running commando, tilting the fuselage to one side. It was a tricky move. Hawkins made a mental note. When he filed his after-action report to the Farm he was going to make sure that Chapman got a medal.

Hawkins unclipped his safety harness and pushed himself from the chopper.

He landed on the deck, hard, and his arrival did not go unnoticed by the Advanced Guard commando. The Korean turned and fired his own AK.

Hawkins slipped sideways, rolling across the deck, and returned fire. Neither man's bullets found the mark. The Korean headed for the superstructure again, and that was his downfall. He had to slow to thread his way through the opening in the maze of steel. Hawkins shot him in the back of the thigh, bringing him down. When he reached the enemy, the Stony Man operative did not give the Korean time to fight, wounded or otherwise. He simply clubbed him in the head with the butt of the AK.

This was the condition in which Hawkins presented the captured Korean, dragging him by one ankle belowdecks to where McCarter was freeing the hostages.

One of the women threw her arms around the Briton and thanked him over and over. Hawkins smiled at that.

"I see you have things well in hand," he said.

McCarter looked at Hawkins's unconscious captive. "Let's get some bandages on that thigh wound," he said. "And while he's out, get a tracker into his boot or something, somewhere he won't notice it."

"Roger that," said Hawkins. He broke out his field medical kit and began bandaging the Korean. The round had gone through, doing a minimum of damage. Fortunately, Hawkins had not hit an artery. There was no way to know just what you might clip when you dumped a round into a man's leg under the stress of combat. Hawkins had gambled and won.

McCarter exhaled, looking tired. The Briton wiped sweat from his forehead. Manning was ushering the hostages out of the cargo space.

"Where do we stand?" Hawkins asked.

"We have a chance, now that we have Soong's man," McCarter said. "I want these explosive backpacks gathered up. We'll take them with us. I need you to make arrangements for one of the launches. When he wakes up, I'm going to have you take him above decks and chain him up. We'll tell him we're planning on killing him and throwing him out to sea, or something suitably ruthless. He'll believe that—they think we're a death squad of some sort. You heard Soong."

"Boy, didn't we all," said Hawkins. "Do you think the Farm can upload new firmware to our transceivers to prevent that from happening again?"

"I'm sure they can," said McCarter. "I'll just pretend I know what you said there, mate."

"Very funny," said Hawkins.

"Gary's going to put a call in to the Farm once all the hostages are squared away," said McCarter. "We'll make sure everyone's accounted for, and make arrangements to get them back to their cruise liner."

"What's our next step?"

McCarter looked down at the wounded commando. "You sure he's out?"

Hawkins peeled back the man's eyelid and touched his eyeball with one finger. The man did not react.

"That's *awful,* lad," said McCarter.

"But effective," said Hawkins. "It doesn't matter how high speed an operator you are, or how much pain you can endure. No man can fail to react when you touch his eyeball like that. Even if it's just a little."

"We'll track the Korean back to his fellows," said McCarter. "It's the only move we've got. Soong almost owned us here. I don't like it, not one bloody bit. He sacrificed the drug ship to keep us busy. That was the point of all this nonsense." McCarter spread his hand, indicating the electronic platform where the hostages had been held. "No doubt when we search the ship we won't find a single ICBM component aboard. Soong will have taken those with him."

"What do you figure *his* next move will be?" Hawkins asked.

"If I were Soong," said McCarter, "I'd be at an accessible port. Assuming he's sitting on a payload of components, he'll need to make his way back to North Korea with the shipment. Remember, this is the North Koreans we're talking about. They'll kill him if he blows the operation. So he'll be looking to establish some credibility at home by bringing the goods to his masters."

"So we track our escaped prisoner to his leader and run him down before he can do it."

"That's the general idea, mate."

"A lot is hinging on this guy," said Hawkins. He finished bandaging the unconscious Korean's leg.

"Fortunately," said McCarter, "they're some of the toughest bastards you've ever met. If there's any way for him to reach Soong, and operating on the notion that these guys have a contingency plan for where to meet if they get separated, you can bet he'll get there."

"All right. Then let's get him up on deck so we can start the show," said Hawkins.

"Mate?"

"Yeah, David?"

"Don't ever do that eyeball thing in front of me again," the Phoenix Force leader said. He shuddered. "Some things are just *wrong.*"

Their laughter echoed through the cargo space.

CHAPTER TWENTY-TWO

New Orleans

"Yeah, I'm betting so," said Lyons into his satellite phone, "and I figure that's what we'll find when we trip this trap. The real question is, how messed up is our system, our domestic intelligence, that stuff like this gets this far under our noses? Multiple firms all working for foreign military interests and it has to turn into a shooting war before we put a stop to it?" He paused, listening. Then he said, "Got it. Thanks, Barb. Able out." He put the phone away.

Schwarz surveyed the old manor house. "This looks like something out of that movie with that guy in it."

"Well, *that* really narrows it down," said Blancanales.

"The instructions for the drop were to bring the cash, enter on the ground floor and wait to be met," said Lyons. "We'll be given a chance to identify Clayton and make sure he's okay. Then we'll make the trade and leave with him."

"Well, that sounds straightforward enough," said Blancanales.

"Yeah," said Lyons. He put two fingers to his ear to activate his transceiver. "You with me, buddy?"

"Roger," said the voice in Lyons's ear. "You say the word, I crash the party."

"Pick one," said Lyons.

"Redemption," said the voice in his ear.

"So be it," said Lyons. He jacked a round into his USAS-

12 shotgun. Blancanales and Schwarz both checked their M-16s.

"Let's go rescue Claridge Clayton," said Lyons. He blew the lock on the door with his shotgun, then stood aside as Schwarz and Blancanales shouldered through the shattered doorway, following behind with the shotgun high.

The entrance to the old manor house was a foyer that boasted twin staircases arcing to an upper balcony. All along the upper balcony stood Sapphire troops in their blue uniforms. They held Uzi submachine guns in their fists. Behind their ranks stood a beautiful, dark-haired woman whom Lyons recognized from the Farm's intelligence briefing: Diana Deruyter, the owner of the security company.

"I suggest you gentlemen drop your weapons," she said. She held a chromed Desert Eagle pistol in two hands. The large weapon looked enormous against her small frame, but she held it as if she knew how to use it. Lyons had no doubt that she did.

"We're federal agents," Lyons warned. "We're here to recover Claridge Clayton."

"You were given specific instructions for delivering the ransom money," Deruyter said. "I don't see any money."

"And I don't see any kidnappers," said Lyons. "If you had any intention of letting Clayton go, you wouldn't be standing there, exposing yourself as the person behind this little money-making scheme."

"True," said Deruyter. "Your people have caused me considerable business difficulty. I need to eliminate you."

"It's not like the government's going to run out of guys," Lyons shot back. He held his shotgun low and was very careful not to raise the barrel. Schwarz and Blancanales were doing likewise. Deruyter obviously thought she had the drop on the team; that she could order her men to shred the three Able Team warriors at any moment she chose. "Do you really want three dead Feds on your record? Things might get a little unpleasant for you in the aftermath."

"No one will know," said Deruyter. "As you say, the fact that I stand in front of you now is proof I don't intend to let you leave here breathing. But there's more to killing you than just eliminating a short-term nuisance. Yes, the government will send more people. Sapphire will probably have to reorganize, reemerge as a new company. You've cost me a lot of time and a lot of profit, and that, by itself, is a good enough reason to kill you. But that's not why I'm doing it. I'm doing it for the power."

"Murdering us doesn't get you any power, lady," said Lyons.

"That's where you're wrong," said Deruyter. "Power is perishable. It must be fed blood to be maintained. You and your organization have hurt me. I must hurt you back to show that I still wield power, that I am not weak. By the way, which agency is it? CIA? FBI? Something else?"

"We're a loosely federated collection of baseball card collectors," said Schwarz. "We heard you had a mint-condition Jose Canseco."

"Your friend is quite the comedian," said Deruyter. "Or at least he thinks he is. He's not actually very funny."

"Marry me," said Lyons.

"Enough of this nonsense," said Deruyter. "Any last words?"

"Just two," said Carl Lyons. "Wait, four."

When Lyons didn't say anything, Deruyter pointed her Desert Eagle at him. "I'm waiting," she said.

"Up yours," said Carl Lyons. "Down! Redemption!"

Lyons put his arms on Schwarz and Blancanales and dropped to the floor, pushing his teammates with him.

The Hughes OH-6 "Little Bird" helicopter dropped into view from somewhere high above the manor house. Through the windows into the foyer, the twin M-134 miniguns mounted on its skids were visible for the briefest moment before both were engulfed in tongues of yellow-orange muzzle-blast. Stony Man pilot Jack Grimaldi had been shot down while on assignment with Phoenix Force only three days earlier. He was looking to redeem himself, he had said, and Able Team was more than happy to let him do it.

At rates of up to six thousand rounds per minute, the firestorm of 7.62 mm bullets tore through the front of the manor house as if it were made of tissue paper. The chopper drifted from left to right as the twin cones of fire ripped through the ranks of the Sapphire men. The air was suddenly thick with a red mist that clung to walls and ceilings, while the floor was awash in blood and body parts. The incredibly powerful fusillade tore through the armed men and reduced them to hamburger before Grimaldi finally stopped firing. Sunlight filtered in through the channel the weapons had carved directly through the facade of the house.

Somewhere at the rear of the upper floor, a door slammed.

"Let's go," said Lyons.

"You sure she's the marrying type, Ironman?" Schwarz asked. "She seems reluctant."

"Har, har, har," said Lyons. He touched his ear. "Thanks for the assist, Jack."

"No problem," said Grimaldi. "I'll just hang around up here in case you need me."

"Good idea," said Lyons.

They came under fire when they reached the midway point in the corridor leading to the upstairs master bedroom. Using the bathroom on one side and the doorway of another bedroom as cover, two Sapphire guards were firing at them with automatic pistols. Lyons returned fire and then ducked to cover behind the corner of the wall. Schwarz and Blancanales took up position opposite him.

"Let's do that thing where the chopper blows everybody up again," said Schwarz. "That part was easy."

"Did you have a lot of sugar for breakfast a week ago?" Lyons demanded. "What *is* it with you lately?"

Blancanales removed a stun grenade from his pocket. "I'll take care of this." He pulled the pin.

"Three," said Lyons.

"Two," said Schwarz.

"One," said Blancanales, tossing the grenade.

They opened their mouths, covered their ears and squeezed their eyes shut. The actinic flash of the grenade left dancing afterimages in their vision, even through their closed eyelids. With Lyons covering them, Blancanales and Schwarz were up and on the move, stalking forward and shooting each of the stumbling, writhing Sapphire guards in the head.

They reached the back bedroom. The door was firmly locked.

"You're pinned down and outgunned," said Lyons.

A trio of what looked and sounded like .357 Magnums punched holes through the door. Deruyter was shooting from the other side.

"I'd call that a no on your proposal, Ironman," said Schwarz.

"Always a bridesmaid," said Blancanales. "Never a bride. Shame."

"I hate both of you," said Lyons. He backed up a step, aimed his USAS-12 and shattered the door lock with a single blast. His roll took him through the door, narrowly missing two more of Deruyter's shots, before he crashed into her. She hit the floor hard, and he slapped the Desert Eagle from her hand.

She stood, dropping into a fighting stance. Lyons braced himself. "You don't want this, lady," he said.

"I'll be the judge of what I want," said Deruyter.

Clayton was sitting up on the bed, his hands and feet duct-taped. He shouted something through the duct-tape gag.

The woman was fast, Lyons had to admit. She leaped for the bed and rolled over it, coming up on the other side with a shotgun she kept in a rack attached to the box frame. She racked the pump and shoved the barrel to the side of Clayton's head.

"You're going to give me safe passage out of here," she said, "or I'll blow his head off."

"You know, I think she might," said Schwarz.

Clayton tried to say something through the tape on his face.

"I know, right?" Schwarz said. He turned to Lyons. "Guess we better let her go."

"I've got a better idea," said Lyons. "We let her pull the trigger, and then we shoot her. In the head. More than once."

Deruyter paled slightly. "You said you were federal agents," she protested. "I'm an American. You can't just murder me."

"You're an expatriate who renounced her citizenship," said Blancanales. "You can't have it both ways."

"Tell me more about power, lady," said Lyons. "The power of this shotgun, for example." He raised the Daewoo to his shoulder. "You get one shot out of that pump. You can use it on Clayton there, or you can try to put a round in me. But here's your problem. As soon as you start to move, I pull my trigger. You're fast, baby, but you're not that fast. And when you move, this bad boy goes off on full auto. I can dump the entire magazine into you in the time it takes you to blink three times. That a bet you want to take?"

"I am not going to prison," said Deruyter. "I'll kill him and let you kill me first."

"Oh, I'm sorry," said Lyons. "Did I give you the impression I was going to kill you? I'm not. I'm loading double-aught buckshot. I'm just going to let my aim drift a little to the right to avoid spraying Clayton too much. That's the problem with shot in a situation like this. You just don't know where it will spread."

"He could be killed. You don't dare," said Deruyter.

"No, again, baby, you're not listening to me. You got the looks, but you didn't get the brains." He said it deliberately. Her face flushed. That was good. Lyons needed her focused on her anger, on her desire to get some payback, and not on anything resembling tactical realities. If you could get into someone's head, make them mad, you could stop them from executing rational tactical decisions. That was behind the entire speech he had given her.

Deruyter sneered. "You almost had me believing you. You wouldn't dare use unnecessary force. The agency you work for will make your life miserable. Your career will be over."

"It's not really that kind of agency," said Lyons. "Do you have any idea what's going to happen when I pull this trigger? The first thing will be that the lamp on the night table next to you there will be blown to pieces. Most of the drywall behind it will be a real mess, too. But when I catch you, at this angle, the way I'm planning... Well, that's going to be just a mess. I'll probably blow off most of your face. Some of your left leg. A bit of your left arm. But mostly it will be your face."

Deruyter spit on the floor. "I'll kill you, too."

"Imagine what it will be like going through life without a face, dragging a colostomy bag around," said Lyons. "You've always been beautiful, haven't you, Deruyter? I'd put money on that. I bet the idea of being disfigured forever leaves you a little cold. I bet right now you're wondering what you'd do if you got messed up like that. I bet you'd put a bullet from that pretty pistol into what was left of your head, if that happened to you."

"Shut up!" she yelled.

"You could be a runway model, looking like you do now," said Lyons. "But after I'm done messing up your looks, you'd be lucky to get five bucks a pop as a street-corner freak show. I hear there are some people who are into that kind of thing."

Deruyter screamed in anger. The pump shotgun came around as she pulled it from Clayton's head and tried to bring it on target with Lyons.

Lyons pulled the trigger.

The single slug that flew from the weapon's barrel struck the shotgun in Deruyter's hands. It was a not a trick shot. Lyons had not been aiming for her weapon. He had simply been aiming for her center of mass, the target that offered the greatest likelihood of putting her down before she could put a bullet in anyone else.

The slug bent the shotgun and punched Deruyter in the gut with it. Air rushed from her lungs as she collapsed on the floor behind the bed.

"Holy crap," said Schwarz.

The members of Able Team moved in. Schwarz and Blancanales collected Deruyter, helping her up and then securing her hands behind her back with a pair of zip-tie cuffs. Lyons, meanwhile, took out the recovered tactical knife that he had found so much use for this trip out. He snapped it open and cut the duct tape binding Clayton's wrists and ankles.

Clayton ripped the tape from his mouth. "You maniac! You could have gotten me killed!"

"Don't go getting all gushy with gratitude, now," said Lyons. "I hate that kind of mushy stuff."

"I will have your badge, you madman," vowed Clayton.

"That would have me real worried," said Lyons, "if I carried a badge. And if I cared what you think. This isn't a cop show, Clayton. You're free and you're alive. Adjust your attitude unless you'd like that to go, 'You're free, and all you have is a broken nose.'"

Clayton sat on the bed. He looked over to where Deruyter was slumped on the floor. "Is she dead?"

"No," said Schwarz. "The impact knocked the wind out of her and I think she struck her head as she hit the floor. She might have a concussion."

"Well, you can't just let her sleep like that," Clayton said. "You're not supposed to let someone sleep if they have a concussion."

Schwarz and Blancanales traded glances. To Clayton, Lyons said, "You seem awfully worried about the well-being of a woman who was ready to make a birdhouse out of your skull."

"She may be…troubled," Clayton said. "But she's still a human being."

"Probably doesn't hurt that she's amazing-looking," said Schwarz.

"There is that," offered Blancanales.

"Knock it off, you two," said Lyons. "Let's…" He stopped. "Did you hear that?"

Lyons stuck his head through the door to the corridor beyond in time to see two more Sapphire guards taking up positions at the end of the hallway. One of them fired a burst of 9 mm rounds from a mini-Uzi, managing to get the trail of fire into the ceiling above Lyons's head. More drywall dust filtered down on him.

"I am getting sick of that," said Lyons as he jumped back to the cover of the doorjamb. "We've got company," he said. "She must have left a couple of guys in reserve."

"If we're lucky, she doesn't have her own helicopter waiting out there," said Blancanales.

Lyons put his fingers to his ear. "G-Force," he said, "we've got some stragglers here. Any chance you can line up a shot from out there?"

Through the walls of the manor house they could hear the agile Little Bird overhead. Right now, Grimaldi would be flitting from window to window, trying to locate the two shooters.

"No can do," said Grimaldi. "I haven't got a shot from here. Can't see them, and can't just fire blind for risk of nibbling all the way through the house and into your position."

"Stand by," said Lyons. He turned to Schwarz and Blancanales. "We're going to have to figure out something else."

"You're always so negative," said Schwarz. He nodded at Blancanales, who took a Beretta 92-F pistol from his waistband and offered it to Clayton.

"Do you know how to use one of these, Mr. Clayton?" he asked.

"Of course I do," said Clayton. He took the offered pistol and held it low at his side, careful not to sweep anyone with its barrel.

"Good idea," said Schwarz. "There's no telling how many hostiles might out there. Giving Clayton the means to defend himself just might save his life."

Lyons bent and hauled Deruyter to her feet. She shook her head as if trying to clear it.

"Come on, Bouncing Betty," said Lyons. "Let's get you to a nice, dank prison cell."

"You're forgetting my men," said Deruyter. "They'll kill you."

"You may not have noticed," Schwarz put in, "but your team of highly trained professionals are about as effective as a kid's action-cartoon villain team."

"You've got thirty seconds!" shouted Lyons at the doorway. "Put your guns down, come out and surrender yourselves to our team. Or you're dead."

More gunfire was the only answer.

"Never once has anyone actually just given up," Lyons said.

"Give us Deruyter and Clayton," shouted one of the two Sapphire guards. "We'll take them and leave. We'll grant you safe passage from here."

"*You'll* grant *us* safe passage?" Lyons yelled back. "Kid, I don't think you quite get that you're the one in trouble."

"Last chance!" shouted the Sapphire man.

"Kid, if you don't take your partner and go home, I will cause you to explode."

"What?"

"You heard me."

Schwarz looked at Blancanales and then to Lyons again. "That's way too far for a grenade. You'll never get it there. The corridor's so long that they'll blow before they get down there."

"We'll see about that," said Lyons. He bent and picked up the metal fire truck in the box of toys in the corner. He placed it on the floor in front of the doorway, took three grenades from inside his gear bag and popped all their pins. Then he wedged the grenades in the metal toy so that the body of the fire truck held the spoons in place.

"I don't believe I'm watching you do that," said Blancanales. He laughed as the Able Team leader kicked the fire truck, sending it rolling swiftly down the hall.

The fire truck stopped just short of the enemy's position. Lyons snapped his Daewoo to his shoulder and fired twice, blowing apart the fire truck and spilling the grenades out. The spoons popped free.

"Clang clang, motherf—"

Lyons's words were drowned out by the explosion at the end of the hallway.

"Wow," said Schwarz. "Just...wow."

"All right," said Lyons. "Let's get these two out of here."

"Hold it right there!" said Claridge Clayton.

He was holding his borrowed pistol on the men of Able Team.

CHAPTER TWENTY-THREE

Naha, Okinawa Prefecture, Japan

Soong stood at the rail of the freighter, whose name in Japanese meant *Sun Fisher*. The falsely flagged vessel would carry him and his men back to North Korea. It would also carry the ICBM components he had managed to obtain through Sapphire before sending his rather brutal message to the company's employees.

It was Soong's hope that Clayton could be made to see reason in the future. The Democratic People's Republic of Korea would gladly accept the equipment his corporation manufactured. It needed the parts for its weapons pipeline. It needed to get its ICBM manufacturing facilities up to speed. But it could not brook interference with its interests.

Soong put a Songbong in his lips, fired it with his precious lighter and regarded once more the words engraved on the lighter's face. Soon he would be home. He did not believe his mission had been a failure, but neither could he report complete success. Two potential pipelines for ICBM parts had been reduced to one, and that one was tenuous. The network for manufacture still was not set up, not completely. There was much guesswork and conjecture remaining. This would have to go into his report. The Leader's son would not be pleased.

All because of the interference of the Western death squads.

North Korea and the Advance Guard maintained a database of intelligence groups, law-enforcement agencies and counterterrorist operatives worldwide. Much speculative information about the death squads of the West was contained in this database. Soong knew that it was further his responsibility to update that database with the details of his encounters with these men. He would spare not even the smallest detail. Anything he put in the database might help some future commander or intelligence operative in dealing with the threat represented by these men.

The freighter's hired crewmen were being paid extra to look the other way where their cargo and passengers were concerned. They were little better than seagoing mercenaries. Soong fully expected to have them murdered when he reached North Korean waters. It would be simpler to do it under the aegis of his own land than to try to do it while in international waters. Besides, he needed the crew to run the *Sun Fisher* until he was close to home. His Advance Guard were no fools when it came to sea travel, and could be pressed into that work, but he preferred to let his men rest and prepare themselves. Should they be confronted by death squads while in transit, he wanted them prepared fully to fight.

He knew of no conceivable way the deaths squads could find him. But that did not mean there was no way. Western technology was quite good and far outstripped much of what was available to Soong. He would have been a fool not to understand that and plan for it. Thus, he assumed that the death squad would search the seas for him and attack him as he tried to return home. They knew that the ICBM parts must go to North Korea. It would be, for them, a simple matter of potential travel routes to harbors in the DPRK.

He wondered, briefly, if it might be possible to use an

alternate port and then move the ICBM components over-
land. There did not seem to be any way to accomplish that
with the resources available to him. He had used most of
his liquid funds to bribe the port officials here in Japan.
There was not enough to repeat the process, or to acquire
the heavy transports they would need to get the parts from
the harbor to the DRPK border.

A commotion on the deck toward the bow caught his
attention. His men were clustered around the gangplank
leading to the deck. He flicked his cigarette into the sea
and hurried to see what was happening. If one of his men
or one of the crew had been seriously injured, it would be
necessary to take certain precautions. Summoning medical attention would require them to permit an outside presence on the freighter. He could not risk being discovered,
not now. The Japanese port officials would not have been
so eager to take his bribe money if they'd known he had a
small army of elite military personnel aboard the vessel.

To his surprise, standing on the deck amid his fellow
Advance Guard soldiers was Kae Sun, one of the two men
he had left behind on the drug ship. There should be no
possible way for Kae to stand in front of them. He was to
have given his life harassing the death squads when they
arrived at the drug lab, thus providing Soong and the others with the time they needed to escape.

"Kae," said Soong. "Explain yourself. Have you dishon-
ored your comrades and betrayed my orders?"

Kae snapped to attention and saluted. "No, Commander!" he responded immediately. "I fought until
wounded. I was captured, but I escaped."

"Explain to me what happened. Be precise," Soong ordered.

"The Western death squad attacked as you foresaw,"
said Kae. "We fought to kill as many of them as we could,

while providing the delaying action you required. I was brought down by a sniper using a helicopter as a shooting platform."

This made sense to Soong. They had proved to the Westerners that their high-tech air support was useless when confronted by a wire-guided missile. The Americans and their allies needed their transport helicopter to leave the craft. They would not risk it in pursuit of Soong, no matter how badly they wished to stop him from leaving with the parts.

Soong bent to examine the now filthy bandage on Kae's leg. "This will become infected," Soong said. "It requires care."

"Yes, Commander."

"You were shot," said Soong. "Tell me everything from that point."

"I awoke chained to the deck," said Kae. "But—"

"Wait," said Soong. "You awoke? You lost consciousness during your shooting and capture."

"I am ashamed to say I did," said Kae. "I was not strong enough to resist."

"I am not concerned about that," said Soong. "How long would you say you were unconscious?"

"I am not sure," said Kae. "I do not believe it was more than an hour."

"And how did you get here?"

"I stole one of the drug ship's launches," said Kae. "I was able to make my way to a shipping lane. I was picked up by a Japanese trawler. They brought me here. I did not know the name of the ship you would be hiring, per the extraction plan we already went over, so I checked each vessel. Finally, I found you."

"Do you mean to tell me," said Soong, "that you have been wandering around this harbor for hours, checking each vessel for Korean crewmen? Have you thought to check to see if you were followed?"

"Sir," said Kae. "I was not followed. I would not endanger our mission."

"Strip!" Soong ordered. He snapped his fingers. "Search him! Search his clothing!"

Kae did as he was told immediately. Advance Guard soldiers did not question the orders of their commander.

"Nin," said Soong. "Bring me the electromagnetic sensor."

Nin nodded and hurried off to do as he had been told.

"You did not follow protocol," said Soong. "You should not have made contact with the unit."

"But, sir," said Kae. "I had valuable intelligence data. I wish to report."

"Then report!" Soong demanded. Meanwhile, Kae finished removing his clothing. He stood, shivering on the deck, as two of his fellow soldiers checked him over for implanted bugging devices.

"There were five of them," said Kae. "One black. The others Caucasian. Highly trained. I believe they carried equipment chosen for deniability. They were extremely effective. They disarmed your explosives and freed the hostages."

"Five men? Only five? How many of them did you kill?" Soong said. "What are their percentage losses?"

Kae hesitated. "Zero, sir," he said finally. "We were not able to kill or incapacitate any of them. I...I barely escaped with my life, sir."

Nin returned with the bug detector and swept it over Kae's clothing. When he got to Kae's boots, he stopped. The green LED on the face of the detector turned red. When this happened twice more, Nin took out his combat knife and used it to pry open the heel of the boot. The heel came away easily. It had been cut and glued back in place.

A small electronic device rested within.

Soong took the bug when Nin handed it to him.

"You fool," he said. "You pitiful fool!" He wrenched the pistol from the holster on his hip and raised it to Kae's face. "You had one task, Kae! One task! You were to die fighting the American death squad! At no time was your assignment to live! And your assignment surely was not to bring the death squad to our door before we were prepared to meet them!"

He shot Kae in the face.

The body fell to the deck. Soong patted himself down, assessing extra magazines.

"Sir," said Nin. "The Japanese authorities will respond to the sound of the gunshot. Firearms are strictly controlled in Japan."

Soong shot him a disgusted look. "Do you think I do not know that? Distribute the automatic rifles among the men. We have no choice but to fight our way out of the harbor now. Kill the crew. We will have to make do crewing the vessel ourselves. They will never cooperate after the battle comes to our decks."

Nin turned around, eager to obey. He raised a hand and opened his mouth to obey.

His head exploded.

Soong felt something warm and wet sprinkle his face. Nin had been standing there a fraction of a second ago. Now there was a crater where the back of his head had been.

Hell came to the *Sun Fisher*.

Automatic gunfire, accompanied by the sporadic thunder of a heavier sniper rifle, pealed from the superstructures of two neighboring vessels. Soong's men on the deck were scattered. They ran for belowdecks to retrieve their weapons

Soong ran. Bullets chased him. He was forced to duck behind one of the deck ventilators, shielded between it and the superstructure of the *Sun Fisher*. Sniper rounds rung the ventilator like a bell. The shots came in a rhythm so steady, so even, that he could only conclude this was deliberate harassment. The sniper was playing with him.

He took the field glasses from the pouch on his belt and risked peering up over the edge of the ventilator, angling himself so that, hopefully, no clear shot would be available. He caught a glimpse of a black man in the superstructure of the neighboring boat. The weapon the man was firing from a prone position was either a Dragunov, a Romanian PSL or some similar sniper rifle.

He was forced to drop to the deck when yet another bullet struck the ventilator.

No. No, it was all going wrong. This was not supposed to be happening. He was supposed to win. He was supposed to return to North Korea in triumph. He was Soong il Yun. His men were the best. This was unthinkable. They could not have made so serious a mistake, could not be facing so devastating an enemy.

Grappling hooks appeared on the railing at the port and starboard sides. Men in Russian camouflage fatigues hoisted themselves up. Soong counted three. He attempted to fire at them, but they returned fire from Kalashnikovs, pinning him down. He had only his Type 68 pistol and very few reloads.

No. He would not die like this. He would not hide. He stood, his pistol in his hand, and ran for the nearest of the death commandos, a man with a narrow face and lean features. He raised his pistol.

"Not so fast, mate," said the commando. He raised a

Browning Hi-Power and fired. Soong tried to dodge but felt something punch him in the temple. He fell.

Roosevelt. It was the one who had called himself Roosevelt.

Pain blossomed in Soong's skull. He was immediately dizzy, then nauseous. His vision swam. He saw colors. The pain pushed from behind his brain and bored into his eye sockets. His head began to throb. Rolling over onto his knees, he retched violently.

He managed to raise one hand gingerly to his head. It was a graze. Yes, that was it. He had been grazed by the bullet. He could feel the furrow in his skin. Red blood coated his fingers when he took his hand away.

"Please, Father," said Dae. "This is not my way."

Suddenly, Soong was in his apartment in Pyongyang, sitting at a table in front of a dour-faced Dae, his beloved son, his handsome, athletic, intelligent boy. Soong had given Dae a sheaf of papers bearing the details of training at the Island. He had written them out by hand. He had spared no detail.

Soong tried to wake from the nightmare. It was one that he had experienced before. But he could not shake the vision, could not return to reality. He was dimly aware of the sounds of a raucous battle around him. Shells littered the deck as the death commandos and his own men exchanged automatic weapons fire. Screams were heard, all of these his troops, as they were gunned down one after another.

The commandos carried canvas backpacks. He recognized those backpacks. They were the very explosives he had wired to the hostages on the drug lab ship. There was enough power in those bags to rip the superstructure from the hull of the *Sun Fisher*.

"But, Father," said Dae in Soong's mind, "you give me an unfair advantage. If I travel to the Island for the training already knowing what will happen and why, and how long each training cycle lasts, I will excel where other students might fail. It is unfair. It is dishonest."

"Why must you forever question my judgment!" Soong heard himself demand of his adopted son. "Have you not considered the dishonor you will bring on me if you fail? Do you wish to make me look like a fool for recommending you? Do you not want to go where I have gone, do as I have done?"

"Of course I do, Father," said Dae. "But… Do you not believe in me? Do you not believe I can succeed on my own merits?"

"Attrition is high at the Island," said Soong. "Many fail. You could be one of them. It is not a question of whether I believe in you or not. Do you think I reached the position I have, gained the Leader's respect and trust, by leaving trivial things to chance?"

"No, Father."

"Then you will do as you are told. You will respect my decision. Have I not already been generous with you? I stopped beating you when you reached the age of majority. This was done out of respect for the young man you are becoming."

"Sometimes I wonder if all of your memories are tainted by the lens of your bias," said Dae suddenly. "Do you rewrite all history as you are rewriting it now?"

The words came back to Soong unbidden, as did the memory of the birthday in question. Dae had been disappointed that his father had done little to celebrate his birthday. Soong had informed him that men did not worry over such trivialities…and to punish his son for these immature feelings, he had begun to beat him with his fists.

Dae had thrown his father off and struck him in the face. Soong, a master of combat arts, could have struck his son and killed him. He could have ended the young man's life in any number of ways. But of course he would not do so.

It was the defiance, the act of raising his hand to the man who was to become his commander, as well as his father, that had so shocked Soong. His son has defied him with physical violence. He had never thought to see the day.

"I swear to you, Father," Dae had told him, "if you touch me again, I will kill you as you sleep. And if you make me become one of your Advance Guard, I will do as you order, but I will do it against my will. It is not my wish to become the puppet of your beloved Leader's regime."

"Never speak about him that way!" Soong had screamed at his son.

"I further swear to you, *Commander*," Dae had said, spitting the last word with utter contempt, "that if you make me go to your precious Island, I will, on my return, take everything from you. I will take your ability to control me. I will take your hold over me. You will lose everything."

Soong even remembered laughing at the empty threat. He had given Dae the notes, yes, even though they scarcely prepared a man for the reality of training to become Advance Guard. Dae would be destroyed and rebuilt. He would become loyal. He would become even more brave. He would have his seditious tendencies and his dissident political views beaten out of him, burned away from him.

The Island would save both of them. It would make Dae an obedient son and a good soldier, squashing the streak of rebellion that had grown in Dae over the past year or two. While Dae was at the Island, Soong would search his room, find every piece of forbidden, censored and otherwise contraindicated material, and burn it. He would take much pleasure in burning the Western propaganda and other books his son read against orders and against the law.

Dae had no idea just how many times his connection to Soong had saved him from arrest.

"You will lose everything." The words echoed through Soong's concussed brain. He heard them in Dae's voice. "You will lose everything."

That was why. He had suppressed the memory. He had willed himself to forget.

Dae had been correct all along. Soong had rewritten history. He had pushed into nothingness the memory of his son's bitter, vicious, vindictive suicide. He had tried to bury the memory, drown it in his revisions to what had occurred. But he could deny it no longer.

His son had hated him.

Tears streamed down Soong's cheeks, mingling with the blood flowing from the wound in his temple. He pushed himself to his feet on the deck, heedless of the bullets flying all around him, uncaring for his own life, unconcerned with his own safety. He had lost his gun. He was not sure when or how. He pulled his combat dagger from his belt

"Dae!" he screamed. "My son! *My son!*"

The fox-faced man, Roosevelt, was walking toward him. Around them both, the gunfight was dying down. He looked to see his Advance Guard, hoping to watch them execute the boarders after first surrounding them. Yes. The death squad commandos would pay. He would have their torture videotaped. He would torture them all until they begged for death, and then he would mutilate them beyond recognition. He would send the video of their disgrace to the American Embassy in Japan before he left.

He would make them all pay.

Roosevelt smiled at him.

Soong lunged with the knife. He made first one pass,

then another. Roosevelt dodged him easily. That should not have been possible, not unless the fox-faced man were superhuman.

Soong stumbled over his own feet and landed on the deck. His knife landed beneath him. He felt the cold shaft of the blade touch his stomach, tried to rise to avoid the danger—

Roosevelt dropped a heavy combat boot on Soong's back. Soong felt his own knife spear him through the guts. Seeping warmth stained his hands.

"No," he said. "Dae. My son. No. It isn't possible."

"You've lost, Soong," said Roosevelt. "My men are wiring the explosives to your ship as we speak. Your scheme has failed. Your cargo, and this ship, are going to the bottom of the ocean. If anyone asks who blew up the boat, we'll tell them it was you, out of spite. The world will never know what you tried to do."

"My son…"

Roosevelt looked troubled. "Not sure what you're getting at there, Soong. But you'll be pleased to know your men performed as you trained them to. They're tough. No one can ever deny them that. But I'll tell you something, Soong. They're not quite as superior as they think themselves to be. Even I was fooled. I expected you buggers to put up a much worse fight…and I'm glad you didn't."

Soong felt himself being rolled over. He stared at the cloudless sky and blinked. Suddenly, Roosevelt's face blotted out the view.

"That's a bad wound," said Roosevelt. "You don't have long, Soong. And we won't be summoning any medical attention for you. Lost cause."

"Leave me…to die…in peace," Soong struggled to say.

"Peace?" Roosevelt said. His face darkened. "Peace? What would someone like you know about peace? You kidnap civilians, wire them to bombs, play sick games with them? Your men are so loyal they seem to want to die above all else. You fight for a corrupt regime run by a madman. No, strike that. A madman's fat son. Your people live in oppression and poverty. You're part of the power structure that keeps them there. No, Soong, don't you dare talk to me about peace, not after you tortured those people on the cruise ship for your twisted amusement. Not with all the blood on your hands, mate."

"There is nothing more you can do to me," said Soong. "Death comes for me. I will know peace…as I lie here, awaiting its embrace." He could feel his voice weakening. His lips and throat were drying out. He was beginning to feel cold.

"Wrong again," said McCarter. The barrel of his Hi-Power pistol appeared in Soong's line of sight. The black hole of the muzzle seemed impossibly large. Soong stared up into the maw of the pistol.

"Shoot me…if you must…" said Soong. "You will be releasing me."

"I may be releasing you," said McCarter, "but I'm not going to make it easier for you." He grabbed Soong's chin and pulled down, yanking the man's mouth open. Then he shoved the barrel of his Hi-Power between Soong's lips.

"Take the coward's way out, Soong. Courtesy of David McCarter."

No, Soong thought. Not like this. Not this way.

There was a flash of light. For the briefest of instants it was the most painful thing Soong had ever seen. He had time to think of his son.

And then he thought nothing more, ever.

CHAPTER TWENTY-FOUR

New Orleans

"I *told* you," said Schwarz. "I told you he would fall for that old movie gag. And that's why it's one of the best action movies ever scripted."

"You're not really going to make me pay you a dollar, are you?" Blancanales asked.

"Of course I am," said Schwarz. "I'm going to add it to the jar of other dollar bets I've won from you."

"I have a gun here," said Clayton. "You idiots shut up. Diana and I are leaving. You'll grant us safe passage."

"No, we won't," said Lyons.

"No, you won't," said Clayton. He looked like a man who had just remembered a good joke. "There's nothing to stop me from just killing you and leaving with her. And after all the trouble you've cost me, after the money you've made me spend, I think I'll enjoy just shooting you."

"Congratulations, Clayton," said Lyons, sounding bored. "You're probably a sociopath."

Clayton pulled the trigger. Nothing happened. He pulled the double-action trigger again and again before he realized his weapon was empty. He ejected the magazine to be sure.

"The first thing I always do when someone hands me a gun," said Schwarz, "is check it to see if it's loaded or chambered. I guess you never got that memo." He took the weapon from the stunned Clayton, who whirled away from him.

"You listen to me, you government errand boy," Clayton said, snarling at Lyons while ignoring Schwarz and Blancanales. "I can break you in Washington. You're going to cut a deal for me. You're going to give me immunity in exchange for my testimony against Diana—"

"Coward," muttered Deruyter.

"Are you listening to me, you brainless oaf?" Clayton demanded. He got in Lyons's face, screaming and turning red.

"Stop yelling," said Lyons calmly. "I'm standing right in front of you. Here, let me introduce you to Mr. Inside Voice." He withdrew his Colt Python and rapped Clayton in the face with the heavy barrel.

Clayton squealed. The bridge of his nose leaked blood. He pointed his finger as he struggled to rise from the floor again.

"I'll *end* you," said Clayton. "I'll *never* do time. Never. I'm too well liked in Washington. I have too many powerful friends. I'll find out where you live. I'll have men come to your home and murder you in your sleep. I'll find out if you have a family. I'll have them killed, too—"

When Clayton suddenly lunged forward, intent on seizing Lyons's Colt, the Able Team leader shot him in the face.

Schwarz and Blancanales looked at their partner.

Diana Deruyter looked on in horror.

As Lyons holstered his pistol, Deruyter was suddenly loose and running down the corridor. Lyons caught a glimpse of the small hide-away stiletto in her hand. She must have been carrying the knife in her sleeve or something. She had used it to cut the zip-ties.

He ran after her.

The intelligence briefing from the Farm had included

the details of Deruyter's extensive training in the martial arts. She was not likely to be an easy target, not unless one of them put a bullet in her, and Lyons was not willing to shoot the woman. It wasn't a case of misplaced chauvinism, either. Deruyter was a valuable witness in the case. Sapphire had been involved in operations abroad and in the United States.

Chances were good that Clayton had given her sensitive information, for only if her company knew Clayton's business could she also safeguard it. Clayton was a menace, but Deruyter was, from all indications, merely self-interested. That was dangerous in and of itself, and for all her raving about power, she would probably take a lot of pleasure in killing the members of Able Team if she had the chance. But she wouldn't have the chance. She was about to go to prison for a long time.

He just had to subdue her first.

She hurdled the dead bodies and ran down the spiral staircase, nimble as a fleeing doe. Lyons came on strong after her, taking the steps three at a time, hitting the floor below heavily and pounding after her in his well-worn combat boots.

"Deruyter!" he called. "I'll put a bullet in your beautiful behind. I swear I will!" As he ran, he withdrew his Python once more. It seemed a shame to scar up a woman as attractive as Diana Deruyter, but he wasn't going to let her escape.

She fooled him, then. She pulled some kind of trick move in which she used her legs to brake her forward momentum, leaning backward. Lyons very nearly collided with her, but she was dropping so low that she was under him. She used her hips to trip him. Lyons hit and rolled, losing the Python in the process.

She didn't try to find the gun, didn't try to fight him

for it. She knew she had a chance to take him and she went for it. She still held the little stiletto. She landed on him, and only his reflexes saved him from taking the slim blade in his kidney. His hand crushed her wrist under his mitt, wrenching her off him. The weight difference between them made it possible for him to throw her around like a rag doll.

She tried to twist her wrist out of his grip, but he was just too strong and too much larger. When she tried to apply leverage, he simply wrenched her back the other way, shaking her like a dog might worry a rag doll. She tried to kick and he brought up his leg, slamming the heel of his boot in her thigh. She hissed in pain.

"You know what your problem is?" Lyons asked. Deruyter tried to kick and he simply covered up, turning his leg in to avoid the groin shot. He ate several more kicks and punches as she tried to find something vital.

"What's my problem?" Deruyter said. She was feigning being game about it all, but he could tell she was afraid. She kept switching styles, chopping away at him with different moves. The lack of success was starting to freak her out. Carl Lyons was a big man, built of muscle and seasoned by years of violence. The day he couldn't take a few punches and kicks from a woman who couldn't weigh more than 120 pounds would be the day he retired.

He grabbed her by the neck and threw her to the floor, pinning her with his free hand. Then it was his turn to twist her wrist. He levered the knife out of her hand and tossed it far from them. When she tried to lunge for his neck and bite him, he slapped her across the face, knocking her to floor. Several more times she tried to get up, and each time, he put her down hard. She was breathing heavily and staring at him with wild eyes by the time she finally stopped resisting.

"Your problem," said Lyons, "is that you still think the martial arts work. They don't. There's really no such thing, Diana. There's only combat. When you train in the martial arts, you learn combat or you don't. If you don't, you walk around thinking you know how to fight. You're a strong woman for your size. You're vicious. You're ruthless. But weight classes exist for a reason. And I'm out of your league."

"I don't have to listen to you bloviate," said Deruyter. "If you must take me in, take me in. But do me the favor of shutting up first."

"You're going away, Diana."

"Help me up," she said. "I'll do what you want."

He guided her back up the stairs, past the shattered windows and scorched walls that Grimaldi's minigun fire had created.

"So this is it?" Deruyter asked. "This is how my career ends? Disgraced and imprisoned?"

"You get a good lawyer," said Lyons, "or cut the right deal, and maybe you'll get out while you're still pretty."

"I can't live caged," she said. "I can't live…powerless. It isn't me. It isn't who I am. I don't deserve that."

"Deserve?" Lyons asked. "You're responsible for a lot of death, Diana. Nobody's ever ready to pay the tab when it comes due. But you're going to have to."

"No," said Deruyter. "I'm not."

She broke free from him again. He blocked the corridor, but she was not trying to escape that way. Instead she went straight for the gaping window.

The manor house was only two stories, but the size of the building put the upper level high enough to be fatal. Especially if she landed directly on her head, deliberately trying to break her own neck…

"No!" Lyons shouted.

Deruyter leaped gracefully through the air, her arms in front of her, as if executing a perfect dive into an Olympic swimming pool. Her lithe body cleared the window—

Carl Lyons snatched the back of her shirt, curling the fabric into his fingers. She wasn't going anywhere.

She dangled from the open window, secure in his iron grip, sobbing openly. Tears ran down her face and disappeared on the neglected lawn below.

"You don't get off that easy," said Carl Lyons.

EPILOGUE

The diner in rural Virginia had seen better days, as far as the upholstery on its counter-front stools went. The linoleum on the floor bore the marks of years' worth of foot traffic. The chipped Formica-topped counter was itself a relic of the Eisenhower Administration, as far as Carl Lyons could tell. But the coffee was the best in town and the chicken-fried steak was just what he was in the mood for. On a television mounted to the wall above the counter, a baseball game was playing. Lyons could not tell, at a glance, if the Yankees were winning or losing.

The man at the booth at the far end of the diner was David McCarter.

"Well, David," said Lyons, sitting across from McCarter. "What brings *you* here?"

"Bloody good coffee," said McCarter. He hefted his cup and took a long swallow. "Black and strong. It was you who introduced me to it."

"Not tea?" Lyons asked, grinning.

"The tea here is crap," McCarter said, shaking his head. "You don't go to a country diner and ask for tea. You don't go to the zoo and ask for a flower arrangement, either."

Lyons signaled the waitress, who nodded and brought him a cup of coffee without asking. "They know me here," he explained to McCarter.

"Come here a lot after missions?" asked the Briton.

"When I can." Lyons smiled at the waitress as she put

the coffee cup in front of him. She was young, blonde and very pretty. McCarter winked at Lyons, who rolled his eyes. "Did you finish Phoenix Force's debrief?" he asked.

"We did," said McCarter.

"Then you heard the news," said Lyons.

"It's rubbish," said McCarter. "You can't let it eat at you, Carl."

But it did. It had stuck in Lyons's craw the moment he'd heard the news.

Some of the fallout from the operation had been much as anyone would expect. The Iranians had clammed up, playing a fairly elaborate game of "this is not happening," disavowing any knowledge of the Revolutionary Path of God mercenaries in the United States or abroad. That was, after all, the point of maintaining such a force. The plausible deniability they facilitated made it possible to cut them loose entirely when they failed. Everyone knew the truth, from the Iranians to the international intelligence community to the President of the United States, but everyone was also going to pretend it hadn't occurred. While Lyons found that kind of political gamesmanship maddening, he understood it.

The Japanese had lodged a complaint with the American government. It was what Price and Brognola called "pro forma." It was expected, but nothing serious. The Japanese government was not thrilled about a gun battle taking place in one of its harbors without its knowledge or forewarning. The Japanese, however, knew precisely what had been prevented. They were no friends to Communist North Korea. That was why they were not pushing the issue, even though an expensive salvage operation was required to clear the wreckage of the *Sun Fisher* out of the harbor.

Sinking the boat had been necessary, however, because

it allowed U.S. Navy divers, working with the cooperation of the Japanese national defense force, to visit the *Sun Fisher* unseen. They had recovered the ICBM components. The parts would be destroyed once they were returned to American soil. The Japanese did not know what the recovered cargo was, and they were smart enough not to ask. Uncle Sam would not have been forthcoming with that piece of news, not given how badly the United States's image had already suffered over the infiltration of its war industry.

The North Koreans weren't talking, but intelligence assets were already indicating a marked drop in drug trafficking in that part of the world. The drug lab scheme had been thwarted, the flow of cash to North Korea interrupted and the ICBM pipeline disrupted. Those were good things, even though the rest of the world would be making a huge mistake to think North Korea wasn't already working on some other means of acquiring intercontinental ballistic weaponry.

The offices of Sapphire worldwide had been cleaned up whenever possible, but most of the employees wouldn't see any jail time. They were cutting deals with the appropriate law-enforcement agencies. There was even the possibility that if Diana Deruyter saw the inside of a prison cell, it would be a minimum security facility. It was anyone's guess how long she would remain there. She had money and influence, and could probably wrangle herself a fairly sweet deal in exchange for her silence about Claridge Clayton and TruTech.

The infiltration, on a massive scale, of this portion of Department of Defense appropriations—and the industry serving it—was under a full Congressional investigation. A good number of the components recovered were indeed very clever counterfeits, which had been duplicated and reverse-engineered from TruTech samples stolen by spies, or sold by inside operators looking for profit. Many more had been of legitimate TruTech manufacture, prompting speculation that rampant espionage had been perpetrated. The fact that this had occurred under the nose of the company's widely known and well-respected owner simply made it that much more tragic.

As for Clayton himself, the beloved patriot and philanthropist had apparently died of a heart attack before knowledge of what had been done to his company could reach him. He had been buried with ceremonial honors in a quiet service attended by the many government officials who had publicly backed his company.

Clayton was inextricably intertwined with the Department of Defense, after all. The patriotic fiction had been perpetrated because, frankly, the country could not afford yet another highly placed political scandal. That was how Brognola had explained it, anyway. It was clear the big Fed didn't like the lie any more than Lyons did.

Ultimately it had been decided at pay grades higher than Lyons's that it was better for Clayton simply not to exist. He would be remembered in death as a loyal American and not a filthy traitor.

Stony Man Farm was better off with Clayton's death. He was a man who definitely had the power, the connections and the willingness to cause great harm to innocent people. Whether Clayton could actually have dug up anything on Stony Man Farm's agents was immaterial. The man was a menace. He did not know Stony Man existed and would not have been able to find any of the staff or their families even if he did, not with the Farm and its computers to watch over his every move. When Lyons had told Brognola that he had shot Clayton, Brognola had offered no comment except to repeat his position that Clayton was a liability. Lyons was okay with that. But he also wasn't celebrating the mission's conclusion. They had done a great deal of good in the world, and acted, as they always did, as a powerful force to justice. But when you got past all that, what was left was politics, and Carl Lyons had no use for politics.

That was why he liked to be alone after missions.

"You've got that hang-dog look, mate," said McCarter. "You're not having doubts about the righteousness of the cause, I hope."

"You know I don't," said Lyons. "I just wish it was all as direct, on the international stage, as it is when we're in the field. In combat, you just deal with the enemy. There's none of this ambiguous puppetry."

"Bone, brains and brawn against the bad guys," McCarter said.

"Yeah," said Lyons. "Something like that." He rested his elbows on the tabletop and sipped his coffee. On the television above the diner's front counter, the baseball game had given way to, of all things, an arm-wrestling competition.

"I think I saw a movie about that once," said Lyons. "It was dumb."

"You've been hanging around Gadgets too much, mate," said McCarter. He turned and looked up at the television.

"Lot of that going around," said Lyons.

"Hardly a sport," said McCarter. "A good SAS man could take those hillocks. No brains to them."

"You think so?" Lyons said. He grinned again. Sliding his arm forward on the tabletop, he offered his big mitt in the traditional arm-wrestling posture.

"I know so, mate," said McCarter.

"Then let's see what you've got," said Lyons.

Their hands clapped together. Immediately sweat beaded on McCarter's forehead. Lyons was shocked to

discover that McCarter was giving as good as he got…
and both men's arms were frozen at the midpoint over the
table. Suddenly the easy victory he had anticipated looked
to be a much more drawn-out battle.

So be it, he thought. Neither of them would give up.
Neither of them would give in. That was why they were
warriors.

That was why they were with Stony Man.

* * * * *

The *Don Pendleton's* Executioner®
VIRAL SIEGE

The sale of a bioweapon to North Korea puts thousands at risk....

A call for help from an FBI agent has Mack Bolan racing to Seattle, but he arrives minutes too late. Hurt during the attack, Bolan can't remember who he is or why he's there. Piecing together the fragments of his memory, Bolan realizes that a deadly virus is about to be handed over to a North Korean client. With his mind working against him, the Executioner is about to put up a fight his enemies will never forget...if they survive.

Available in September wherever books are sold.

GOLD
EAGLE®

TAKE 'EM FREE
2 action-packed novels
plus a mystery bonus

NO RISK

NO OBLIGATION
TO BUY

James Axler
Outlanders®

COSMIC RIFT

Dominate and Avenge

Untapped riches are being mined on Earth—a treasure trove of alien superscience strewn across the planet. High above, hidden in a quantum rift, the scavenger citizens of Authentiville have built a paradise from the trawled detritus of the God wars. A coup is poised to dethrone Authentiville's benevolent ruler and doom Earth, once again, to an epic battle against impossible odds. Cerberus must rally against a twisted—but quite human—new enemy who has mastered the secrets of inhuman power….

Available in November wherever books are sold.